DIRTY LITTLE MIDLIFE MESS

HEART'S COVE HOTTIES
BOOK 2

LILIAN MONROE

Cover design: Qamber Designs
Editing: Shavonne Clarke
Proofreading: Jane Beyer

Published by Method and Madness Publishing PTY LTD
PO Box 168 Subiaco, WA, Australia 6008

Print ISBN: 978-1-922986-42-9

ONE
SIMONE

MY TOE NUDGES the edge of the rug as I fold my hands on my lap, clasping them tight to stop myself from fidgeting. I shouldn't be nervous; I'm repaying a favor for a favor. It's business.

This house smells of wood smoke and cedar and a hint of the scent that is purely man, purely Wesley Byron. I breathe deep, wondering how it would feel to wake up in a bed of rumpled sheets and inhale this scent deep in my lungs, a heavy male arm draped around my waist, the heat of his big body at my back.

Wait.

No.

No, I'm not imagining that.

I'm imagining repaying this favor and getting out of here with my dignity intact, for once.

Ugh. This was a mistake. I shouldn't be here. I shouldn't have agreed to this stupid bargain. If simply being in his house makes me feel like the world has turned sideways, how am I supposed to survive a whole week in his presence?

We made a deal, and I'll stick to my end of it...but right about now, as I try to banish the thoughts of Wes's strong, powerful body curled around mine, regret is my close companion. Someone is going to end up making a fool of themselves and —spoiler alert—it's going to be me.

A few months ago, I arrived in Heart's Cove for a two-week vacation with my best friend. Fiona had finalized her divorce a number of months prior, and I could tell she needed a distraction.

She got a distraction, all right. She also got a business, fell in love with a swoonworthy hunk of a man, acquired a teenage kid, and enjoyed the promise of a happy future. I couldn't be happier for her. Fiona deserves every minute of joy the town of Heart's Cove has brought her.

My role in it all?

Apart from masterminding the original vacation, I'm the one who made sure her—well, *our*—new business venture had a home. I convinced a burly beast of a man to lease us his parents' old café space. Wesley Byron's parents owned the old café in town, but it had been boarded up since their death last year and he wasn't exactly keen on letting four forty-something women use it to live out our new dream.

A bargain was struck right outside this house.

I still remember the way Wesley's eyes glimmered in the

morning light. How the dappled sun shone through the trees, gilding his light-brown hair a complicated shade of bronze. I remember him rubbing his jaw, two-day stubble looking more delicious than it had any right to.

We made a deal.

I needed the lease to his parents' old café space. He needed someone to work as a housekeeper while his uncle was in town. Seven days spent in Wes's presence. Seven days in exchange for the lease. Seven days of cleaning to ensure my new business had a chance.

I thought it was a good deal.

I agreed.

I was a fool.

I was so wrapped up in the need to help Fiona, to save her from disaster by providing a space for the new café, that I didn't think things through.

I'm paying for that now.

See, I can do the maid part. I can clean, and I'm fairly certain I can do it without embarrassing myself. But doing it for Wesley? Spending seven whole days in his presence and pretending I'm not affected by him? That poses a problem.

Wes turns from the kitchen counter, holding a glass of water in one hand and two beer bottles in the other. His biceps flex against the fabric of his shirt, a fact I noticed as soon as he opened the door, and again when he gestured to the couch, and once more when he ran his fingers through his hair and offered me a drink. One word: *yum*. The olive-green cotton clings to his shoulders and chest and falls loose around his waist.

I clench my thighs, cursing the hormones running riot in my blood. It's got to be hormones. What else could explain the effect this man has on me?

He hands me a beer and the glass of water. I take the drinks, careful not to touch his fingers when I grip both items. Who knows what horrors physical touch would inflict on my poor body? I might not survive it.

And I'm supposed to work in this man's house? For *a whole week?*

Stupid, stupid, stupid.

I'm going to embarrass myself. I mean, look at him! That body belongs in a magazine, or at least a sexy calendar.

"I was starting to think you'd back out of our deal." Wesley folds his tall, powerful body as he sits across from me. Stretching his legs across the rug, he surveys me. His green eyes look nearly black in this light, sharp and curious as they sweep over my body. My nipples tighten under his gaze, and I praise the genius who invented padded bras.

We're in his house. More of a cabin, really. His grandfather built it out of local cedar logs that he chopped and shaped himself, little more than a large room with a loft space for a bed. I can see the edge of the mattress on the floor above us. The whole place is tidy, utilitarian, lumberjack-chic.

Twisting a strand of orange-red hair around my finger, I tuck it behind my ear and force myself to lean back. A casual expression paints itself on my face, but judging by the arch in Wesley's eyebrow, I'm not exactly being very convincing. I shrug. "I'm a woman of my word."

"I hope you know what you've signed up for." His voice is a rumbly growl.

"Cleaning up after the best and brightest of the Byron clan for a week? How hard could it be?"

"If by 'best and brightest' you mean 'vile and conniving,' then yeah. My uncle is...difficult."

I want to laugh. Difficult? Please. I was married to a man with a difficult family for eleven years. I did my best to be the perfect wife, the perfect daughter-in-law, the perfect little homemaker for my big, strong, clever husband. Then we grew apart, and he tossed me out like garbage. His family didn't blink an eye.

Yeah, I can do *difficult*. Given the opportunity, I might even have fun with it.

"My uncle will most likely ignore you. He doesn't usually notice the staff." Wes's lips curl into a slight snarl. "Still, he might want to test you. You need to be ready for that." Wesley's eyes dart to my lips. Heat lances my core, and it takes all my effort to keep my body loose. He looks away from my mouth as his brows tilt downward in annoyance. At me? Or his uncle? Or himself? I'm not sure.

"Test me?" I scoff, shaking my head. "He can try." I have more than enough experience dealing with in-laws suffering from a superiority complex. This won't be much different. I'll still be running around cleaning up after people who think they're better than me. Being invisible to them will be a bonus.

Wesley's face twists into an expression somewhere between a smile and a grimace.

I shrug. "They won't even notice me, Wes. I'll be a quiet

little mouse scurrying around with a duster in her hand." I pick a piece of lint off my shirt. "Did you invite me over here to ply me with alcohol and tell me Uncle Dearest is going to rip me apart? Give me some credit, Wes. I'm not a little girl anymore."

No, I'm forty-four years old. Divorced, independent, and more than a little attracted to the man sitting across from me. It's purely physical, though. The man is built like a Greek god with a face that would fit right in on a Hollywood red carpet. Wide, green eyes that do this sexy flashing thing whenever I say something he doesn't like, which is often. Body corded with lean muscle, stacked broad shoulders that taper down to a trim waist. His thighs always strain against the fabric of whatever pants he happens to be wearing, which are usually faded jeans.

Yeah, it's physical. I'm a woman in my sexual prime with no outlet for all this brimming energy. He's all slabs of muscle and buckets of testosterone. Being attracted to him is inevitable.

Too bad every time Wesley opens his mouth, he acts like he wants to jam a fork in my eye. Not exactly a Heart's Cove friendly local, if you catch my drift. He seems to have one mood whenever I'm around: annoyed. It doesn't exactly promise rumpled sheets and lazy mornings.

Wes sucks in a long breath and tries to stamp out the frustration from his eyes. "I know you're not a little girl, Simone."

My heart skips, even though he's just repeating my words. See, when he says it, it sounds like pure sex. He speaks the words, then growls my name, drops his eyes to my lips then lower, and I just sit here like a mute idiot. His eyes do that flashing thing again, and I resist the urge to touch my bottle of beer to my heated forehead.

I shift in my seat. "Look, Wesley. I can handle your family. You told me you needed help while you host your little family reunion thing—"

"'Little family reunion thing?'"

"—and I needed you to give us a lease for the new café. It's a simple exchange. I'll do my best not to embarrass you—no promises, though—and you do your best to pretend you don't hate my guts. Or don't, I don't care. I'm just the maid, remember?"

"Simone, this isn't just a family reunion. My uncle and his new girlfriend will be coming to town looking at this land and house and counting down the days before it gets transferred to his name." He lets out a long sigh, staring at a spot on the carpet. He closes his eyes for a moment and takes a deep breath. "Before they died, my parents created a trust containing the property and most of their wealth. They put...conditions...on my inheritance. Conditions I can't meet. Once I fail to meet the conditions, this property gets transferred to my uncle's name. It's just a matter of time before my uncle gets this place, and we both know it. This 'little family reunion thing' is basically his victory lap. He's going to be gloating the whole time."

I frown. "What conditions? You can't access your inheritance?"

He ignores my questions. "My uncle will be an ass. You need to be ready."

"Ready?" My eyes narrow. "If I remember correctly, when you first proposed this little exchange, you said, 'You'll just have to clean, smile, and keep your mouth shut.' Now, after I got over the absolute horror of a man saying that to me and reminded myself that I needed that café lease, I agreed. Clean and smile with my mouth shut. Those are the terms. If I need to be ready for anything else, we need to renegotiate."

"I'm starting to think this was a bad idea," Wesley growls.

That growl does something to my insides. I feel it everywhere.

"Do I get a sexy maid outfit?" I blurt, then immediately insert my foot in my mouth. Why would I say that? *Why?*

Wesley gives me a flat stare. He's about my age—mid forties—but he could easily pass for ten years younger. His hair has no grey in it that I can tell, but a few lines around his eyes and mouth betray a life lived, including two big frown lines between his brows that seem to appear anytime I'm around. Thick brown hair gleams in the low light of his house when he runs his fingers through it, obviously trying to gather all the scraps of his patience before he responds.

I bet those silky strands would feel good between my fingers, too. If I tugged his hair, would he snarl?

Focus, Simone. Focus.

"Look, Wesley, I get it. It'll be fine. A deal's a deal. You signed the lease for the café over to us, and I'm pretending to be your loyal servant for the week. Easy."

He snorts, eyes on mine, and his lips tilt up ever so slightly. His elusive dimple ghosts over his cheek and another thrill spirals through my stomach.

I give him what I hope is an encouraging grin. "Everything will work out fine."

A tight slash of a smile is the only response I get, and I can tell Wes isn't convinced. We make plans to meet up in a week, then I gather myself together and head for the door.

I step out into the woods, inhaling the crisp scent of moss, pine needles, and cedar. Wesley's property is on the coast of the Pacific Ocean, thick forest surrounding his little log cabin. Even though we're walking distance from the neighbors, who happen to be Fiona and her new man-friend Grant, there's nothing but trees and grass and ocean around us. It's peaceful, quiet, solitary, and exactly what I'd imagine a grump like Wesley would like.

"Hey, Simone?"

I turn. Wes has one hand on the door frame and the other on the handle. His shirt rides up ever so slightly, revealing a strip of bronzed flesh and a peek at his underwear. I snap my eyes back up to his face, but a glimmer in his eyes makes me think he saw me ogling.

He tilts his head. "If I bought a sexy maid outfit, would you wear it?"

My cheeks heat. "In your dreams, Wes."

His grin widens, both dimples making an appearance. Wow. He's stupidly handsome, and this little arrangement feels like an increasingly bad idea. He's also mocking me, which stings more than I'd like to admit.

It's silly, really. I'm not insecure. I shouldn't care if Wesley Byron finds me attractive or not. We're two adults fulfilling a bargain that was agreed on a bit too hastily by both parties. Once it's done, we'll move on with our lives.

I know I will. The last thing I need right now is an arrogant man with an overbearing family. Eleven years of that was more than enough for me, thank you very much.

Wesley holds my gaze, something unreadable crossing his eyes. "I'll be in touch."

"A BLACKSMITH!" I pound my fist on the square café table for emphasis. "That's what Fallon reminds me of."

Satisfied with myself, I suck down a big gulp of iced coffee and immediately regret it when a monster brain freeze attacks the space between my eyes. Pinching the bridge of my nose, I groan as I wait for it to pass, then lean back in my metal chair and arch my eyebrows at Fiona. "Don't you think?"

She just frowns. "What are you talking about?"

I jerk my head toward the back of the café. A rectangular opening gives a view of the chefs moving around the kitchen, along with the smells and sounds of all the delicious things they're concocting. Both Fallon and Jen, one of the four of us women who invested in this café a few months ago, are moving around the kitchen like they were born to do it, dutifully ignoring each other. "Look at him. Dark hair, pale, almost icy blue eyes, a barrel chest down to a trim waist, biceps the size of basketballs. Can't you imagine him in some blazing-hot forge with a hammer, banging a steel sword on an anvil? It's so hot in the forge he's only wearing gloves and a leather apron, sweat glistening on every inch of muscled flesh..."

Glancing at Fiona, and seeing no encouragement from her, I shift my gaze to Candice. As the original owner of the café down the street, the three of us—Fiona, Jen, and me—could thank Candice for giving us a new lease on life. She's the one who wanted to start this new café, wanted to expand, wanted to make it into a place where the whole community gathers.

Combined with my little bargain with Wesley to let us use this space, and investment funds from Jen, Fiona, Candice, and me, we did it. I did have to drain all my reserves from the sale of my old house, but hey. At least I have a quarter of a café in a small town to show for it. I'll deal with my cash flow problems... somehow.

The Four Cups Café means a lot to the four of us. We spent weeks scrubbing, painting, and renovating this space, just like Fiona and Candice had done to the old café. The walls are studded with local artists' works for sale, with a big timber bar where Sven, the barista, makes coffee after coffee. He's wearing a pink shirt with a glittery "Heart's Cove Hottie" written across the chest, and big, black gauges in his ears that highlight the inch-wide hole in his lobes. He looks right at home in here. The tables and chairs are eclectic but somehow cohesive—Candice's design eye—and the whole place fits right into Heart's Cove. It's artistic, calming, and has quickly become a meeting place in town.

Candice spins around in her chair to look at the kitchen, the blond tips of her ombré hair brushing the table as she flicks her ponytail over her shoulder. She purses her lips, narrowing her eyes, then dips her chin once. "Definitely. I see it."

"You're both lunatics." Fiona dumps another spoonful of sugar in her coffee.

"Don't pretend you're not imagining it. A man with a body like Fallon's wearing nothing but an apron? Dirt smudged on his forehead, hammer banging down on the anvil with so much force you feel it rattling your bones? Just because you have Grant satisfying all your womanly needs now doesn't mean you can't look at another man and appreciate a good view."

A bang in the kitchen makes us all jump. Jen glares at us through the opening in the wall. "We can hear every word you're saying, you know."

"No, no. Don't stop them." Fallon glances over his shoulder, pale eyes shining with barely-suppressed glee. "Go on, Simone. You were saying I'm wearing nothing but an apron? What happens next? Do you enter the forge in need of my *services?*"

"Men just have to go and make everything into a porno, don't they?" I grumble, but I can't quite keep the grin off my face. I need *someone's* services, otherwise my week with Wes will end with me embarrassing myself.

Don't think of sexy maid costumes. Don't think of sexy maid costumes. Definitely don't think of Wes removing a sexy maid costume from my body...

Candice giggles as Fiona hides a smile behind her mug. I suck on my iced coffee to cool my heated cheeks, giving Fallon a coy wink. He just laughs, and Jen mumbles something as she bangs around the kitchen.

"I was thinking of hosting Thanksgiving at my place." Candice glances at Fiona before shifting her gaze to me. "We opened the café just over a month ago and I thought we could celebrate. Boyfriends and kids invited, too."

"Fiona's the only one with either of those." I grin and open my mouth to tell them I won't be able to make it. Thanksgiving is smack bang in the middle of Wesley's little family reunion, and I'll be in full-on maid mode with Wes—but what can I say? *Sorry, can't make it, I'll be playing servant to a grumpy loner and his uncle to make sure we can keep the café!*

Yeah, that would go down well. None of them know how I convinced Wes, and I don't feel like explaining. This is my present to Fiona for being my best friend and for giving me a fresh start in this town. If I have to be a maid for a week, who cares?

The other thing is secrets don't last long in Heart's Cove. This little town on the northern Californian coast is a bustling center for the arts, and also the home of the biggest rumor mill I've ever witnessed. Even Dorothy, one of the women who owns the Heart's Cove Hotel, and Agnes, her sworn enemy, will put down their swords to share a juicy bit of gossip. Last week, I saw Agnes duck into the hotel. Thinking there would be trouble, I followed. All I found was Agnes telling Dorothy that one of her neighbors was seen sneaking out of another woman's house while his wife was at work. He'd done it *ten minutes* prior. Then Agnes left with a spring in her step. No violence. No projectiles. Just a friendly conversation between two elderly women who make feuding with each other a professional sport.

If I were to tell my friends about my deal with Wes, his family would probably know we were faking the whole maid thing within minutes of arriving in town. They'd know he doesn't have a full-time staff. They'd know he usually lives in the cabin on his own. They'd probably use that as leverage to force him out of that will, or whatever it is he's got going on. None of my business.

No, in order to fulfill my end of the bargain, I need to keep this to myself. I'll either have to think up some other excuse to miss Candice's Thanksgiving dinner, or I'll have to tell Wes I need the day off.

"Dinner sounds great," Fiona says to Candice, and I have no choice but to nod along.

The conversation continues, we finish our coffees, but my mind stays stuck somewhere on the edge of town, thinking of a man with forest-green eyes.

One week is doable. Any longer, and my hormones might get the best of me.

TWO
WESLEY

THE SHRILL SOUND of my phone ringing cuts through the silence of the woods. I stand, tossing the weeds I've plucked into the waiting wheelbarrow. It's been two days since Simone came to talk about our upcoming week together, and I haven't been able to shake the uneasy feeling that it's a bad idea.

When she pounded on my door and begged for the lease on my parents' old café, I didn't want to agree. Apart from the house, that café was the last thing I had of them. Letting someone else take over the café that had been Mom and Dad's pride and joy felt like the end. The real end. My parents passed away nearly a year ago, but letting go of the café still felt hard.

But Simone stared at me with those wide, pale blue eyes, and something shifted inside me. She said she'd do anything. The desperation was painted all over her face, and I had a moment of weakness.

I'm already regretting it.

Her voice was hoarse. "I'll help you with anything. You need online marketing? Social media management? Copywriting?" Her eyes had widened then, and she'd clasped her hands in front of her. Oh, God. She was begging. "Someone to help you around the house? Landscaping? Money? Daily aromatic massages with essential oils? Come on, Wes."

I shook my head, but one of her suggestions had stuck. Help around the house was exactly what I needed.

She'd leaned toward me, her sweet scent invading my space, shoving itself up my nostrils. Citrus and lavender. Her face was so earnest, so free of her usual sass. "We can't lose the café, Wes. It would kill Fiona. She needs something good to happen in her life."

Their original café space a few doors down from my parents' old place had suffered from an unfortunate flood. A Heart's Cove municipal plumbing trademarked disaster, complete with a weeks-long underground leak. The building was condemned, and the women's fledgling business looked like it would be no more. Heart's Cove would once again be left without a café of its own.

Maybe it was the way Simone looked at me, with that spark of hope in her eyes. The way she came to beg me to help her friend. She promised me anything within her power to give, and I could tell she meant it. I've never had anyone do something like that for me.

So, I told her the one thing I needed: a maid.

I still remember the way her lips dropped open, hope flaring in her eyes. It was early morning, and the woods around my place were quiet apart for the calls of a few happy birds. Sun glinted off her red hair, a wild mane around her head, and she looked like some sort of goddess sent down to test me.

"A maid?" She tilted her head to the side. "You want me to clean up after you? What, like, once a week or something? For how long?"

"My uncle is coming to town. I need some help while he's here." That wasn't the whole story, but it was enough.

How could I explain that my parents had put my inheritance in a trust, and there was no way I could access it unless I got married? My parents meant well. They really did. The conditions they put on the trust were probably meant to push me to look for a partner to share my life with. My parents had a great relationship, and they wanted the same for me.

Too bad I tried that, and my ex-fiancée Alina broke my heart.

I don't know if my parents forgot to change the trust's conditions after Alina and I broke up, or if they really meant for me to find someone else. But either way, they passed away and it was written and notarized: I need to be married in order to access my inheritance. If it doesn't happen by the time I'm forty-five, the trust's contents are chopped up and handed out to all remaining family members and charities my parents supported. I'll get a fraction of what I would get were I married, and I'll lose the house and land. That'll go to my uncle, Sean.

Probably why he's coming here—to gloat.

What Sean doesn't understand is that I've accepted it. I'm okay with not getting what's in that trust. Deep down, I know I don't deserve my inheritance. I lied to my parents about who I was, I lied about my business successes, and I never had the courage to tell them the truth about all my failures.

No, I don't deserve their money. They worked hard for it, and it shouldn't come to me.

Something still stings in my chest when I think about losing the house, though. It's the last thing I have of my parents. It's where I grew up. I turn forty-five in eighteen months, and I intend to enjoy the last of my time on this property. It's my final goodbye to this place.

But that day last month, when Simone looked at me and nibbled her lip, I felt something like regret. I didn't want this to be the last year I spent here.

She stuck out her hand. "Fine."

That handshake was the first time I touched her. After she left, my palm tingled for hours. Her skin was criminally soft. I felt like the whole world got brighter, somehow. I had something to look forward to, and my uncle's visit didn't seem so bad.

A moment of weakness, that's all it was.

My phone rings again, and I shake the memories of that day away. Pulling the phone out of my pocket, I see Fallon Richter's name on my screen and swipe to answer. "Yeah?"

"Hey, Wes. You mind coming down to the café? There's a problem with the roof."

"The roof? What's wrong with it?" I peer at the blue sky through the trees. It can't be a leak—the sun is shining.

Fallon clears his throat. "It's probably easier to explain in person."

Wonderful. Not only do I have to spend a week pretending

to be Simone's boss, but I also have to deal with all the joys of being a landlord. Yeah, agreeing to this was definitely a mistake.

FALLON CROSSES his huge arms over his barrel chest, lifting a hand to comb his fingers through the beard hugging his jaw. I plant my hands on my hips, staring at a puffy white cloud floating across the sky.

Thing is, I shouldn't be able to see a cloud from here. I'm standing in the café's back storage room, and a chunk of roof the size of a refrigerator is currently sitting on the floor.

"Huh," I say.

"Yeah." Fallon scrapes his beard some more. "Came back here this morning and saw it. Must have collapsed last night."

"Purlins look rotted." I squint at the crumbling pieces of wood that used to hold up the roof. "We probably shouldn't be in here until we get someone to look at it."

Fallon grunts, and the two of us head back to the main café space. It's busy—just like it was when my parents were running it. A barista behind the counter smiles at Agnes, the local bookshop owner. Agnes inspects a pastry in a brown bag and gives a curt nod. The woman has a withering glare, and I mostly try to stay away from her.

Candice, the woman who ran the original café down the street, walks toward us. Her brows are drawn together in concern. Her hair is piled on top of her head in one massive loop that flops every time she walks. "I'm cursed, Wesley.

Cursed! First, water damage in the other place, and now this?" She shakes her head. "So? What's the verdict?"

"There's a hole in the roof," I answer.

Someone snorts behind me, and I see Simone walking in from the back door. "Thank you, Captain Obvious." She arches a brow. "Any other revelations for us from that massive brain of yours? Please, bless us with another piece of wisdom. Maybe you can tell us that coffee is brown and sugar is sweet."

I ignore her. "I'll call Grant. He should be able to fix it, or at least patch the hole temporarily. He knows all the contractors around here who'll be able to give me a quote."

Simone moves closer, her arm just brushing mine as she walks past. I inhale the scent of her, feeling as off-balance as I did the first day she stepped out of the woods and into my life. There's something wild about her. She doesn't give a damn what people say about her, what they think, how they might perceive her. It's like she's lived through hell and came out the other side, determined to enjoy herself.

I wish I could relate.

I've lived through hell and ended up battered and alone, soon to be homeless and broke, too.

"Grant is just finishing up his class at the hotel," Candice says. "If you head over there now, you should be able to catch him."

"I'll walk with you," Simone says. "I need to talk to the twins."

The twins, Margaret and Dorothy, are two older ladies who run the Heart's Cove Hotel.

We step outside together, and Simone inhales a deep breath

of salty coastal air. Most things in Heart's Cove are either on the main street, Cove Boulevard, or just off it. Properties along the ocean are prized, but there's plenty of wooded, beautiful land away from the ocean too. Trees line Cove Boulevard on both sides, and in the summer their branches braid over the road in a dappled green canopy.

This time of year, in early November, spindly branches shed the last of their leaves. It won't get that cold here, but we can expect grey skies and rain for the next few months.

Simone and I say nothing to each other until we're halfway to the hotel, a short walk away. She tilts her head up to the sky, unbothered by the clouds and naked trees. She walks like she doesn't have a care in the world.

"You still want to come to work for me next week?" I finally ask.

"Define 'want.'"

I huff a laugh, then catch Simone glancing my way. "What?"

"I like it when you laugh." She glances at me from under thick lashes, searching my face. "It takes you from Broody McBrooderson to sex on a stick."

Sex on a stick, huh. "I don't brood."

"Really? That's the part of that sentence you choose to focus on?" She shakes her head. "That actually says a lot about you. You focus on the negatives."

I fight a grin. "How am I supposed to react? If I responded by smiling at you, you might not be able to control yourself."

"You're right. Better keep that scowl on your face lest I lose control and tear your clothes off." She says it like it's ridiculous, but a spark of heat ignites in my gut. I douse it immediately. Not going down that road.

We turn onto the path leading to the Heart's Cove Hotel entrance, crossing over a patch of new asphalt where an unfortunate geyser tore up the parking lot a few months ago. Stealing a glance at Simone, I watch her lick her full bottom lip and tuck a strand of hair behind her ear. When I pull the door open for her, she gives me an exaggerated surprised look and tells me she didn't know I had it in me to be a gentleman.

"Careful, Simone," a woman's voice says from inside the door. "That tongue will get you in trouble one day."

"Are you speaking from experience, Dorothy?" Simone saunters inside the hotel lobby, flashing a grin at the woman behind the desk.

Dorothy is the town's crazy aunt. She was my mother's best friend, and I could fill a whole book with the nutty things she's said and done. No raspberry bush is safe from her. Today, her long silver hair is braided in a thick plait lying on her shoulder. An animal-print scarf is tied around her neck, but the rest of her outfit is surprisingly subdued. Just a plain black dress. Dorothy steps out from behind the reception desk, and I spy a pair of sparkly animal-print shoes. Ah, all about the accessories today.

"Honey, you don't want to know how much trouble my mouth has gotten me into." She spreads her arms and gives Simone a hug, then turns to me. "Darling boy, come here. You've been avoiding me."

Dorothy has been calling me 'darling boy' for as long as I can remember. My heart tugs at the old nickname, and I fight the tidal wave of memories threatening to overwhelm me. This is why I stay away from town most days. Ever since Mom and Dad died, it's too hard being around people who knew them so well.

Dorothy wraps her arms around me and pulls away, squeezing my bicep. "What can I do for you?"

"I'm looking for Grant."

"He should be out in a minute. We had great attendance for his class today," Dorothy says.

"Well, yeah. It was the life-drawing class." Simone snorts. "Who wouldn't want to show up when Grant takes his clothes off? I only stay away out of respect for Fiona."

A pang punches me in the gut. It feels suspiciously like anger. Or jealousy. Where the hell did that come from?

Dorothy waves a hand. "She wouldn't mind. It's art." She tilts her head at Simone. "And you? Are you here to see Grant, too?"

"I wanted to talk to you about the social media strategy for the next few weeks. Have you had a chance to look through the proposal I sent over?"

"Margaret did. Marge!" Dorothy calls out toward the back room, and Margaret's face appears in the doorway. Dressed in a navy pantsuit with her hair wrapped into a sleek French twist, Margaret has the exact opposite style to Dorothy's artsy-fartsy one. "Ah, Simone! I was just going to call you. We've had lots of people interested in the latest advertisements you put out on social media. I need your help to answer them all. We're inundated."

I take a seat on one of the floral wingback chairs in the corner of the lobby and wait for Grant to emerge. Simone leans

over the reception desk as she points at something on the twins'
computer screen, and my eyes drift over her body. Generous
curves, a trim waist, pants that hug her hips and ass like they're
painted on. The kind of body that makes me ache.

I shake my head. She's going to be working for me. Sure,
she's attractive, but I need to keep my distance. That's the whole
point of this business arrangement. I'm helping her out with the
café space; she's helping me out while I host my uncle.

Simple. Clean.

No attraction. No dating. No sex. Just work.

I don't want to get involved with anyone. I *can't* get involved
with anyone, because I know how it'll end. With me chasing
after her like a lost puppy and her laughing in my face when she
finds out how little I have to my name—and how much less I'll
have in eighteen months.

It happened with Alina, and I won't let it happen again.

My ex-fiancée was supposed to be the one. We met after
college, when I had stars in my eyes, a clever business idea, and
investors at my back. I was going to build a business. It was
going to be great.

Then it wasn't.

She left, and I floundered.

No, I'm not dating anyone. I'm not getting close to anyone
who can make me feel that way again. Simone's already
mentioned the fact that she's broke. She'll see my parents'
house, she'll see my uncle flashing his cash around, and she'll
think I can provide for her.

Would she still be as sassy as she is now? Would she still

treat me like she thinks nothing of me? Or would she get dollar signs in her eyes until she found out the truth about me?

I know the answer to that already.

That's why I can't get close to her. This has to remain a simple exchange of services. The café lease for a week as my maid.

No strings. No emotions. No sex.

Simone laughs at something one of the twins says, then glances over her shoulder at me. "I don't know, Dor. I think Wes enjoys cultivating an air of mystery. That's why he's perfected the sexy scowl."

I scowl harder, which only makes the women laugh. Thankfully, Grant chooses that moment to walk out of the studio at the back of the hotel. With his arm slung over Fiona's shoulders, he stares down at her flushed cheeks, her shining eyes. She leans her head on Grant's shoulder, a smile playing over her lips.

I don't know if a woman has ever looked at me like that and really seen me. The real me. Not the man trying to run a new business. Not the man who's supposed to inherit a chunk of money from his parents. I've never had someone look me in the eyes and smile because they were beside *me*.

Standing up out of the chair, I jerk my chin at Grant. "Hey. You got a minute?"

"What's up?"

"The café roof caved in," Simone interjects.

"*What?*" Fiona freezes, staring at her friend, then at me.

I shrug. "It's fixable." I glance at Simone. "See you on Friday?"

Her face turns a lovely shade of red. Fiona takes a step forward, frowning. "What's happening Friday?"

"Oh, we're just meeting up to talk about work." Simone waves me off. "I'll see you guys back at the café."

I hold her gaze for a moment, long enough to see her eyes widen slightly as if to say, *Don't tell them.* Interesting. She never told anyone how she got me to agree to the café lease. Embarrassed, ashamed, or considerate? I'm not sure.

I walk out the door with Fiona and Grant, feeling Simone's gaze on my back.

AFTER GRANT and I take a look at the roof and he promises to get a few specialized contractors to prepare quotes for the repair, I find myself in front of a plain brown door just beside the café. My keys jingle in my hand as I move to unlock the door, my heart thundering so hard I can barely think.

A musty smell greets me, hiding a familiar scent of lemon and verbena. My mother's imprint is all over this place, even the creaky stairs leading up to her sanctuary. I open the interior door and pause, casting an eye over the dim interior. This one room occupies the front of the building, with a view to the back showing off the large hole in the roof below.

Old, comfortable sofas are arranged around a coffee table. A small kitchenette still has a million and one boxes of my mother's favorite teas beside an electric kettle, an open shelf holding an eclectic collection of mugs—her favorite was the one shaped like a cow complete with legs and udder sticking out the side—a small space for a fridge, and a sink. One entire wall of the small room is dedicated to books, thousands of them.

Mom used to come here when she needed to get away. She and Dorothy hosted a book club together for years, back before the feud with Agnes started. The floorboards creak as I walk toward the bookshelves, choosing a title from the vast array. A romance novel—Mom's favorite.

My eyes bug as I open a page at random and land on a scene that I did *not* expect my mother to be reading. There's... touching and...throbbing and...thrusting and—

I slam the book shut. I don't need to be reading that while I think about my mother. My eyes drift to the bookcase, to the thousands of books before me, and I wonder what my mother and her book club really talked about.

Nope. Not going to think about that.

The throw blanket on the edge of the sofa feels soft beneath my fingertips as memories flood my mind. Mom loved this place —a space that was hers and hers alone. My father had the cabin, and she had this little library. Being in here...it's hard, but it's also comforting.

The Four Cups ladies never asked me about this space when they requested the lease, and I never mentioned it. But now, with contractors coming to fix the roof, I wonder if I should...do something about this place. Use it for something.

Sighing, I retreat. The lock snicks shut, and I set the thought aside. I'll deal with that space later. For now, I need to prepare for my uncle's arrival.

THREE
SIMONE

OLD BOXES that haven't been opened in years spill their contents on my couch and living room floor. I stand in the middle of the carnage, doing a slow circle, trying to ignore the squeezing of my heart.

Memories assault me, one after another after another.

The red gown I wore to a fundraiser, bought at the last minute when my ex-husband sprang the event on me the same day. He then ignored me the entire evening. The black, square-neck gown I'd wear to his business events when I was expected to play the dutiful wife. The sequined silver gown was a New Year's dress, one I wore while I cried at midnight because I was half-drunk and my ex was nowhere to be seen.

Yeah, memories. They were better stuffed in old boxes.

Nate still lives in L.A., and I would have stayed too if Fiona and I hadn't found Heart's Cove last summer. She fell in love, and I decided to tag along. I sold my house and moved up here in the hopes of giving my budget some breathing room, only to sink all that cash into Four Cups and end up right where I started: flat broke.

I'm clever like that.

Now I'm trying to sort through all my old junk and let go—for real this time. No more clinging to the past. No more meeting up with Nate when I feel like falling back to something familiar. No more looking at these gowns and accessories and thinking about the lifestyle I willingly gave up.

I've been divorced eight years. It's time to get rid of all this stuff. I'm sick of carting it around everywhere with me, a literal weight dragging me down. I don't have Nate's big mansion to store these clothes in, with all the walk-in closets and personal stylists. I don't have his credit card to replenish my outfits when the gaping void in my heart screamed at me to fill it with something, anything.

Moving to Heart's Cove has been a big change for me. I sold the house that was left to me in the divorce—the first home we bought as a married couple. I've committed to my online business, and I've invested in Four Cups. I'm here to stay.

That means it's time to get rid of my old life once and for all.

My new apartment—well, new to me—is small, but comfortable. I believe real estate agents refer to these types of places as "cozy." I live above the local hardware store in a studio apartment with a kitchen the size of a postage stamp. The floors are covered in worn brown carpet everywhere except the kitchen and bathroom, where linoleum reigns supreme. The ceilings are sprayed with popcorn and the walls probably used to be white at some point in the very distant past. Now they're covered in canvasses I've painted in my various amateur art classes at the hotel, and every horizontal surface has at least one candle on it. Before hauling these boxes out of storage, I lit my favorite candle—a limited-edition gingerbread scent—in the hopes it would help calm me while I sort through all my old clothes.

This place is home, at least for now. Sure, sometimes I miss my house. That place was full of memories too. You don't spend eleven years as someone's wife without a few good memories to make walking away just a little bit harder.

Planting my hands on my hips, I push thoughts of the past down and take a deep breath. I met up with my ex-husband last time I was in L.A., before selling the house and moving up here. It was the last time I'll ever do that. I mean it this time. I'm not giving Nate any more of my time.

Now I just need to get rid of all the remnants of our marriage. The *stuff*. The presents, the jewelry, the clothes—all the things Nate bought me when I thought presents meant he loved me.

My hands tremble as I grab my knife and reach for the last box. Smaller than the others, I know exactly what's inside. Jewelry and a bag.

No, not just a bag. A Hermès Birkin bag in paradise blue. My second anniversary present from my ex-husband, because he said the color reminded him of my eyes. This thing is worth more than twelve grand, and I remember fawning over it like it was sentient and would fix the early cracks in my marriage.

It didn't.

I haven't been able to get rid of it. I've worn it exactly four times, every time completely terrified of damaging it, losing it, or having it stolen. After the divorce, when the proceedings drained my savings and my copywriting and online marketing business wasn't yet making a livable wage, I considered selling it. I considered it many, many times. Twelve grand goes a long way when you're broke. Every time I got sick of eating beans and rice for the tenth week in a row, I'd pull the bag out, run my fingers over it, feel my heart splinter and crack, and stuff it back into its protective plastic bag to dump it at the back of my closet again. I've lugged it around with me for eight years since the divorce, never looking too closely at it, never being able to get rid of it.

Well, I'm looking at it now, and it's beautiful.

I still remember what Nate said when I told him it was too much. *You deserve the best, Simone. I want you to wear that bag and remember that you're my wife, and you can have everything you want.*

At the time, I thought it was romantic. I thought he bought me things because he loved me.

I was an idiot.

The gifts had nothing to do with me. He bought me things because it made him feel like a big man. Because he could parade me around to all his rich friends, dress me up in designer labels, and show them just how successful he'd become. *Look, my wife's outfit is worth more than you make in six months. Aren't I great?*

The blue leather feels soft under my fingers. It smells exactly how I remembered. The buckles and clasps still gleam and the lining is unmarred. This bag is *beautiful.* My heart squeezes into a painful rock in my chest.

Still, after all these years, it's hard to get rid of it. Does that make me shallow?

Probably.

It's not just the fact that this is a designer bag. Nate gave it to me when I thought our marriage would last forever. When I was in love with him and blinded by the lifestyle.

Don't get me wrong—I liked the clothes and bags and jewelry. I liked the first-class flights. I liked the restaurants and cars. I never turned my nose up at all the luxuries I'd never had access to before I married Nate. Being rich didn't make me happy, but it sure did make me comfortable. Luxuries are *nice*, and I enjoyed every minute of them.

In the end, though, the money wasn't enough. Never again will I sell myself to be someone else's wife. Never again will I go through hell trying to make another man's family think I'm an appropriate match. It's not worth it. Not even a little bit. You could buy me a thousand Birkin bags, and it still wouldn't be enough.

Having my own online business, investing in the café with my friends, living in a tiny apartment that would be too small for a broke student—that's what makes my self-worth soar higher than it ever did when all I was was someone's wife.

The buzzer makes me jump. Gingerly, I place the bag down and hop over a stack of clothing to get to the intercom.

"It's me," a young voice says. Clancy—Fiona's kid. Fiona's new boyfriend, Grant, didn't know he had a daughter until a few months ago when Clancy showed up on his doorstep. Now Clancy's here permanently, terrorizing the town with her best friend Allie, Candice's daughter. The two haven't left each other's side since Clancy came back to live in Heart's Cove at the start of the school year.

"Come on up." I buzz her in, then flick the lock on the door and crack it open.

Her steps are deafening as she stomps her way up the steps, breathing heavily, then crashes through the door with all the grace of a fifteen-year-old who just went through a growth spurt. "Hey."

I look her over, arching a brow. "You want something to drink? You're looking a little parched."

Clancy tucks a strand of golden-blond hair behind her ear and nods, dropping her backpack on the floor next to the door. She sinks into a chair and looks around the room. "Are you packing for something?" She grabs one of the scented candles on the table and sniffs it, then looks at me, waiting for an answer.

"Just sorting through old stuff." *And finally letting go of my old self.*

"Oh." She reaches over to the nearest box, plucking my twelve-thousand-dollar bag from it and sliding it over her shoulder.

I resist the urge to lunge at her and rip it away. It's just a bag. She can touch it. Just a bag. Just a bag. If I keep reminding myself, it'll sink in, right?

Clancy frowns, looking at the collection of evening gowns laid out in their garment bags. "Why do you need all these fancy clothes?" Her eyes flick to mine, intelligence sparking in them. "You've been acting weird. This has to do with Wesley, doesn't it? I saw you leaving his cabin driveway the other day when I got home from school."

Damn it. I was hoping I could get through the week with no one even noticing I was at his place.

I ignore her, fetching a glass of water. I weave my way back through the room, around the clothes and boxes, and extend the glass to Clancy.

"What's going on? Why wouldn't you tell Fiona?" Clancy asks, running her finger along the edge of the bag. She arches a brow, finally reaching for the glass of water.

"Hush. Nothing's going on. This has nothing to do with Wes. I'm just getting rid of old stuff before I move to a more permanent place."

"*Wes.* You called him Wes, not Wesley. You guys are dating!" She takes a sip of water, ice cubes clinking against the edge of the glass as Clancy meets my eyes over the rim. "I'll tell Fiona."

I freeze. "We are *not* dating. Stop trying to blackmail me."

"So why were you at his house?" Mischief gleams in her eyes. Looks like the Heart's Cove rumor mill has another willing participant.

Crossing my arms, I cock a hip to the side. "What do you want, Clancy? You're threatening me with this false gossip about me and Wes to get something, so just spill it."

Clancy's eyes gleam, a smile tugging at the corner of her lips. Evil, evil girl. She places the glass down and looks at the bag on her shoulder.

I grunt. "You can't have the bag."

Clancy's shoulders drop and she slides the Birkin off her

shoulder, extending it toward me. "Fine." She sucks her bottom lip between her teeth, and I can hear the gears in her mind gnashing from across the room. Finally, the teen speaks. "There's a party next weekend."

I throw my palm up. "Absolutely not."

"I didn't even tell you what the party was for!"

"After what happened at your birthday, I won't be complicit in anything party-related."

A few months ago, when Clancy first arrived in Heart's Cove, her dad and Fiona threw her a birthday party. Clancy and Allie ended up sneaking away with a few bottles of alcohol to have a party of their own, and Grant spent the night in the hospital next to Clancy. It was terrible.

I shake my head. "Whatever you're going to ask me, I'm not interested. You can tell Fiona that I'm packing for a trip to the moon with Wes for all I care. I won't be encouraging you to go to any parties."

Clancy slumps in her chair, letting out a sigh so long I'm afraid she'll pass out from lack of oxygen. Finally, she flicks her eyes up to mine. "There's a boy."

I slide into a chair across from her, arching a brow. "And this boy is going to the party?"

Clancy nods. "He's in my math class."

"What's his name?"

"Alec."

Chewing my lip, I try to find the right words to say what I want to say. I'm not used to talking to teenagers, especially not ones who have been through as much as Clancy. "Did he ask you to go to the party with him?"

Clancy nods. "He's never spoken to me before." Another long sigh. A strand of blond hair flutters toward her face. "The party is at his friend's house a half hour away, and Allie and I don't have driver's licenses. We just need a ride over. We'll find our own way back."

Uh-huh. Right.

I reach over to put my hand over hers. "You know I can't encourage you to go to a party, Clancy. Your dad would rip my head off, and I won't lie to Fiona."

"I know." She tugs at the toggles on her hoodie, then slumps in her chair. "I wasn't even going to drink at the party. I just wanted to go for a few hours. Alec..." She sighs.

"Have you asked your parents?"

Clancy grumbles. "They said no."

"Well, there's your answer."

"It's not fair!"

"Life's not fair."

Clancy groans. She looks at all my old clothes strewn around the place. "So why are you going through all your stuff? Why were you at Wesley's house?"

"That's none of your business, kiddo. I wasn't born yester-day. I know you'll use any information I give you as blackmail to get me to bring you to this party of yours."

Clancy's lips finally tilt into a grin. She rolls her eyes, stands up, and gives me a little wave. "I'll see you later."

"Stay out of trouble, Clancy."

Her eyes just sparkle in response. Grant and Fiona will have their hands full for at least a few years with that girl. When the door closes and I'm alone again, I turn back to the explosion of clothes in my living room. With a deep sigh, I get to work.

Might as well get this over with and send most of this stuff to charity. Time to let go.

As I put my old evening gowns into big bags, saying goodbye to each of them, my thoughts drift to Wesley. His family is probably the same type of people as Nate's. I'm glad I'm just the maid, because I don't ever want to feel the way I did when I was Nate's wife—like I wasn't my own person, like all my worth was derived from Nate's success.

Everything will be fine. It's just a week at Wes's house with him and his family. I can stay out of the way, silent and smiling with a feather duster in hand. A week in the lion's den. I was married to Nate for eleven years—I can do seven days.

Right?

FOUR

WESLEY

SIMONE GLANCES up and down the street before hurrying out her door, hauling a huge box of cleaning supplies into the bed of my truck.

I arch a brow. "Are you that worried someone will see you?"

"I never told the girls how I convinced you to let us use the café space. I don't intend to tell them now."

"Why not?"

"Fiona would feel guilty. I'd never hear the end of it." She rushes over to the passenger door and slides in. She slumps down in the seat, glancing in the side mirror before scanning the street. You'd think she was going into witness protection.

"You're *that* worried about Fiona feeling bad?" I start the car and listen to Simone let out a relieved breath as I drive onto a side street.

"Fiona needed a fresh start. She came here and found happiness, and if she knew I'd made this ridiculous deal with you, I wouldn't be able to handle the look on her face. She deserves to be happy, and I don't want to saddle her with any guilt. Her ex-husband did enough damage. Plus, word would get out and someone in town would definitely slip up and tell your uncle all about this little arrangement. How would your uncle react if he knew you didn't *actually* have staff? I'm sure he'd think less of you."

I chew my lip. She's withholding information from Fiona in order to save her friend from guilt. Simone has a big heart—I wonder what I'd have to do to earn that kind of loyalty from her. "Don't you think lying to Fiona would cause just as much damage, though?"

"You know what? Take your logic and shove it where the sun don't shine."

My lips tug into a grin and I drive toward the coast. In order to get to my property by car, I need to do a large loop around Heart's Cove. As soon as we get away from the busy parts of town, Simone relaxes and sits up in her seat. We drive in silence until I pass the driveway leading to my grandfather's cabin, where Simone and I first met.

"You missed it." Simone points to the driveway behind us.

"We're going to my parents' house."

"There's another house?" She leans forward, searching the thick forest.

"Did you really think my uncle, his girlfriend, and I would be sleeping in that one-bedroom cabin?"

Simone doesn't answer.

I take the next turn. The drive to my childhood home is winding, the gravel road snaking around trees big enough it'd take two people to reach all the way around their trunks. Old growth. Old memories. I haven't driven here in months. The last time I was here was after my father's funeral. Dorothy organized a caterer and had everyone come over to the house, and I just sat in the corner, catatonic. After everyone left, Dorothy and Margaret cleaned up and fawned over me like I was their son, then they too walked out the door. I got in my truck and drove to the cabin.

Being in that house is too painful. I lost both my parents within six months of each other, and I never got to tell them the truth about myself. I never admitted to all my failures, and they went to the grave thinking I was someone I'm not. I regret it every day. I don't deserve this house. I don't deserve the money in the trust. I don't deserve any of it, and I just want to savor this year and a half before I get what I *do* deserve—nothing.

Simone sucks in a breath when the house comes into view. It's not huge, but it sits so naturally in a small clearing it looks like it sprouted from the ground. Deep, forest-green siding and a cedar shingle roof, an A-frame design, and windows large enough to see straight through the house to the ocean.

"Wesley Byron," Simone whispers, eyes wide. "This place is like a woodland fairy castle. You grew up here?"

I grunt. My throat is too tight to say anything.

Parking the truck, I grab Simone's cleaning supplies and lead her to the front door.

Simone's eyes are glued to the huge windows on the far end of the house. She weaves through the living room, past the huge stone fireplace, through the massive kitchen, over to the dining area on the far end of the house. She stands in front of the windows that look out on the patio, watching the sun setting over the ocean, her face the picture of awe.

Turning to face me, she arches her brows. "I get it now."

"Get what?"

"Why your uncle would want this place. Why you're so sad about giving it up."

I freeze. She could tell how much this place meant to me from the two or three sentences I said about it?

Shaking my head, I clear my throat. "My room is upstairs. My uncle will be staying down here." I point to the guest bedroom near the front of the house. It has its own bathroom and enough privacy that I won't have to hear him and his girl-friend doing anything...private. "No one's staying in the master. No need for you to clean it or go in there at all." It's full of my parents' things, and I don't want anyone setting foot in there. Judging by the nod Simone gives me, she understands that without me having to say it.

"Got it." Simone turns away from me, putting one hand on her waist and the other on her forehead. Yoga pants cling to her legs and ass, and her feet are clad in flat sandals with two white straps. Her toes are painted green.

I look away, cursing myself for noticing. This is a business arrangement. Who cares what she's wearing or what color her toes are? She's the maid.

We walk back through the kitchen, where Simone runs her fingers over the marble countertops, admiring the huge gas range and massive stainless steel fridge. This house might be small, but it's packed with top-of-the-line finishes. My parents worked their whole life to build their wealth, and I'd hoped to do the same. I wanted to make something of myself. Do them proud.

That didn't happen.

I walk ahead of Simone, leaving her cleaning supplies on the kitchen counter, and I gesture for her to follow me up the timber steps to the second floor. Ignoring the master bedroom to the left, I turn right. My room.

Simone steps through the door and glances around. Queen bed pushed into the corner, a two-seater couch on the other end of the room with an old TV on the opposite wall, small walk-in closet, bedside table, and a lamp. Just the way I left it when I moved out.

"Well, you certainly have a style." Simone arches an eyebrow, grinning. "Utilitarian bachelor." She sweeps her hands in an arc for emphasis.

I grunt, heading back downstairs. When we make it to the kitchen, I rap my knuckles on the countertop. "You can start doing a general clean. It's pretty tidy, but we need to make it look like I've been living here the whole time. Help yourself to whatever you need."

She tilts her head. "You don't want your uncle to know you've been staying in the cabin? Why?"

Because he'll gloat. He'll tell me he doesn't want to wait eighteen months. He'll push and push until I either snap or let him move into this house early.

I just need *time*. Time to come to terms with Mom and Dad's death, time to say goodbye.

"I'll go grab my things from the cabin."

By the time I get my bag from the cabin and stop in town for groceries, I come back to see Simone wiping down the counter-tops in the kitchen. She has a bottle of wine open and two glasses poured.

"You've made yourself at home." I put grocery bags on the counter, my side brushing against hers. My chest compresses, and I'm not sure why. Is it being here, or seeing someone else in this space?

"Perks of the job." She gives me a mischievous smile. "Or were you not serious when you said to help myself to whatever I need?"

"You need wine?"

Simone frowns. "Is that a serious question?" She pats my bicep and gives it a gentle squeeze. "Silly boy."

I stare at the touch, trying to ignore the heat of her hand through my shirt.

Simone doesn't even seem to notice; she looks at the bags of food and starts unpacking the groceries. Opening the refriger-ator and keeping it propped against her hip, she gets to work putting things away like she's lived here for years.

That's a good thing, I guess. It'll make it easier for her to do her job.

Still, I curl my hands into fists and try to stop myself from saying something rude. All I want to do is leave this house, run away, lock it up, and never come back. Instead, I grab the wine and take a sip.

Simone glances at me over her shoulder and grins. "See? Better."

I look at the glass in my hands and let my shoulders drop. "Better," I agree.

Being in this house makes me want to peel my skin off. This is where I grew up. Where my parents tried to shape me into a man worthy of their love. It's where I came back to care for them for the last few weeks of their lives, and didn't have the guts to mention how I'd come up short of their expectations. I'm a dud. I failed. Couldn't get my business off the ground, couldn't convince my fiancée to marry me, couldn't make anything of myself.

I'm almost glad they put that stupid clause on the trust. If I'd inherited all this, I would've felt like an even bigger ass for not telling them about my failures.

"Earth to Scowly McGrumperson," Simone sing-songs, reaching for her wine. "You look like you're about to hurl."

I grab the non-perishables and start putting them in the pantry. "I was just thinking of my parents."

"Here." She extends the bottle of wine toward me and holds out her hand for my glass. "A top-up will help."

Her fingers brush mine when I hand her the glass, and a pulse of heat rushes through my arm. First my bicep, now my fingers. Everywhere she touches almost burns. Taking the glass back to gulp down a swig of wine, I nod. "Yeah. Helps."

Her grin electrifies me. She nods. "Right. Now, are you going to tell me what to expect from this week, or am I supposed to just go with the flow?" She tilts her face, the big messy bun of red hair like a live flame atop her head.

"My uncle is coming to visit. He's bringing his girlfriend."

"And I just smile with a feather duster in my hand?" She arches a brow.

"What else do you want to know?"

"How can I make this easier for you? Duh." Simone shakes her head as if it's obvious she'd want to help me.

I stare at her like she just sprouted another head. I hadn't considered her helping me. I just thought she could clear the table and make sure the house stays tidy.

Simone takes a deep breath. "Right. Okay. What about his girlfriend?"

"What about her?"

"What's her story?"

I shrug. "I've never met her. My uncle owns a chain of sporting goods stores. He did really well for himself, and he usually attracts younger women who like the finer things in life."

"Gold diggers."

I nod. "I don't see why that would have changed, so I'm expecting someone who fits that mold." My voice sounds bitter, even to my ears. Thinking of gold diggers inevitably reminds me of my ex-fiancée, Alina. She treated me like a king when I started my business. When investors signed on and things were looking promising, she fawned over me like no one had before. We were going to be rich together. She'd be by my side forever.

Then it all fell apart, and she dropped me so fast it took me weeks to realize it was really over.

That's exactly the type of woman my uncle attracts. She'll walk into this house and catalogue every square inch of it with a discerning eye, evaluating everything in here by some fucked-up parameters of wealth and status. I'm not looking forward to it.

Simone chews her lip. "My ex-husband was a successful

businessman, too. I've traveled in those circles. I don't envy you this week." She gives me a sad smile.

She's traveled in those circles? So...is that what she's looking for in a man? Someone to provide?

"All right, give me a tour. I want to know where everything is so I can pretend to be a qualified employee of the house. This is my domain." She sweeps her hands as she says the last words, dropping her voice as she does it. Then she giggles.

God, she's cute.

Kill me now. This was a bad idea. Bad, bad idea.

My uncle won't believe she's a professional cleaner for a second. He'll be like a shark scenting a drop of blood in the ocean and unravel this whole charade within minutes. He'll see this place, see the cabin, and know I can't even stand to be here. With my luck, he'll weasel his way into my mind and convince me to give up my right to the trust before I even turn forty-five.

Simone hunts through the cupboards until she finds a feather duster. She whirls, brandishing it at me like a magic wand. "Ah-ha! Found it." With a wine glass in one hand and the duster in the other, she starts moving through the living room. She leans down to look at a few photos of my childhood, dusts them, and moves on.

I didn't expect Simone to be so...comfortable. I feel like I'm preparing for a week of daily root canals, but she just waltzed in here like she owns the place. Frustration winds through my core as Simone's red hair disappears around a corner, and all I can do is grab my glass of wine and follow.

"This is the guest room for your uncle and his partner?" Simone looks around the room. It's a good size with big windows looking out onto the forest. There's an attached walk-in closet and en-suite bathroom. It smells a bit stale, but that's to be expected from a house that's been closed up for months.

I grunt.

Simone purses her lips. "We should freshen this place up. They'll be judging me when they walk in here."

"It's my house."

She waves a hand. "But it'll be *me* they'll judge. Trust me. The condition of the house will be a reflection of my suitability as your employee. Then, when they judge me, they'll pass that judgment onto you."

"That doesn't make any sense."

"I didn't say it made sense." She drains her glass and extends her other hand.

I stare at it. "What?"

"Keys. I've only had one glass of wine, I'm fine to drive."

"Where are you going?"

"I quit. I'm not doing this. I'm going to take your truck and drive myself home."

I flinch as if she just slapped me across the face.

Simone just laughs. "I'm kidding. I'm going to buy some new sheets and bring some smelly candles. This place will look like a luxury hotel by the time I'm done."

"The room is fine."

"Wes, trust me. This isn't good enough." The way she says it makes me pause, and I find myself reaching into my pocket to take my keys out. She flashes a feral grin and plucks them from my fingers. "Good boy."

Good boy? Anger flashes through me. "You seem very sure of yourself."

"I've dealt with your kind of people for many years, Wes."

"My kind of people?"

"Men with money. The kind who expect women to fawn over them just because they have a few zeroes in their bank accounts." Her eyes meet mine, two shards of ice. *Men like you,* she seems to be saying.

"You seem to think you know me." For some reason it bothers me that she's painting me with the same brush as my uncle. Yeah, my family has money. But I'm not like that.

"I just know the type. I'll be back in an hour. You should give that bathroom a clean while I'm gone."

"Ordering me around now, huh?"

She rolls her eyes. "I'm starting to think I got the raw end of the deal. Working with you is going to be hell."

"*For*, Simone. Working *for* me."

"Potato, po-tah-to. Still think I got screwed here."

"It's only a week."

"Time is relative, Wes." She hands me her empty glass and glides toward the front door.

As she slings her purse over her shoulder, I watch her walk away, moving to the window to keep my eyes on her. I can't help myself. That little purse bounces off the swell of her hips with every step. Her top is loose, but when she turns toward the truck, it snags in her strap and clings to every curve. I stand very, very still, watching Simone slide into my truck like she owns it. Her eyes gleam, that wild mane of hair not quite tamed in a messy bun.

She's fucking gorgeous.

Not in a rich heiress kind of way. Not in the perfectly groomed, nipped and tucked way of women I've been with before. Simone is barely contained energy. She's wild and feral and she makes me want to tear every strip of clothing off her with my teeth, just to hear her gasp beneath me.

Being around her makes me think of sex. Sweaty, hot sex with someone who'd enjoy it as much as I would, who wouldn't be worried about what she looks like or what I think, she'd just want and need and burn. It makes me think of nails carving red lines along my skin, of lips dropped open with silent screams. Simone doesn't have a generic kind of beauty—objectively speaking, her eyes might be too big for her face, hair too wild, bottom lip a little too fun compared to the top one—but it's the sum of all her features together that makes her stunning, almost otherworldly. She has sharp, intelligent eyes that miss nothing and promise mischief. Easy confidence with a sharp tongue. I can't help but look at her and think of taking her to bed. Sex with Simone would be really, really good.

Closing my eyes, I grip the windowsill. My wine tastes bitter as I drain it. Sleeping with her is the last thing I need to think about. We're going to survive a week with my uncle and his new girlfriend, then forget this ever happened.

FIVE

SIMONE

MY FIRST STOP is my apartment, where I grab a selection of scented candles from my obscenely large collection. I even splash out and grab the unused ones stacked ten deep in my linen closet. Yes, I have a problem. No, I don't want to talk about it. I toss a few throw pillows and blankets into bags for good measure, then head to the local department store. I buy sheets, pillows, and a duvet cover, then stop at the florist to grab some plants and fresh-cut flowers. I stop by the café, using my keys to unlock the door and step into the dark space. I take some pastries and desserts that Jen made, putting them in a big white box, and leave a note itemizing what I've taken. Fiona won't mind. I hope.

My last stop is the bookstore. Agnes is perched behind the front desk, her short legs swinging off the edge of a chair, a pair of reading glasses balanced on the edge of her nose.

She looks up as the door opens, then frowns. "What do you want?"

"Lovely to see you too, Agnes."

The old woman rolls her eyes. "I haven't got all day, Simone."

I glance around the empty bookstore, wondering what could possibly be taking up all of Agnes's time, but wisely choose not to comment on it. Instead, I lean my hip against the counter. "I need some beautiful-looking books about interior design. Coffee table books, reference manuals, magazines—anything you've got. Something that will look good displayed."

She frowns. "You rent a tiny apartment."

"Maybe I'm starting a new business."

"And maybe I'll transform into a twenty-five-year-old super-model at the full moon."

We stare at each other for a beat.

I crack first. "Have you got the books or not?"

Agnes gives me a long-suffering sigh, then hops off her chair and waves a hand. We weave through the stacks to the back corner of the bookstore, and Agnes points to a shelf. "There."

"Thanks." As she walks away, I start reading the titles on the spines. Choosing half a dozen books, I haul them over to the front desk.

Agnes says nothing as she rings my purchases through, but I glance around the store. "Would you be interested in having a small display of books at the café?"

Agnes pauses, her hand hovering over one of the books I've chosen. Her eyes narrow. "Why would I do that?"

"You could have the display branded with the bookstore

logo. Maybe have bookmarks with your address and phone number, put out some classics and bestsellers. People would come in, browse the books while they wait for their coffees, maybe buy one. We'd keep a small portion of the sale and you'd get more exposure and business for the bookstore."

Agnes stares at me for a moment, pursing her lips. Her face is so wrinkled, most expressions look pinched, but I can see the wheels turning inside her head. Finally, she bags my books up and meets my gaze. "That's not a bad idea, Simone. I'll talk to Rudy about getting it organized."

Rudy is Agnes's grandson. He's in his thirties, handsome, and is the apple of Agnes's eye. Straight white teeth, blond hair, and easy charm. You could plant him next to a stack of books and watch sales skyrocket.

I nod. "Let me know what you decide." I take my books and scamper back to the truck in time to see Fiona exiting the hotel. She's wearing yoga clothes, which means she was probably at one of Candice's classes. Shit.

"Simone?" She walks toward me, her eyes moving to the truck. "Is that Wes's truck?"

"I, uh..." I clear my throat. "Yeah."

"Why do you have it?"

"I'm, um, helping him out. I told him I owed him a favor when he gave us the lease to the café, and he needs help hosting his family in town next week."

"Oh." Fiona smiles, waiting for me to elaborate.

Not gonna happen. Instead, I tell her about my conversation with Agnes.

Fiona's eyes brighten. "See, this is why you're a marketing

guru, and all I can do is day-to-day management. The café wouldn't be the same without you."

I smile, placing the books next to the bouquets of flowers in the passenger seat of the truck.

Fiona watches me, still obviously waiting for an explanation.

"Well, I'd better get going." I smile awkwardly.

"Simone, there's something you're not telling me." She crosses her arms.

"You've really got the mom thing down, Fi. I feel for Clancy."

"Simone."

I take a deep breath. What's the big deal about this whole working-for-Wes thing? Why am I keeping it secret? I know Fiona, Jen, and Candice would feel weird about me giving a week of my life for their sake, and I just... I'm sick of people questioning my decisions. I don't want the whole town to know. I don't want rumors. I don't want people wondering what *else* I might have promised for this lease. I'm sick of being judged for anything other than who I am.

And...I'm embarrassed. Fiona came into town and met Grant within about ten seconds. The only man I can get a real date with is my ex-husband, which is about as much fun as it sounds. For the past eight years I haven't gotten past the second date with anyone, and I've slipped up and slept with Nate half a dozen times, the latest of which was six months ago.

Not good.

Here's Wes, this gorgeous, muscle-bound hottie, and he doesn't even see me as a woman. No, he wants to hire me to be the damn maid. He'd never want to actually *date* me. I'm past my use-by date. Forty-five, divorced, and broke. What a catch.

It just... If I don't tell anyone, I can pretend it doesn't sting. I can tell myself it's a simple business arrangement. A means to an end. The cost of getting the lease.

Fiona lets her lips slide into a smile. "Fine. Keep your secrets. Will you be at the café tomorrow?"

"Yep."

She wraps her arms around me. "When you see Wes, tell him Grant got a temporary board up on the roof. He's going to get a few quotes from roofing companies to fix the damage and check the rest of the building. Should have some options for Wesley by the end of the week."

"Will do." I give Fiona a little salute and slide into the truck. I drive back to Wes's place, already looking forward to the day when his uncle leaves and I can go back to living life on my terms.

I WALK into Wes's house and smell bleach. Wes exits the guest bathroom with a bucket dangling from a rubber-glove-clad hand, his eyes widening as he looks at my multitude of bags.

"You owe me two hundred and seventy-three dollars," I say. "And sixteen cents."

"Is that right?"

"I kept the receipts."

"And the fact that these purchases were your idea doesn't factor into that calculation?"

"These purchases are going to help us weave the illusion you're trying to achieve, boss. Now help me with the bags."

Within minutes, we've got the flowers in vases, candles lit, throw pillows artfully displayed on the living room couch, and new sheets spread over the guest room bed.

Wes puts his hands on his hips and nods. "You were right."

I cup my hand to my ear. "Come again? What's that?"

The dimple makes an appearance as Wesley grins. My poor lady-parts quiver with delight. "You were right, Simone." He takes a step toward me, eyes darkening. "I eat my words. The place looks better now than it did before. Looks lived-in and classy and like I'm here to stay. You are wise and all-knowing and I was a fool to ever question you."

Another step shrinks the distance between us, and pretty soon we'll be chest to chest. I can't handle that much Wesley in my space. If he gets close enough that I can feel the heat of his body, I'm not sure I trust myself not to lean into him and run my fingers over that broad expanse of muscle.

I'm working for him. That's all.

So, I extend my hand, palm up. "Pay up, buddy."

His grin widens and the second dimple shows up. My lady-parts jump for joy and start a party in my panties. Shoot me now and put me out of my misery. It'll be better than the torture of being in his presence for a whole week.

My body hasn't exactly gotten the memo about this being a working relationship.

The doorbell rings before I manage to melt into a puddle of female need, thank goodness. Wesley stiffens, his gaze taking on a hard edge. "They're here."

I'm half a step behind Wesley as he opens the door. A man in a crisp black suit greets us. It looks suspiciously like a uniform. His hair is streaked with silver, and he holds himself tall. A car idles in the driveway behind him. I throw Wesley a questioning glance, which he dutifully ignores.

"Mr. Byron." His voice is a deep baritone, his eyes bright and intelligent. He glances at me for no more than a second or two, but I have a feeling he misses nothing. The driver gives Wes a deep nod that teeters on the edge of a bow.

Oh, give me a break. Wes'll need a little wagon to cart around his own ego after this.

"Hi, Eli." Wes glances at the car. "Are they in there?"

"We wanted to make sure you were home. I'll grab the bags." The man spins on his heels and heads for the car as the two rear doors open.

"They brought their own driver?" I whisper as I paint a smile on my face. "No wonder you needed a maid. This is keeping up with the Joneses on steroids."

"Eli's basically a personal concierge, assistant, and driver all in one. He must have thought I wouldn't have staff. We'll need to find a place for him to stay. I told you my family was well-off."

"You told me your family was difficult."

"Same thing, no?" His eyes glimmer in that way that always makes me want to tear his clothes off.

"Wesley!" An older gentleman exits the car and spreads his arms wide.

"Uncle Sean," Wes says, his voice oddly flat. "Good to see you."

Uncle Sean slides his meaty hand over his salt-and-pepper

hair, his dark-green eyes assessing. He's built like a man who worked out most of his life, and even into his sixties, he's still carrying a decent amount of muscle. A hard stomach bulges slightly over his pressed trousers, but he doesn't look fat. Just solid. And scary.

This was a terrible idea. *I'm going to hate this.*

Then Sean's new girlfriend exits the car, and everything turns to shit. Wes freezes beside me, his face a dull mask of rage. Something's very, very wrong.

The young woman gives Wes a smile that says a thousand things. It's triumphant and gloating and cruel. She's tall and thin, built like a model—except for the massive tits. Her nipples poke through the pale yellow fabric of her dress like two headlights. The clothes hug her flat stomach and generous hips. She has long, chocolate-brown hair styled in loose waves that were definitely done by a professional. Deep, olive skin is set off by the yellow of her dress, and dark eyes flash under finely groomed eyebrows. A tailored jacket is thrown over her shoulders like a cape, rich-person style.

Yeah, I feel frumpy as hell, old, and worried that I'm missing some crucial piece of information. Does Wes know her?

"Alina," Wes says through clenched teeth.

"Hello, Wesley." Her voice is a purr.

Wes looks like he's about to shoot flames from his eyes. He turns to his uncle. "What's going on, Sean? What is she doing here?"

"Don't be rude, son."

"I'm not your son." He turns to Alina. "Why are you here?"

Oh, shit. He definitely knows her. He...dated her? Am I

reading this right? Some sort of sick drama is unfolding right before my eyes. If I stand really, really still, maybe no one will notice me. Where's my feather duster when I need it?

Eli grabs suitcases out of the trunk, oblivious. Either that, or he's used to it.

Alina ignores Wes's question and turns that plastic smile to me. "Who's this?" Her eyes drop down to my leggings, my sneakers, my loose top.

Wonderful. I meant to change before they got here, and I feel more than a little sweaty and disheveled after my shopping trip and rush to set up the room. Honestly, a sexy maid's uniform would be better than this.

Then, Wes hooks his arm around my waist and drags me closer to him with a hard tug. I crash into his hard chest with a low *oomph*, barely catching myself against his pecs as the edge of the porch looms closer. He stops me from falling with another yank in the opposite direction, his side a hard wall against my front, his arm wrapped around my waist. What the...?

"This is my girlfriend, Simone," Wes says, his hands gripping me with iron strength.

His *what*? Excuse me? What the fresh hell is going on?

Frantically, I stare up at his face. He meets my gaze, his lips stretched in a tense smile. I'm still pressed against his side, smelling wood smoke and cedar and Wes. Another tug, and I'm even closer. Breasts crushed against his chest. Legs tangled with his. In literally any other situation, I'd be over the moon with this development. Except for the fact that *none of this makes any sense.*

Wes's lips skate over my cheek, his breath tickling my ear. "Play along."

Play? Along?? That's the explanation I get? Are you freaking kidding me?

Fine. *Fine.* You want me to play along? I'll play along, you big burly oaf. I'll play along so hard you won't know what the hell hit you...you mongrel. You little shit. Maid, my ass. Did he plan this? Was this his idea the whole time?

Play along. *Pfft.* Right. Sure.

I spin in his arms, leaning against his chest. "Welcome." *I'm the woman of the house. Welcome to my domain. This is my lover, Wesley. Nothing to see here. This is all perfectly normal and expected.*

My lips curl into a smile. I nuzzle and spin against Wes, grabbing his hands to hook both arms around my waist, my back leaning against his front. I grind my ass into him for good measure.

Wes freezes. Ha! Play along with that, asshole.

Recovering quickly, Wes puts an inch of space between his crotch and my ass. His arms hold me in place so I can't back into him again. Damn his strength. He deserves to be uncomfortable.

"Looks like we'll be able to double date!" Alina bares her teeth, eyes flicking between the two of us. She's...mad? Is she psycho? Why would *she* be mad Wes is dating someone when she showed up here with his uncle? Whatever family drama is going on, I don't even want to know. I did *not* sign up for this.

Wes's voice is low when he speaks again, rumbling through his chest and along my spine. "How great. Come in."

Alina somehow manages to walk gracefully on six-inch

heels through gravel to the front of the car. Dang. I would've broken my ankle a dozen times trying that.

Sean slides his thick arm around the younger woman's waist, his eyes almost predatory as they meet Wes's. "I wanted to tell you in person. That's why I didn't warn you when we spoke on the phone. I thought it would be better this way."

Wes still has his arms around me, holding me between him and his uncle like a shield. Great. Exactly where I want to be right now—in the middle of some family boxing match that I have literally no desire or right to be witnessing.

I glance back to see Wes's face. Totally blank. His voice is frigid. "Tell me what." A muscle feathers along his jaw, his arms stiff by his sides. Oh, no. This is very, very bad.

And I'm in the middle. Literally—in the middle.

Oh, Wes is going to hear about this. He is going to get a very large piece of my mind. I'm *not* going to take it easy on him. This wasn't part of our deal. Nuh-uh.

"We met at a fundraiser last year." Alina's voice is like velvet. She turns to look at Wes's uncle, a flirty smile playing over her lips. "It was—"

"Don't say love at first sight." Wes is shaking now, the length of his body trembling against mine. I need to do something.

I turn toward him and slide my hand over his arm. He nearly jerks his entire upper body away from me. Smooth. Real convincing, loverboy.

Wide-eyed, he glances at me and lets out a long breath. He clasps my hand in his much larger one and with visible effort, clamps down the rage flaring in his eyes. Then he turns back to our guests and inclines his chin. "I'm happy for the two of you. Please come in."

As we turn around, I glance at Wes and speak out of the corner of my mouth. "You dated her?"

"I was engaged to her." He doesn't look at me when he speaks, his gaze turned inward. His body feels stiff beside mine, his control obviously a hair away from slipping.

Alina was his fiancée, and now she's dating his uncle. We're supposed to host them for a *week* and pretend that everything is okay. Oh my goodness. And now...I'm his girlfriend? I close my eyes for a brief moment to gather myself. *Difficult* is right. Vile and conniving never seemed so accurate.

With a deep breath, I rearrange my face into a placid smile. I survived eleven years as Nate's wife. I can do one week as Wes's girlfriend, fake or not.

It's for Fiona, Candice, Jen, and me. For the café. It's so I can hold my head high and keep my word, and continue to live life on my terms. I'm doing this because I need to do it, and I won't let a bit of family drama drag me down.

I pat Wesley's arm. "Why don't you go crack open a bottle of champagne in the kitchen? I'll show them to their room."

Wesley nods and turns on his heels. His movements are jerky, as if some puppet master is yanking his strings all wrong.

I turn to the guests, pointing Eli, bags in hand, to the guest room. He drops the bags and does that weird nod-bow thing that will *definitely* make me uncomfortable if he does it all week, then heads back to the car.

"In here," I say to Sean and Alina. "I'll give you a few

moments to freshen up, then you can join us for a drink on the patio." I turn my smile to gigawatt-blinding levels and close the door on the two of them.

Eli slips into the driver's seat, and I don't have the bandwidth to ask him where the heck he's going to stay.

Scampering to the kitchen, I find Wes staring at two bottles in his hands, seeing nothing. "Hey," I whisper.

He jumps when I touch his arm again. We're going to have to work on that. "His new girlfriend is my ex-fiancée."

"He's a dog," I whisper, glancing over my shoulder. I clear my throat. "So...what's the plan, here?"

The sound of my voice seems to jog something loose inside him, and he shifts his gaze to meet mine. For the first time since Alina stepped outside of the car, I see the Wes I recognize. He lets out a long sigh. "We have to pretend we're dating."

"You say that like it's a totally normal thing to do. Just pretend we're dating like two regular people would do when hosting your family." I lean in. "You do realize this is insane, right?"

"Please, Simone." His brows draw together, desperation nipping at the edges of his voice.

Something softens inside me. Anger flees from my heart and my shoulders drop. I'm way too nice a person for this. I bite my lip and glance over my shoulder. "Fine. Just for the week."

He lets out a breath, gaze returning to the two bottles in his hands.

I point to the bottle in his right hand. "Champagne, definitely. I'll get a cheese plate ready. Go sit on the deck, stare longingly at the ocean, and look pretty. You're good at that. Okay, babe?"

"*Babe?*" Those pine-green eyes meet mine again, face blank. Damn this man. He's handsome even when he's overwhelmed and confused.

I shrug. "Would you prefer honey? Or sugartits?"

"I would prefer nothing."

"Sugartits it is." I flash him the kind of smile that always makes him scowl.

His brows arch a fraction of an inch, fire flaring within his eyes. Finally, a reaction.

I shoo him away and get to work.

DRINKS on the balcony are tense. Wesley mostly just sits there —and fine, he *does* looks pretty—and I natter on about Heart's Cove and the locals and the wildlife. Uncle Sean and Alina pick at the food and scan the house and surroundings like they're assessing cattle at a country fair.

Finally, we all decide to get freshened up before dinner. We're going to go to the restaurant Jen works at during the week —the one in the next town over with a Michelin star. Rich people love fancy food.

I drag Wesley toward the staircase. He walks a step behind me, his presence a solid wall of warmth at my back. Throwing the door to the bedroom open, I usher him in and let out a sigh. "Okay. We have an hour or two before we have to go down for dinner."

He nods. "Thank you. For everything."

I wave my hand. "You want me to pretend I have *woman troubles* so we don't have to go downstairs? I can talk about being premenopausal and include lots of gory imagery about blood."

Wes glares at me, and I grin. There he is. "You should go home and pack a bag."

I freeze. "Excuse me? Pack a bag for what?"

He spreads his arms. "If you were my girlfriend, you'd be staying here. You wouldn't be in that shithole apartment in town."

"*Shithole apartment?*"

He rakes his fingers through his hair. "That's not what I meant." He sucks in a breath. "Look. This is...complicated. It would be better if we pretended to live together. My uncle will be looking for weaknesses in our relationship."

"Well, I can think of one weakness: it's not real. We're not dating, Wes. You just sprang this on me this afternoon with zero warning and no explanation."

Wes leans back on the bed, laying sideways across it. He groans, scrubbing his face. "Fuck. Fuckety fuck, fuck!" Then, pulling himself together, he sits up. "The terms of our deal have changed, so it's only fair we renegotiate."

My frown deepens. "Renegotiate." I taste the word, trying to understand what he means.

"I'll pay you."

I pause. We're on opposite sides of the room. He's sitting, I'm standing with my arms crossed. I consider his words, chewing the edge of my lip.

Money *would* help. I sold my house a couple of months ago,

but then sank all those funds in the Four Cups Café. My copy-writing business is keeping me afloat, but I'm not exactly comfortable. My car, Bertha, died last summer, and I need some cash for new wheels.

I can't believe I'm actually considering this. "How much?"

"Three grand for the week."

Let's see how desperate he is. "Ten."

He scoffs. "Five."

"Deal." I grin and extend a hand. "Nice doing business with you, sugartits."

He shakes, his large hand swallowing mine. "I'm going to regret this, aren't I?" He flops back down onto the bed.

The...bed. The bed we're supposed to share. Something I must have realized when I agreed to this, but haven't had time to completely internalize.

I'll be sharing a bed with Wesley for a whole week.

Gut clenching, I gulp. I can handle holding Wes's hand. I can deal with his hand on my lower back. I can grind my ass against him to make him regret putting me in an awkward situation. I can probably deal with a peck on the lips to make it seem like we're together. But sharing a bed?

My body will riot. My hormones will go on a rampage.

Wes must read my mind, because he jerks his chin toward the other side of the room. "I'll take the couch." He starts grabbing a couple of pillows off the bed.

"Okay," I squeak. I duck down the hall into the bathroom. My reflection stares back at me, just as frumpy and tired-looking as I'd expected. My hair is pure frizz, like an orange-red halo around my pale moon of a face. Lovely. I look down at my chest. No headlights to speak of, at least. I splash water on my face and head back to the bedroom, poking my head inside. "I'm going to head to my place to grab some clothing. Be right back."

WHEN I GET BACK, Wes is lying on the couch in his bedroom, feet propped on the armrest and phone in hand. I managed to make it out and back without Sean and Alina seeing me, which is some kind of miracle. Wes looks at my little suitcase, then at me, and his chest seems to cave in. "We're really doing this."

"Don't blame me," I say. "This brilliant plan was your brainchild, not mine. I need to get ready for dinner."

After a quick shower, I find a blow dryer and do my best to tame my hair, swipe some makeup on, and look around. I left my clothes in the bedroom. Shit.

Wrapping the towel around my body and tucking it under my armpits, I exit the bathroom.

Wes looks up from his makeshift bed on the couch, dropping his phone into his lap. His eyes widen slightly as he takes in my face, my shoulders, the towel, my bare legs.

I just...stand there.

His eyes are hungry. When his tongue slides out to swipe his bottom lip, fire ignites deep in my core. When was the last time a man looked at me like that? When was the last time I stood in front of a man feeling like I deserved to be wanted?

It's been a long, long while.

That's my excuse for standing rooted to the floor. I'm just not used to that kind of attention. That kind of hunger. Neither of us moves, and a small part of my brain wonders what would happen if I dropped the towel.

As soon as the thought pops into my brain, I stuff it down somewhere very, very deep, and shuffle over to my suitcase. Wes mumbles something unintelligible and when I turn around again, his nose is pressed up against his phone screen. I scurry to the walk-in closet to get changed.

Dressed in a pair of jeans and a flowy white blouse, I emerge from the closet to find Wes wearing jeans and a white shirt.

"Damn it," I say.

He turns around, buttoning the shirt. I catch a glimpse of his chest, the edge of his tattoo peeking over his pectoral muscle. He arches a brow. "What?"

"We match."

He looks at me, then at himself, then back at me. "I'll change." With his fingers moving in the opposite direction, it only takes him a few seconds to unbutton the shirt and slide it off his broad shoulders.

Unlike Wes, I'm not polite enough to pretend to look at my phone. When there's a sexy piece of man-meat forced to share a room with me, and when he happens to be changing in my vicinity, I stare. I ogle, even. I might even drool a little bit.

Wes's eyes flick up to mine as he chooses a dark burgundy shirt instead. "Enjoying the view?"

"Very much, thank you." I give him a grin. "There may be a

lot of things wrong with you, Wes, but your body isn't one of them."

Still holding the shirt, his brows tug closer together. "What's wrong with me?"

I let out an exaggerated sigh that would rival one of Clancy's. "Gosh. Where should I start?"

He levels me with a stare, then slides his arms through the sleeves of his shirt. It's hard not to notice the way his shoulder muscles strain against the fabric, or how his hands move deftly to work the buttons closed from bottom to top. I ignore the pang of disappointment when his bare flesh disappears beneath his clothes. He leaves the top two buttons undone, then combs his fingers through his hair. "I'm still waiting for all the things that are wrong with me. So far all you've done is stare at me like a wild dog stares at a juicy steak."

I tilt my head. "Did you just compare me to a dog? Although I don't know if that's more insulting than referring to yourself as a juicy steak."

His lips crack into a smile—the first full smile I've seen since his uncle and Alina arrived. It does something to my insides. Liquifies them completely, turns my knees to jelly. The man is attractive on a regular day, but when he smiles, he turns from handsome to divine. It takes all my self-control not to throw my panties at him.

I'm just here to honor my end of the deal and make a bit of cash while I'm at it. I'm building up my car fund, that's all. Sleeping with him would be a bad idea. A really, really bad idea.

He extends his hand toward me, and I slip my palm against

his. His hand is warm and comforting, the heat of it sending a jolt through my body. I glance down at my blouse and yep, I've got headlights now. Great.

Wes starts walking to the bedroom door. With his other hand on the doorknob, he glances at me. "Ready?"

I shrug. "Sure. How bad could it be?"

SIX

WESLEY

SIMONE and I walk downstairs to find Eli in the kitchen with my mother's frilly pink apron on. He's cracking pepper onto a plate full of steaks when he lifts his head to see us approach.

"Wesley," he says in a deep baritone voice. "Mr. Byron thought he'd rather stay in tonight and asked that I prepare your meal. I hope you don't mind me helping myself to the groceries in the refrigerator?"

I glance at Simone, whose face is completely neutral, then shrug. "Sure." How typical of my uncle to change plans for a full group of people on a whim. I don't mind, though. I'd rather stay home today.

I reach for a bottle of wine, then pause. "Hey Eli, where are you staying? Did my uncle mention it to you?"

The only room available in the house is my parents' old room, and it remains closed at all times. I haven't been in there since the day of the funeral, and I have no intention of letting my uncle's butler stay there. I'll pay for a hotel if I need to.

"Mr. Byron mentioned there was a lodge I could use." Eli nudges the lever on the faucet with his elbow and starts washing his hands. He glances over his shoulder at me. "I hadn't realized he didn't discuss it with you beforehand."

My eyebrows inch upward. Simone looks at me, tilting her head. My uncle told Eli he could stay in Grandpa's lodge. As soon as he steps inside, it'll be more than obvious that I've been living there. Alone.

This whole charade could fall apart before it even begins.

Simone puts her hand on my arm, and I ignore the heat of her palm and how it makes my heart beat a little bit harder. Her touch makes my body react a little too violently, and I don't want to acknowledge what that means. She smiles at me. Damn, this woman is gorgeous. She nods to the door. "I'll go over there and get it ready. I'll be back in no time."

My shoulders relax ever so slightly, and I give her a small nod. "Thank you."

With her hand on my arm and her side almost touching mine, it's easy to forget we're supposed to be pretending. It would be so simple to lean down and brush my lips over hers. Wouldn't that be the natural thing to do if we were really dating? I could slide my arm across her lower back and give her a kiss that shows my appreciation, my gratitude, my affection.

Instead, Simone clears her throat and nods at the two of us before slipping out the front door. I watch her leave and try to ignore the sensation of the walls closing in on me.

"She's not your usual type."

I turn to see Alina entering from the back porch. She's changed out of her skin-tight yellow dress and sky-high heels into a sort of gauzy, easy ensemble that's loose-fitting and somehow refined and sexy at the same time. After being in Heart's Cove for so long, I'd almost forgotten how wealthy people dress and carry themselves—like they own everything in sight.

Alina nods to the bottle of wine on the counter, and I find myself pouring her a glass. Damn it. I'm not sure it's me playing the host or some holdover of another life when I was happy to serve her in whatever way she pleased.

"I wasn't aware I had a type," I answer as I hand her the glass. I pour myself one as well, if only to ignore her searching stare.

"You used to. Tall, thin, willowy. Someone that would fit into your family's social circle." *Someone like me*, she leaves unsaid.

I snort. "My family's social circle isn't what you think it is." If only she knew Dorothy and Margaret, she wouldn't be talking to me about fitting in. Simone was probably born to fit in with those crazy old ladies, if only because they seem to collect eccentrics and artists like Alina collects suitors.

My ex-fiancée leans against the counter, casting her eye over the living room and kitchen. She sips her wine, every movement graceful. I wonder if it's innate, or if she learned it growing up. Did her fancy prep school teach her how to move through the world? Or is it just some deep sense of knowing that your superiority is absolute?

My heart squeezes to a painful ball in my chest. I remember meeting her when we were both in our thirties, working professionals in tech. I met her at a conference, where she was perpetually surrounded by panting men. She was so unbelievably beautiful, and I thought I was the luckiest man in the world. When she deigned to date me, I felt like I'd been blessed.

She encouraged me to pursue my dreams, to make my business work. She charmed my investors and probably had as much to do with them signing on as I did. Then she turned her back on me as quickly as the investors did, too.

"You look sad, Wes," Alina says, pulling me from my thoughts. "Your eyes are dull." She takes a half step toward me, her hand reaching for mine. When her fingers brush my palm, an electric jolt zips across my skin, like an elastic band snapping. Unpleasant.

I pull back. "When did you and Sean...?"

"About a year ago." Alina holds my gaze but makes no move to touch me again. "I wanted to tell you, but I thought it would be better in person."

"Right. Showing up on my doorstep is a much better tactic. Can't react, otherwise I look like an asshole."

"That's not what I meant." Alina's brows draw together, and I can feel her charm weaving around me like a drug. I want to forgive her. I want to walk toward her and let her put her arms around my neck. She's the kind of woman who makes you forget yourself in an instant. Tilting her head, she gives me a mournful smile. "I want you to be happy, Wes. Even if it didn't work out between us, I still want the best for you."

Her words are sweet and sad and they sound sincere, but

how true are they? When she left me, she said I was dragging her down. I'd taken a chance on building a business—an app that was supposed to be a massive platform for all kinds of services. A virtual phone book for hair stylists and barbers and personal trainers. I had angel investors and business plans and I was living in Silicon Valley like the rest of them. It was going to be the next Uber, the next AirBnB. I had the support of my parents, my fiancée, and all the right connections.

But I didn't have customers. The app didn't take off the way I wanted it to, and I ended up hundreds of thousands of dollars in debt with investors pulling out at every turn. Doors that were once wide open were shut in my face.

I was disgraced.

An oily feeling slicks over my skin as Alina tilts her head, tucking a strand of chocolatey hair behind her ear. Her eyes look into mine, and if I were still a fool in love, I'd think she were being sincere. She's not, though. It's an act. As soon as she saw my ship was sinking, she ran for shore. Then, what? A few years later, she found my uncle by chance?

"There you are!" Sean walks into the room, shoulders back, steps sure. He slides his arm around Alina's waist and accepts a glass of wine from Eli. "Have you two put the past behind you now? We can move on and have a good vacation?"

"Sure," I answer, pinching a smile. A few words exchanged under duress, and the past is water under the bridge. At least that's how it works in my family. I motion to the living room and take a seat in an armchair, watching them sit side by side on the sofa.

My uncle and my ex-fiancée, happy together.

I want to be sick.

Sean looks around the room. "I've always loved this house, but I told my brother he could do better. This piece of land is worth a fortune now that Heart's Cove is growing. It could be a real moneymaker. A hotel, or maybe vacation cabins. A bed and breakfast..." He glances at me, arching his brows. "Now would be the time. Heart's Cove is growing, and in a year and a half it might be too late."

Is he seriously trying to get me to give up this house right now? He can't wait eighteen months to let me grieve in peace? Thunderclouds gather over my head.

"Straight to business," Alina says, swatting his thigh. Her delicate laugh shakes loose a thousand memories. How many times did she do this when I was sitting next to her? Soften the blow of business proposals, charm the opponent, close the deal.

"I'm not interested in developing my parents' land," I say through clenched teeth.

Sean's eyes narrow. "Things with you and Simone are serious, then?"

Oh. My uncle thinks I'll get married. Of course he does. He thinks Simone will be the one to fulfill the conditions on the trust, and he won't be able to get his grubby little paws on this land after all.

Shit. Oh, shit. I didn't think this through.

When I put my arm around Simone, it was because I saw Alina and I didn't want to be the loser who ended up alone. It was my dumb, misplaced pride. I didn't consider what they'd think—that they would see it as a direct attack on the inheritance they'd been counting on.

Stupid—I've been stupid. I've put Simone in an awkward position.

Sean leans back, putting his arm around Alina's shoulders. He pulls her close and she leans into him, a little show for my benefit. My uncle's eyes glint. "Wes, think about it, son. Just because your little app didn't work doesn't mean you can't start over with another successful business. You and that woman"—he waves a hand dismissively toward the door—"it's not what's best for you."

Blood boils in my veins as I do my best to contain the anger threatening to spill from me. *That woman?* I won't give him the satisfaction of acknowledging that. Instead, I respond through clenched teeth, "My little app?"

"You know what I mean. It was a venture, and it flopped. Move on. Real estate has been around forever, and you and I could do big things here. You just have to think clearly about the situation."

"Simone and I live in this house."

"Hmm." Sean leans back on the couch, a muscle feathering in his jaw. "You need to have some ambition, Wes. Your parents' passing was tragic, but there's real opportunity here. Don't let your pride or some piece of ass cloud your vision."

Don't punch him in the face. Don't punch him in the face. Don't punch him in the face.

The front door opens and a burst of cool air washes over me. Simone steps through, her cheeks ruddy and hair as wild as usual. A piece of ass, huh. She's so much more than that. She closes the door and stomps her feet, shedding her jacket.

"Getting chilly out there!" she calls out as she walks toward me. Her hand lands on my shoulder and she grabs the wine glass from between my fingers, taking a sip. She glances at the glass with an approving nod. "I have to hand it to your parents, Wes. They had great taste in wine."

"You're still drinking from their collection?" Sean's eyes move from me to Simone. "I thought you'd have made it through their bottles within a month or two. It's not like they had a full cellar."

"Keeping it for special occasions," Simone cuts in smoothly with a smile. She hands me my glass and walks to the kitchen to pour her own. I watch her walk away, missing the weight of her hand on my shoulder. She's handling this much better than I am.

I catch my uncle following my gaze, his eyes riveted on Simone's ass. Protective, possessive fury whips through me before I can snuff it out. Where the hell did that come from? Alina's presence and my uncle's comments have me twisted up in knots.

When Simone returns, the room is quiet. She perches herself on the arm of the single-seater where I sit seething, her hip touching my side, arm slung across the back of my chair, smiling at our two guests. A standoff.

Alina breaks the silence first. She leans forward, her arms pressing her breasts together in a move I've seen a thousand times, and picks up one of the books on the coffee table. "Are you an interior designer, Simone?"

"Oh, those." Simone smiles at the brand-new books on the table. "Wes and I have been thinking of remodeling the place. Small changes, you know. Make the place our own."

My uncle's gaze shifts to Simone, then me. His eyes narrow.

Simone puts her glass of wine down on the coffee table and picks up a book, flicking through it. "We've yet to agree on a style, but it's fun to think about, don't you think? We both love this house so much, we don't want to change the bones, but it would be great to modernize it just a bit."

Sean's eyes dim as he leans back on the couch. Alina glances back at him, an unspoken conversation passing between them. The tension in the room heightens.

With just a few sentences, some candles, throw pillows, and a couple of books on the coffee table, Simone has been more effective in discouraging my uncle than I could have been by arguing for hours. She's made it clear that this is our home. But she bought those books before we agreed to pretend. How could she have known?

I glance at Simone, renewed admiration flowing through me. If she feels my gaze, she ignores it. Eli enters the room, topping up everyone's wine. When he leaves, Simone shakes her head. "I have to say, I'm jealous of Eli. I need someone like that in my life. Wouldn't mind a man to drive me around, organize all my affairs, cook for me... every woman's dream."

"You have Wesley, don't you?" Alina's eyes are sharp as she stares at Simone. "Is he not spoiling you? I seem to remember he was good at that, at least when he was dating me. Maybe he doesn't feel the need to be as doting with someone who's...more experienced."

Older. The word she's looking for is older.

Simone returns my ex's gaze, death sparking in her eyes. She sits down on the arm of the chair again, leaning ever so slightly against me. "Experience is a good thing, sweetheart. And I don't need Wes to drive me around. He's good for other things."

My body grows stiff. Was that sexual innuendo? Blood pumps through my body, hot and thick. Simone puts her hand across my shoulders and I lift my gaze to hers, seeing something unreadable in her pale blue eyes. We stare at each other for a long moment, so long I nearly forget about my uncle and ex-fiancée.

There's something so fucking erotic about her, especially when she looks just like this. Visions of sweat and sex and screaming flash through my mind. Red hair twisted around my fist. Simone panting my name, telling me she needs me to—

Eli appears at the edge of the room. "Dinner is ready."

Simone looks away, and the spell is broken.

I tug at my shirt collar, trotting behind her toward the dining room. Who's the panting dog now? In the minute before my uncle and Alina arrive at the table, I lean toward Simone. "How did you know to get those books?"

"You mentioned something about the house. I figured it would make you look like you intended to stay. Easy enough to make it sound like it was a project for both of us."

Clever. Very clever.

My eyes flick to her lips as warmth floods my chest, then Alina's hand ghosts over my shoulders and Simone stiffens beside me. Alina sits across from us, shaking her napkin out and laying it across her lap in prim, tidy movements.

I slide my hand over Simone's thigh—I don't even know why. To make sure she's still there. To feel the heat of her body under my palm. To my surprise, she places her hand over mine and squeezes before starting a polite conversation about the local attractions my uncle might have missed since he was here last.

SOMEHOW, I make it through the meal. When the plates are cleared away, Simone gets up from the table and follows Eli into the kitchen, re-emerging with a platter of pastries that had to have come from the café. Did she get those during her outing earlier, too?

"Dessert by the county's best pastry chef and my very own good friend. Jen and I are part-owners of the café in town, along with two other friends. Please, help yourselves." She puts the plate down and takes a seat, smiling like a gracious hostess.

She's damn good, I'll give her that. Even I'm almost convinced that Simone has lived in this house with me for months.

Simone's eyes glimmer, and after a few more minutes of tense conversation, we finally make our escape. It's not until we're in our room behind a closed door that Simone lets out a long sigh. "I can't believe I agreed to this. No wonder you're a grump. I would be too if I had to deal with family members like that."

My fingers work to unbutton my shirt as Simone frees her hair from its thousand and one pins. Grinning, I arch an eyebrow. "You did surprisingly well."

"I've had lots of practice, sugartits."

"Was it really that bad?"

"What, dinner?" She sits on the bed, leaning against her elbows. I try—and fail—not to notice the way her shirt tugs against her breasts as she angles her body back. "It was fine."

"I meant your marriage. You were so good at pretending that I was almost convinced we were really dating." I pull my shirt off, and maybe I flex a little as Simone's eyes drift down to my chest. She snaps her eyes back to the wall and lets out a huff. "Like I said, I've had a lot of practice pretending to belong beside snooty rich people."

I sit next to her, and we're silent for a moment. Then I let out a sigh. "Thank you."

"It's nothing." She waves a hand. "We made a deal, and I told you I'd do it. You're paying me for this."

"I meant for everything. For the candles and pillows and books. For sorting out my cabin while I entertained them. For being so great at dinner."

Simone holds my gaze for a moment, and the space between us seems to shrink. There's that look in her eyes again, the feral need brimming just below the surface.

She's the first to break away, shaking her head as she sighs. "Thank goodness it's only for a week. That was exhausting. Oh, that reminds me." She looks at me again. "Grant has a few things to talk to you about regarding the roof. He'll be at the café tomorrow. Maybe we can all go there for breakfast in the morn- ing. I've got some work to do anyway, and it'll be a good time to let your uncle and Alina roam free in the town for the day."

"Get rid of them while getting our own stuff done." I laugh. "You really are an expert."

"Never underestimate me again, sugartits." She pats my

thigh and stands up, heading to the bathroom to get ready for bed. When she returns, Simone climbs into bed, flopping back on the mountain of pillows with a happy groan.

I follow her lead and get ready for bed in the bathroom. When I come back, Simone has a silk eye mask propped on her forehead, her mane of red hair stark against the white pillows.

I head for the couch and take a seat. When I try to curl on my side and fold my legs to make them fit, I feel Simone's gaze. "Wes."

"What?"

She takes a deep breath. "Look, we're both adults. You won't sleep on that sofa, and you'll need all the rest you can get this week. That couch is way too small and you look like you'll break it if you turn around. Just sleep in the bed. There's more than enough room."

I hesitate, my eyes drifting down her body. Her thin T-shirt clings to her breasts, the outline of her nipples visible beneath the grey fabric. Her long legs gleam in the moonlight, stacked one on top of another. Her little booty shorts aren't exactly modest. I shouldn't get in bed with her. Not because I wouldn't be able to control myself, but because I haven't slept beside a woman in a long time. It would be crossing some invisible line in my mind that I have no business crossing.

She pats the bed again, giving me a pointed stare. "I promise not to jump your bones, Wes. I just want you to get a good night's sleep. I'm considerate like that. Plus, we're not twenty years old anymore. Sleeping on sofas should be a crime once you're out of college."

I huff a laugh, hesitate, and finally stand up. The pillow I'd carried to the couch lands beside her with a thud, and she holds my gaze for a few moments before turning her back to me. I allow myself one moment—just one moment—to let my eyes drift down the curves of her body, then I climb into bed and turn to face the other way.

SEVEN
SIMONE

WELL, that was really clever of me. *Here, sexy man, come lie down in bed next to me. No big deal, we're both adults. I'm not currently picturing all the things we could be doing other than sleeping.*

Right.

Except as soon as Wesley's weight dips the mattress next to me, my heart feels like it's about to jump out of my chest. I roll over onto my side, if only so Wesley won't see how red my face is.

I need to get laid.

Last time I had sex was six months ago, when my ex-husband invited me out to lunch. I had a few too many glasses of wine and he had his charming smolder on full blast. The smile I fell in love with all those years ago.

Yeah, that was a mistake. I conveniently forgot to mention

that little tidbit when I told Fiona about meeting up with him. She was worried enough about me having lunch with Nate.

Now I'm lying in bed next to a man about a million times hotter than my ex-husband, wearing nothing but a loose T-shirt and sleep shorts. He's shirtless, as usual. If I rolled over, I could lay my arm across his muscled chest and feel his heartbeat under my palm. I could run my fingers over his pecs and lay my cheek against his skin. I could move my head lower and hear what kind of growls he makes when he's turned on. I bet his arms would feel really good wrapped around me.

Squeezing my eyes shut, I try to regain control over my rioting body. It's not going well.

My phone buzzes from the nightstand on Wes's side of the bed. I must have put it there before going to the bathroom. He lifts his head and glances at the screen. "Who's El Bastardo?"

Speak of the devil...

"No one. Pass the phone over, I'll put it on silent."

Wesley's fingers brush mine as he hands me my phone, his eyes gleaming with interest. He rolls over onto his side, facing me. "Is that your ex-husband?"

"Mm."

"What's my name in your phone? Mr. Sex on a Stick?"

Oh, he remembered that comment, did he? I tap on my phone screen and turn it his way.

"Scowly McScowlerson?" His eyebrows inch together.

I grin. "I think it's appropriate, no?"

Wes's scowl deepens.

I laugh. "I rest my case." Flicking my phone to silent, I slide it onto the nightstand and blow Wesley a kiss. "Night-night, sugartits."

A rumble sounds from his side of the bed, sending a hot thrill rushing down my spine. It takes a long time for sleep to come.

MY BIRKIN BAG in paradise blue looks pristine when I slide it over my shoulder. It feels weird to be wearing the bag for a simple breakfast in town, but I know Alina will notice it. Maybe it's the way she touched Wes at dinner last night, or just some latent feeling of insecurity I've carried over from my marriage, but I want her to know she's not any better than me.

I run my fingers over the bag's straps, glancing at myself in the mirror. With a fitted shirt-dress and classy flats, I look like I belong next to Alina and Sean—but I feel like an imposter.

I mean, I *am* an imposter. I have no money, my online marketing business is barely making enough to keep me afloat, the café needs at least six months to start turning a profit, and I'm pretending to date the man I'm sharing a bed with. Everything about me is false.

If it weren't for Dorothy and Marge hiring me to run the hotel's marketing, I'd be living off ramen noodles and condiments. But sure, I'll wear a bag worth twelve grand.

"You sure you want to do this?" Wesley walks into the bedroom rubbing a towel over his wet hair. "I can make an excuse for you to skip breakfast. Going into town together might raise some questions. I'm sure Agnes will have told half the town we arrived together by the time we have our coffees ordered."

I shake my head. "If I don't go, it'll leave a bad impression. I told you I'd do my best to pretend to be your girlfriend, and if we were really dating, I'd be going to breakfast with you all. Plus, I need to talk to Candice about the café's social media pages, and Grant needs to talk to you about the roof. If we were a couple, we'd go down to the café together to take care of business and have a meal. Anything else wouldn't make sense."

"You're taking this surprisingly seriously. I expected you to be flippant about the whole thing. You haven't said anything sarcastic to me all morning." He frowns. "Did you hurt your head? How many fingers am I holding up?"

"Quiet, you." I roll my eyes to hide my grin. "Let's get this over with."

Even though I slept surprisingly well last night, considering the hunk of man meat who took up three quarters of the bed and hogged all the covers, I can't shake the nerves. There's so much tension between Alina, Sean, and Wesley, and I feel like I owe it to him not to make his life more difficult than it already is.

Call me a fool, but I actually like him. Even though he's gruff and scowling most of the time, I still want to help him. Fiona and I would have left town if not for the café lease, so I owe him a bit of effort at least. This town is my fresh start.

I shouldn't care. He's our landlord at the café—nothing more. But something about the way Wesley's teeth ground at dinner last night, the tension in his shoulders, and then the way he relaxed with me afterwards...it makes me want to stand by him. I know how difficult it can be to feel like the odd one out at family events. I can help him through it.

We walk downstairs together. Alina is waiting in the front living room, tapping her fingers over her phone screen. She's wearing a tight cream sweater complete with headlights on full blast, and a brown leather skirt that hits her mid-calf. Her hair is coiled into a bun on top of her head, with a few delicate tendrils framing her oval face. She looks classy and sexy and so much more elegant than me.

Wes stiffens beside me as Alina sets her phone down to look at us.

I don't know why it bothers me that she's so much more attractive than I am, or why I care that he notices. We're not even dating. It's fake. It's only for a week.

Still, when Wesley rolled over and looked at me in the dim light of the bedroom last night, I felt like I was the only woman in the world. I felt like he could *see* me, and he liked what he saw.

Now, I'm standing beside his modelesque ex-fiancée and I remember that I'm not in her league, Birkin bag or not. Wearing this purse was a stupid idea. I should have sold the damn thing years ago.

"Simone," Alina says, her face splitting into a wide smile. Her eyes take me in from head to toe, judging. They linger for just a moment on the bag before flicking up to my face. "How did you two lovebirds sleep?"

She says *lovebirds* like a jab, and I wonder if she can tell we're not actually together.

Wesley grunts something, his body leaning away from me,

as if he, too, wants to confirm that we're not an item. It hurts, even though I know it shouldn't. I stuff that feeling away, too, along with all the others that have sparked since last night.

"Slept great, thanks." I force a smile. "You?" I slide my hand over Wesley's bicep, hating that I crave the feel of his muscles under my fingers. It's a possessive move, and by the gleam in Alina's eyes, she noticed. She can tell their history bothers me.

I'm a grown woman, damn it. I shouldn't care about Alina or Wesley or how much money his family has. This is a simple business exchange. Five grand and the café lease for a week as his girlfriend. I should be ecstatic. It's a great deal for me.

I walked away from this lifestyle when I divorced Nate, and my life has only improved since then. Sure, I have fewer luxuries, but I'm happier. I'm independent. I do what I want, when I want.

But there's a certain female part of me that would love to be wanted by a man like Wesley. Everything about him makes my core ignite. Every time he's near, I can feel the heat of his body. I can sense his movements, no matter how slight, as if I'm tuned to his exact frequency.

It's not how I ever felt with Nate. With my ex-husband, it was fresh and exciting at first, and then it felt like we were going through the motions. He proposed after dating for a year, and we got married a year later. We bought a house, tried for kids, and did all the things we were supposed to do. But the sex was mechanical—even more so as the years went on. When I saw him in L.A. a couple months ago, it was honestly some of the worst sex of my life, but it scratched an itch and reminded me that I don't want to be with him. If there was any hope of igniting some fresh flame after all these years, our last romp together confirmed that it's well and truly dead.

In all honesty, I think our relationship was over when I had a miscarriage at thirty-two. Nate never looked at me the same after that.

But with Wes... Oh, I don't know. I feel more alive when he's around, even if he drives me crazy. I like seeing his frustration bubble over when I say something he doesn't like. I like the surprise in his eyes when I'm not what he expects.

I can't compete with women like Alina, though. I can't be the trophy wife.

"Slept like a rock," Wes growls, sliding his hand across my back. His touch sends sparks dancing across my skin. I lean into him, freezing when his mouth dips down toward me. He brushes his lips over my cheek, his breath warm and minty. If I turned my head a fraction of an inch, I could kiss him.

Wes pulls away, holding my gaze for a moment. "I'll be right back. Bathroom." He turns around, but it's not until he turns the corner that I realize both Alina and I were watching him walk away.

I take a seat, smiling awkwardly at Wes's ex-fiancée.

Six more days. I can do six days.

"He's such a dear, isn't he? He's always been a sweetheart." Alina braids her fingers over her crossed legs. Her eyes flash, and I hear the unspoken words: *I had him first. I know him better than you do. You can't compete with the memory of me.*

My smile feels like a grimace. "He sure is."

. . .

AGNES'S FACE looks like thunder. "Get your dirty paws off my books, you hag."

Dorothy rears back, her hand on her chest. "I'm trying to *buy* one of them, Agnes. Last time I checked, they were for sale. Isn't that the whole reason you have a display next to the cash register?"

Agnes pulls herself up to all her four-foot-nine glory. "I wasn't aware you could even read, Dorothy."

"Ha-ha." Dorothy rolls her eyes. "Just let me buy the damn book, you troglodyte."

"Huh. That's a big word. Maybe you can read after all." She turns to her grandson. "Did you know Dorothy knew words with more than one syllable?"

Rudy bites his lip. He glances beside him at Candice, whose face is in her hands. Her hip is leaning against a tall banner with the bookstore's logo and address on it. They must have been setting up the new display. That was quick.

Rudy reaches over to put a hand on Candice's shoulder. There's softness in the movement—but before I can examine it further, a growl makes me turn back to the feuding women.

Dorothy's face grows nearly scarlet. "Are you going to stand there all day scaring customers away? How have you managed to run the bookstore for so long without driving it into the ground?"

Dorothy's dress is an explosion of floral print. Her hair is wrapped in a polka-dot headscarf, and her chunky jewelry swings with every movement of her head. Agnes, in head-to-toe brown, looks like she's about to explode.

Uh-oh. I need to stop this before they come to blows.

I wave my hands toward a table, and Wesley leads his uncle and ex-fiancée over to it. Sven, our barista, is cringing behind the counter looking shell-shocked. Allie and Clancy are wiping down a table on the other end of the café, making no secret that they've been watching the whole thing without any intention of intervening.

Guess it's down to me. Simone McMaster, human fire extinguisher. Specialties include averting interpersonal disasters and pacifying all types of feuds. Family, neighbor, retiree...

"Ladies!" I paint a smile on my face. "Good morning."

"This colorblind witch is tampering with my book display," Agnes says, whirling on me.

"Colorblind witch?" Dorothy's lips pinch together. Oh, no. That's the expression she makes right before things start flying across the room. Shoes, books, coffee mugs—we could have projectiles in moments.

"Look at the way you're dressed, Dorothy. You're either colorblind or you're in denial about it. Have they taken your driver's license away yet? I might need to make a phone call to the DMV."

I take a deep breath. Defusing this situation will require delicate diplomacy. Both ladies have egos the size of a football stadium and enough righteous anger to fill every seat. I glance over my shoulder for a moment to see Wesley watching me, a smile playing over his full lips. Clearly, he has no intention of helping. Jerk.

Okay, be diplomatic. Nice and easy, keep everyone happy.

"One more word out of either of you and you'll be barred from the café for life," I snap. There. Diplomatic.

Agnes and Dorothy whirl to look at me, looking offended and furious—the full weight of their anger directed right at me.

"Excuse me?" Agnes plants a hand on her hip. Her body is short and squat, but I've seen her move. She's fast. I bend my knees sightly, ready to dart out of the way if she chooses to take a swing at me. "Did you just threaten to throw us out?"

"We were just discussing the latest bestsellers, Simone. No need to be rude." Dorothy smooths her hands over her hips.

"Discussing the latest bestsellers?" I arch my brows. That's one way of describing the potential war that was brewing a moment ago.

Agnes picks up a book from the display. "This is ridiculous. Where's my coffee?"

"Here," Clancy says, an angelic smile on her face. "I put an extra sleeve on it so you wouldn't burn your fingers."

"You're a sweetheart." Agnes chucks Clancy's cheek. "At least someone in here has some manners."

Allie gives Dorothy her drink, and the two old ladies grumble some more as they make their way out of the café. Agnes exits, then Eli appears in the doorway.

Dorothy startles back, looking the silver-haired driver up and down. He clears his throat, bows—a real one this time, not the piddly half-bow Wes and I earned—and steps out of the way. The two of them exchange a lingering glance as Dorothy walks out the door. There's an extra swish in her hips as she turns toward the hotel, and Eli definitely notices.

I shake my head. This is too much for me so early in the morning.

Clancy's eyes shine as they meet mine. "You should become a mediator, Simone. You have a talent for it."

"Quiet, you."

Clancy giggles. She exchanges a glance with Allie, then takes a step toward me. Her eyes gleam with teenage mischief. "Alec's party is tonight. The way I look at it, you owe me a favor for getting Agnes out of here when she wanted to rip your head off."

I hold up a hand. "I'm going to stop you right there. Not going to happen."

Clancy pouts, jerking her head toward the back room, and the two of them scamper away.

I take a deep breath, letting my shoulders drop.

My nerves are frayed. Between pretending to be Wesley's girlfriend, managing the café's social media, trying to keep my online marketing clients happy, fielding blackmail attempts by a fifteen-year-old, and stepping into vicious town feuds, I'm not sure I'll survive the next week. Next thing, my ex-husband will walk through the door and beg me to give him another shot. With my luck, he'll drop to his knees and let everyone know we slept together a few months ago, and my charade with Wesley will be ruined.

The bell above the café door jingles and I whip my head around, then let out a sigh when a woman in her thirties walks through with two kids in tow. Not El Bastardo. Thank goodness.

"You look like you need a long, hot bath and a massage just to get through the rest of the day," Wesley's voice says next to my ear.

I spin around to see him standing there in all his muscled

glory, light playing in his green eyes. I cross my arms, popping a brow. "Are you offering your services?"

His lips tug, those pesky dimples making an appearance. My knees feel weak. Just what I need now—a sexy man turning his charm up to the max when I'm vulnerable. This isn't going to end well.

"Let me buy you breakfast first." His voice is a low growl that makes something tighten in my gut. His eyes linger on mine, then drop down to my lips for a brief moment.

He needs to stop doing that. Every time he looks at my mouth, my whole body is bathed in flames. I won't be able to make it through the week if I have to change my underwear every five minutes.

I let out a breath. "Fine. Breakfast and a very large...coffee." I almost said penis. I literally almost said penis right then. What the hell is wrong with me?

He moves to the counter and orders our food and drinks. He grabs a number for the table and turns to look at me, winking. He *winks*. Broody McGrumperson has smiled *and* winked at me today. The world has gone mad.

Just when Wes and I turn to our table, a deafening crash sounds from the back of the café, and I know I won't be able to enjoy my breakfast and coffee after all.

EIGHT

WESLEY

SIMONE LOOKS like she's about to snap. I put my hand on her lower back again. I can't help touching her. "I'll go check it out," I tell her, my breath ruffling a strand of her hair. "Grant sent me a text this morning, it's probably him back there messing with the roof."

She lets out a long breath. "You're just trying to avoid your uncle and Alina. Even Eli's sitting at a different table."

I grin—been doing a lot of that lately—and shrug. "So what if I am?"

"Fine. Go." She leans into me slightly, and for a moment I think she's going to kiss me.

We both freeze and take a step away from each other. A flush creeps over Simone's cheeks as she shakes her head, mumbling something I don't quite catch. Maybe this pretending is going to our heads. It's too easy to feel like it's real.

Without another word, I stalk to the back of the café. Even

though I didn't want to lease this space to anyone, it feels good to be here again. My parents loved this place. They poured their everything into it and made it someplace special for the whole town.

I thought letting other people set up shop in here would feel like a betrayal, but it's the opposite. I think my parents would be happy that the space is being used. It's honoring their memory by continuing the business they started all those years ago.

Plus, it feels like home. I walk down the narrow hallway toward the back room and notice an old photo of my parents and me when the place first opened. They kept the old photos up. My heart squeezes, and it takes me a moment to pull myself together. I push open a door marked *Staff Only*.

Grant looks up at me from his spot on the floor, boxes and bags of coffee strewn around him, a wire shelf tipped over beside him. He grimaces. "Oops."

I extend a hand and help him to his feet. "What happened?"

"I was trying to clear this space out so we can get to work on the roof. The shelf wasn't secured to the wall and when I grabbed a box off the top shelf, it fell over. Missed crushing my leg by a hair."

"Maybe Candice is right. This place is cursed." I grin. "My parents might be haunting it."

"Don't tell her that. She's superstitious enough as it is."

I laugh, grabbing a few big bags of coffee beans off the floor. When I follow Grant outside, I see a temporary shed set up at the back of the building. Grant hauls a few boxes from the storage room into the shed and I follow, making quick work of the mess. Within minutes, the storage room is clear, the shelf righted, and both of us sweaty and covered in dust and coffee particles.

Glancing up at the patch of plywood covering the hole, I let out a grunt. "Simone told me you had a few quotes to discuss with me?"

"You got time to jump on the roof for a second? I know your family's in town…"

"Sure." Any excuse not to go back out there and sit across from Alina and my uncle. A twinge of guilt hits me in the chest, but it's not because I'm not spending time with my family—it's because I'm leaving Simone to deal with them on her own.

Grant grabs a ladder out of the shed and props it against the back of the café building. He goes up first, and I follow. The pitch of the roof is fairly gentle, so we're able to stand around the damaged section to survey the damage. Grant lifts the plywood off the hole and slides it across the shingles before straightening up next to me.

"A few purlins have quite a bit of dry rot. We might be able to fix them by laminating them with healthy wood, but it looks like at least one of them will have to be completely replaced. The major support beams and columns for the building are intact, and it looks like localized damage. Must have been a dip in the roof that collected water in this area."

"How long and how much?"

Grant grins. "No bullshit with you, huh." He tells me he's talking to roofing companies. They're all busy right now, but he's confident it'll get done within four weeks—and definitely before Christmas.

I nod. "Fine. It's got to be fixed, so I don't have much of a choice."

"The joys of being a landlord."

I snort, taking one last look at the hole. I take a step toward it—I'm not even sure why. Walking on rotten roof supports is a very dumb idea. As soon as I do, I regret it. My foot goes straight through a portion of the roof and my body jerks downward. I yell in shock and pain. My heart jumps to my throat as my stomach bottoms out. I slide down to my chest, head and arms poking above the roof, legs dangling below.

The whole thing takes half a second, then I'm stuck. I've just made a second hole in the roof. Great. "Shit."

Grant holds out his hand and tries to pull me out.

I grunt and stop him, watching a bit of blood soak through my shirt. "Something's poking me."

Understatement of the year. It feels like my entire torso has been scratched to shit.

"What the hell is going on here?" A voice comes through the original hole in the roof. A second later, Simone's red hair comes into view.

I give her a smile and a wave. "Hey, babe."

Grant gives me a knowing grin. Huh.

Simone points in my direction. "Your feet are dangling through the roof."

"Are they? Wow. Go figure."

"Your lack of concern is disconcerting." She crosses her arms, lips pinched together. Her eyes are wide though, betraying worry. She sucks her bottom lip between her teeth, the movement catching my eye. Even as I dangle stuck halfway through a rotten roof, I still can't help but notice her lips. Not good.

"I'm going to get a ladder. Is the roof strong enough for you to pull yourself out if your legs are supported?" She frowns, glancing at my lower body. "You're bleeding."

"I'm fine."

"I'll stay up here to help pull him out. The ladder's out here," Grant calls out, staying far away from the hole in the roof. Smart man.

A second later, the ladder moves from the edge of the roof. I wince, a piece of wood jabbing my side. Swinging my legs slightly, I try to reduce some of the pressure on the wound. There's a large piece of wood poking my side. I'm going to be sore as hell after this. Not to mention the mountain of teasing Simone will shovel my way. I'll never hear the end of it.

I struggle again, trying to relieve some of the pressure on my side. The rotten wood of the roof is in bad shape, though—much worse than I realized. When I push against it to relieve some pressure on my wound, a chunk comes off in my hand. I don't have time to react as wood and shingles crumble around me, the world rushes past me again, and I fall through.

Simone screams as I drop, the ladder clattering to the floor a second before I hit the ground. My ankle crunches and pain shatters through me. I cry out, my eyes watering, body crumpled on the ground. Fuck.

In an instant, Simone's beside me, her hands on my face, my chest. Her eyes are wild, panicked. "Wes. Oh no, oh no. Are you okay?"

I groan, swallowing down pain-induced vomit. I gasp. "Fine.

I'm fine." I suck in a breath as I try to lift my leg, a sharp pain stabbing my ankle. That doesn't feel good.

"I'm calling an ambulance."

"I don't need an ambulance."

"Quiet, you idiot." Simone jumps to her feet and rushes out the storeroom door.

I lie back, letting out a breath.

Grant's voice comes through from the roof. "You okay, buddy?"

"Never been better."

A chuckle answers back, Grant's face poking through the new, smaller hole in the roof above me.

Simone enters the room, her brows drawn so close she looks like she's about to start crying. She scans my body, clutching her phone.

"I don't need an ambulance, Simone. Just drive me to the hospital. I think my ankle is broken."

She pinches the bridge of her nose. She's not faking this. Maybe she does care about me for real, even a little bit. Her shoulders drop and she shakes her head. "You stupid, idiotic, moronic man."

"I'm guessing the name-calling means you care." I flash her the type of grin that always makes her blush.

"Hey, Simone?" Grant calls out from above our heads. "Would you mind bringing the ladder back here so I can come down? I'll help you load the invalid up in his car." His eyes dart from me to Simone, a sparkle in his gaze.

Simone stands up again, her eyes lingering on me. "Sure. The invalid can lie on the floor and think about his mistakes."

My grin widens, and Simone rewards me with a blush.

TEN MINUTES LATER, I've hopped my way to the passenger seat of my truck, one arm slung around Grant and the other around Simone. There's a bag of ice strapped to my ankle and a wad of gauze taped to my side. The pain is so bad I think I might pass out, and I sit back in the truck with a groan. My uncle and Alina are standing next to the truck as I roll the window down, their eyes wide.

Simone bursts through the café door and launches herself into the driver's seat. She puts a takeaway container on my lap and slides two coffees in the cupholder. "You ruined my breakfast, you knucklehead."

"Glad to hear you're so concerned for my health."

"Next time you go traipsing around on rotten roofs, try to wear a harness or something, yeah? Or better yet, use that peabrain of yours and try *not* traipsing around on half-collapsed roofs."

My uncle chuckles, shaking his head. "I'm glad you've found someone who cares about you, Wesley. Even though they can nag your ear off, a good woman will always be by your side." He slides his arm around Alina, and I don't know if it's a jab or a genuine compliment. I choose to ignore it altogether.

"Sorry about this. If you need a ride back to the house, Grant offered to take you. Otherwise the hotel is next door—they should be able to give you a map of the town and surrounding attractions. It's not far to walk back, and the forest is nice this time of year. They can call a cab for you otherwise."

"We'll be fine." Alina's fingers curl over the window next to me. "You take care, okay?" Her eyes are wide, worried. The weak part of me likes that she cares.

I grunt at them, nod, and Simone starts driving.

She says nothing for a few minutes, then finally glances over at me and shakes her head. "You're an idiot, you know that? What were you thinking, going up there? You and Grant could have broken your necks. Fiona would have been heartbroken!"

"So you're more worried about Fiona losing her new boyfriend than you are about me?"

"Yes." Her eyes shoot flames. "I'm mad at you."

"Cute. Our first fight."

Her fingers tighten on the steering wheel.

I reach for one of the coffees and flip open the container on my lap. A breakfast wrap stares back at me.

"That's mine," Simone says. "If you need surgery, you won't be allowed to eat."

"I don't need surgery."

"I wasn't aware you were a doctor, Wes." Her eyes do that fiery thing again. "No eating until they clear you. You shouldn't even be drinking coffee. Which reminds me—those are both for me, and they still won't be enough. Don't touch."

"Yes, ma'am."

"Call me ma'am again and I'll break your other ankle."

A grin tugs at my lips. "I like you like this."

"Like what? Mad at you? Setting aside all the responsibilities and important things in my life so I can babysit you at the hospital?"

"When your walls are down. It was weird seeing you behave so appropriately last night. Threw me off."

"I always behave appropriately." She grinds her teeth, which only makes me smile wider.

"Yeah, sure. Like when you told Agnes and Dorothy you'd bar them from the café for life."

"Nothing unites people like a common enemy."

I laugh, drawing Simone's wide-eyed gaze. She shakes her head and turns to the road again, clamping her lips shut until we arrive at the hospital. I don't protest when she rolls a wheelchair to the car, and I accept her help when I hop my way into the seat.

In all honestly, my ankle is killing me. It's throbbing like crazy, and it feels like my shoe is so tight it might explode. The wound on my side has leaked through the gauze, and I feel weak and sweaty.

Simone leans down and extends the leg rest on the wheelchair, then puts her hand on my shoulder and lets out a sigh. "Let's get you fixed up."

"You should be thanking me, Simone."

"Uh-huh." A pop of her brow. "Why's that?"

"I shaved a whole day off the week. You won't have to interact with my uncle and Alina for at least a few hours."

"Are you planning on breaking a bone every day for the week? Because there are better ways of dealing with difficult family members."

I chuckle, leaning my head back against the edge of the wheelchair. Simone's body is just behind me, close enough to feel its heat. Citrus and lavender. Mm.

She wheels me through the sliding glass doors and gets in line for the triage nurse, glancing back at me every few minutes.

I take back what I said about Alina. I don't care if she's worried about me or not. The flash of concern in her face when she stood outside my truck doesn't compare to the feeling of Simone's worried anger, her gentle touch, and the time she's taking to make sure I'm okay.

When she sits down next to me and plucks the takeout container from my lap, the scowl she throws me only makes my heart thump harder. "This was so not part of the deal," she says, flipping open the top of the container to grab half her breakfast sandwich. "I might have to renegotiate the rent on the café space by the end of the week."

"I'm open to renegotiation." My voice comes out like a growl, and I clamp my lips shut. I didn't mean that to sound so... sexual.

Simone holds my gaze for a moment, her breaths shallow, body completely still. Finally, she shakes her head and turns to her breakfast.

MY ANKLE IS BROKEN. It takes thirteen hours of waiting, x-rays, pain meds, and air cast fittings before Simone and I leave the hospital again. She looks exhausted, her red hair a frizzy halo around her face. My stomach grumbles so loud she turns her head toward me. "Food?"

I grunt in acknowledgement.

Simone nods, helping me into the truck. We pass a twenty-four-hour diner and Simone pulls in, coming around once again to help me out of the vehicle. I have crutches now, and Simone hovers near, holding them, until I'm ready to start swinging my way to the door.

She doesn't complain. Doesn't give me shit about being irresponsible and reckless. Doesn't do anything except stand next to me and make sure I don't stumble and fall.

We slide into a booth and order an obscene amount of food. Simone's stack of pancakes gets drowned in enough syrup to fill a lake, and I eat a truckload of bacon and sausage. We don't speak, but in a way it feels more intimate than any date I've ever been on.

When I lean back, sated, the pain in my ankle nothing but a dull throb, Simone gives me a tired smile. "Ready to go home?"

I nod. It feels good to hear her call my house home, but I'm too tired to examine that thought as closely as I should. I just hobble to the truck and let her drive me back to Heart's Cove.

NINE
SIMONE

WES IS SNORING when my phone rings. I grab it, cringing, and press the side button to get the ringer to quiet down, but Wes hasn't even twitched. He's dead to the world. That's good. I could tell by the lines in his face today that he was in a lot of pain. I hated seeing the sharpness in his eyes and the winces he tried so hard to hide. Idiot man. Who goes up on a roof when they know the support beams are rotten? Does he have a death wish? He and Grant should know better.

My phone vibrates in my hand, and I finally manage to read the name on the screen. Clancy. Why is my best friend's fifteen-year-old kid calling me at nearly midnight?

Frowning, I swipe to answer and put it to my ear. "Clancy?"

Music thumps in the background and something rustles, as if she's walking away from the noise. Snarky, teenaged, and with a rebellious streak the size of a semi-truck, Clancy is more than a handful—and she obviously decided to go to the party she told me about. Did she call me to gloat?

When she speaks, though, her voice is small. "Simone, I need help."

I sit up straight, glance at Wes's prone body, and slip out of the bedroom. "Tell me."

Turns out Clancy did go to that boy's party. She and Allie told their parents they were sleeping at each other's houses and met up in town, got a lift from an older girl, and went to the party without telling anyone. Things at the party are getting out of hand, and she needs someone to come get her. Since Grant and Fiona would lock her up in the house and never let her leave for lying to them, that someone is me. Lovely.

"I'm on my way."

"Thank you." Clancy's voice cracks when she speaks, and something softens in my chest. She's a good kid. Hell, I did worse than sneaking out for a crush's party when I was her age. I was an absolute terror, and I had wonderful parents and a stable upbringing.

Clancy grew up thinking her father abandoned her while she watched her mother slowly poison herself with alcohol. It wasn't until she showed up in town, demanding answers from Grant, that things changed. The girl has been through more than any fifteen-year-old should, and a few bumps are expected.

Now she's Grant and Fiona's kid, and I'm apparently her get-out-of-jail-free card.

"Heading out again?" Alina says as I slip on my shoes.

I look up to see her leaning a shoulder against the wall, arms crossed. I hadn't heard her approach. I grunt in response. Wes must be rubbing off on me. "It seems I'm running a taxi service now."

She takes a step closer to me. "How's Wesley? You two went straight upstairs when you got home. I didn't get a chance to see him."

As if it's her right to see her ex-fiancé whenever she wishes. As if she's the important person in this situation. Give me a break.

"His ankle is broken in three places. Serves him right for stomping around on a half-collapsed roof."

"That's not very kind of you," she admonishes, her perfectly groomed brows drawing together. "He could have been seriously hurt."

You know what? I'm about done with this conversation. I straighten up and give her my hardest stare. "He's fine. He's sleeping. I need to go rescue another poor soul from themselves now, otherwise I'd be sleeping, too. Is there anything you need?"

She rears back as if I slapped her, then shakes her head. "No."

"I'll see you in the morning, then."

"Goodnight."

I might have slammed the door a bit too hard just there. Oops. Wes's truck roars to life and I back out of the driveway, glancing at my phone to confirm the address Clancy sent me. Half an hour later, I pull up on a house pulsing with light and music in a quiet suburb. How the neighbors haven't called the cops yet, I have no idea.

Two blond girls stand up from their spot on the curb. One curly head, one pin-straight. Allie and Clancy.

I stop the truck and jerk my head to say, *Get in.*

The two girls clamber inside and slam the door. I wait until they have their seatbelts on before I start driving.

Silence settles like a thick blanket in the cab of the truck. I let it drag on for a minute, then two...

"Thanks, Simone."

Finally.

"Like pulling teeth getting that out of you," I grumble. I'm tired and grumpy and I've been running around saving people all day. Still, I grip the steering wheel and force myself to slowly inhale and exhale. There. Slightly better.

"So," I start, my voice nice and neutral, "what happened? Did you have a plan for getting back to Heart's Cove?"

"Alec said he'd drive us." Clancy stares out the window as Allie crosses her arms beside me. This is an older-style truck, with one long bench in the cab. Thankfully Wes keeps it clean, otherwise there'd be no room for the three of us. Allie's pressed up against my side as it is, Clancy against hers.

They're obviously not in a chatty mood. Maybe a bit of prompting will help. "But?"

"But he was drinking when we got there, and I could tell he was drunk when he grabbed his keys to drive us back. I didn't want to get in the car with him."

A sigh escapes my lips. It's hard to be mad at a fifteen-year-old when she made the right decision. I nod. "Okay. Then what happened?"

"He threw us out. Said we were losers." Clancy's voice wobbles, and my heart breaks. Stupid boys. They turn into stupid men, and whether you're fifteen or forty-five, they somehow end up ruining a perfectly good day.

"Oh, Clancy. He's not worth the dirt off your shoe."

"Yeah." She lets out a sigh and shakes her head, then looks over at me. "Please don't tell my dad."

"Clancy..."

"Please, Simone. That's why I called you!"

"I have to tell Grant. I can't lie."

"It wouldn't be lying. It would just be not volunteering the information."

"That's lying by omission, Clancy."

"I'll tell them you're dating Wes!"

I whip my head to stare at her. "What?"

"I talked to that chick you walked in with. She asked me how long you were dating, and it all made sense. You leaving Wes's cabin, driving around in Wes's truck..."

"All right, Sherlock." I grind my teeth. This situation is complicated enough as is. I don't need Clancy adding fuel to the flames. "I don't negotiate with terrorists, and I'm not keeping secrets like this from your parents."

"My dad won't understand, Simone. We go to therapy together every week, and still he won't let me anywhere near parties or alcohol."

"You think he might have a reason for that?" Okay, now *I* sound like a snarky teenager. I need sleep.

"Simone, I didn't drink at the party. Neither did Allie. I don't *want* to drink alcohol, and I don't want to party, but I just wanted to hang out with my friends. Dad won't understand that. He'll think

I'm like my mom and all I want to do is get drunk. I don't! But he's so worried about me, he won't let me explain. I didn't drink. I didn't get in a car with someone who was drinking. I called an adult."

"She didn't have any alcohol, Simone," Allie says. "Neither of us did. We're not stupid."

It's been a long day. That's my excuse for even entertaining this ridiculous plan. I know if I keep a secret from Grant and Fiona, it'll blow up in my face. I *know* that, yet I'm considering it. I don't want to punish Clancy and Allie for making good decisions and calling me. I don't want them to hesitate to call someone next time they're in trouble.

"So, whose house am I dropping you off at?" I look at Allie. "Yours?"

Allie bites her lip, looking at me with big blue eyes. Give her four or five years and she'll be an absolute heartbreaker. Candice won't know what's hit her when boys start lining up outside her front door to drool over her daughter.

"My mom thinks I'm at Clancy's place," Allie says.

"And my dad thinks I'm at Allie's."

I make a low noise at the back of my throat. "Right, you told me that. Classic. I did that once or twice, too."

"Can we sleep at your apartment? You're not even there, are you?" Clancy's eyes bore holes in the side of my head. "I saw you driving toward Wes's house, and that's the direction you came from this morning. You're staying with him, aren't you? Are you really dating him? Since when?"

This is ridiculous. I should drive both girls to their respective homes. I shouldn't let two teenage girls dictate this situation

—but I'm so, so tired. This day has lasted about three years. If I drive them to each other's house, I'll have to explain the situation. I'll have to deal with two sets of parents demanding answers, and who knows how long that'll take?

I need sleep. Badly.

"You can sleep at my apartment for one night. I'll be there at seven o'clock tomorrow morning, and then you need to go home. If you touch any of my stuff, I'll cut off your fingers." I really need to stop threatening people with bodily harm. I take a deep breath. "Tomorrow, you go home and you tell your parents the truth. I'm trusting you to do that, okay? You have to tell them where you went and what you did. I won't keep this secret for you."

The two girls exchange a glance. Tension unwinds from their bodies, and they slump against the seats. "Okay."

This is a bad idea. I'm not being a responsible adult. Fiona will kill me when she finds out—but the girls are safe, they made a good decision, and the least I can do is give them a night to sort out their plan for coming clean to their parents.

A short while later, I unlock my apartment and herd the girls inside. They jump into my bed without hesitation, giggling, and I plant my hands on my hips. "Seven o'clock."

"We won't touch anything."

"And you'll tell your parents where you were."

"We promise." Clancy smiles at me, angelic. Right.

Sighing, I nod. "Fine." I say goodbye and head back to the truck. By the time I climb into bed beside Wesley, my whole body is sore. Knees, back, neck—everything. I feel about four hundred years old. I groan as I sink into the pillows, and Wesley turns toward me. He wraps his arm around my waist and pulls me to him, my back to his front.

Everything inside me goes still. I freeze, heart thumping, eyes wide open.

His breathing is steady. He did that in his sleep.

Slowly, my heartbeat returns to normal. The weight of Wesley's arm across my waist is comforting. Safe. His body at my back is impossibly warm and nice.

It's been a long time since I shared a bed with a man. Since I cuddled. I should probably fight this feeling, but my eyelids are heavy. I'm so very tired, and this is so very comfortable.

It means nothing, though. He wanted a warm body next to him while he slept. I want the same.

Just because we fit together like two jigsaw pieces doesn't mean this relationship is real. It doesn't mean my worry for him today gnawed at every frayed nerve. It doesn't mean I care about him. Not at all.

TEN

JEN

AS THE BAKER of the four-woman circus that created the Four Cups Café, I feel a huge amount of responsibility to do my job well. So, I always get to work early. It gives me time to get set up without anyone else around. Space to set out my equipment, to plan my bakes, to be as precise as I want to be.

The other restaurant where I work—a true foodie's place with an ever-changing degustation menu and a Michelin star to boot—is a hive of activity and shouting. Four Cups has been my haven for over a month, a place where I can just do what I do best. Bake.

But then...there's Fallon. That smiley, muscular, bearded beauty of a man. A man who, for some unknown reason, has decided that he, too, likes to get to work early. I'm only here three days a week! And he does all his prep work in the afternoon, yet as soon as I unlock the door, I hear his music, his banging, his chopping and frying, and *voice*.

Ugh.

Candice, Fiona, and Simone don't seem to understand when I say he's a damn nuisance. They just see how much customers love his food, but they don't have to work with him.

The man who crowds the kitchen, eyeballing every recipe and prancing around like some sort of two-hundred-and-fifty-pound ballerina. Ballerino? Whatever.

This morning, I thought I'd get here even earlier. Five-fifteen. The sky is grey, the sun not poking above the horizon yet. The days are getting shorter. It won't be up for another hour. Most people are asleep.

But you know who isn't asleep like he should be?

Fallon freaking Richter. I push the café door open and hear his stupid folk-rock music blaring through the restaurant. Flicking the button on the speaker, I cross my arms. "Would it kill you to let me have a few minutes here by myself in the morning? You don't even need all this extra time. All you end up doing is waiting around for the first people to show up for breakfast at seven or eight o'clock. Your prep is done from yesterday. You don't need to be here before six."

"But then I wouldn't get the pleasure of seeing your scowling face every morning." He flashes a smile at me that I'm sure makes women weak in the knees.

He probably thinks it works on me.

His straight, even teeth and tightly cropped beard do nothing for me. Yes, he's big and strong and he looks like he could throw me over his shoulder without an ounce of effort, but there are so many things about him that turn me off.

Like his stupid, cheeky grin and the way he makes fun of

my baking process. It's too precise for his taste, apparently. He thinks weighing ingredients is ridiculous, but he doesn't seem to understand that baking isn't the same thing as frying an egg and putting it on a piece of sourdough.

Fallon leans his hip against a stainless-steel countertop as his eyes track my movements through the kitchen. "I took out your kitchen scale. It needed a new battery, so I replaced it."

My hands freeze as they work to tie my apron, my back to Fallon. "You didn't have to do that. I'd rather you not touch my stuff."

"That's a funny way of saying thank you."

I throw him a glance over my shoulder, hoping it conveys how much I resent his presence.

He starts whistling in response.

Sighing, I grip the edge of the worktop and count to ten. I make it to eight, then let out a breath and get to work. I've got sourdough proofing in the refrigerator, so I pull it out, shape it, and set it aside for its final rise. Before I know it half an hour has passed, and a mug appears next to me.

Fallon's arm is ridiculously muscular. The cup looks like a child's toy in his hand. I let my gaze crawl up his tattooed forearm, over his muscular bicep, and all the way to his face.

He really is quite handsome. Objectively speaking.

"Here. A peace offering. Does it really bother you that I'm here early every morning?"

"Yes, it really does."

"Tomorrow, I'll come in at six. You'll have a whole forty-five minutes to yourself."

I nod. "That would be nice."

He moves away on silent feet, grabs a knife, and starts chopping chives into teeny tiny pieces without even looking. I think he might be showing off.

I stare at the mug of hot liquid, inhaling the scent of spices—cinnamon, cloves, cardamon. This is milky, sweet chai. I glance at Fallon's broad back, frowning. How did he know?

I don't drink coffee—never liked the stuff—but masala chai is my drink. I rarely have it while I'm in the kitchen, and the tea bags we sell at the café taste watered down and weak, but once in a while I bring my own in a travel mug. Fallon must have smelled it.

My bread needs another few minutes to rest before it goes in the oven, so I lean against the counter and give in. This chai smells incredible, and when it hits my tongue—whoa. I must make a noise, because Fallon turns around with a grin on his face.

"Good?"

"Really good," I answer, eyebrows inching up. "What brand is this? It's not the stuff we sell out there." I jerk my head toward the front of house.

"Richter brand." He winks.

"Where did you learn to make tea like this?"

"My mom's half Indian," he answers. "Grew up on the stuff."

I tilt my head. He does have deep brown, almost black hair and his skin is darker than mine. Blue eyes, almond-shaped. The color must come from the other side of the family. Full lips, a burgundy-brown shade. I'd never really noticed the color of them before. They're nice lips. They look soft. His cropped beard hides a defined jaw, especially with the hair net he hooks around his chin.

"Are you dissecting my facial features right now?" He arches a thick, dark eyebrow.

A blush creeps over my cheeks. "No." I put the delicious tea down and pop my bread in the oven, make some excuse to escape the kitchen with my drink, and head out the front door just in time to see Allie and Clancy exiting Simone's apartment. Huh. Weird.

I stare at them through the window, watching them carefully close the door and lean their heads close together. The two teenagers hug, then head in opposite directions. I wonder what they were doing at Simone's. I'll ask Fiona when she gets here.

Glancing at the clock, I realize it's already past six. Sven will be arriving to open up the front of the café any minute, which means I need to get cracking on brownies and cheesecake to replace what we've sold already. I shuffle back to the kitchen, steal a glance at Fallon as he glides through the space, and get to work.

The man makes good tea. I'll give him that.

Doesn't mean he doesn't drive me crazy.

ELEVEN
WESLEY

I WAKE up with my arm around Simone's waist and my hard cock pressed up against her ass.

Shit. Damn. Shit.

My pulse takes off as my eyes snap open, my erection merrily throbbing against her body with every heartbeat. Simone's snoring softly, which means she's asleep. Thank God.

Slowly, I pull my arm away and put some space between our bodies. Simone lets out a small whimper of protest, angling her body against mine. Her hip brushes my cock again, which bounces in response. I pull away, wincing when pain lances through my leg.

Right, my ankle's broken. How could I forget? I glance down at the massive cast propped on a stack of pillows, then roll away a bit more. Hooking my hands under my knee, I swing my injured leg off the bed and pause, catching my breath. My crutches are propped next to the bed, and a glass of water with pain medication is waiting for me on the nightstand. Simone must have done that last night.

I glance over my shoulder at her sleeping form. Her hair is splayed over the white pillows, fiery and wild. Her heart-shaped face is totally calm, lips slightly open as she sleeps. She looks... Never mind. It doesn't matter how she looks.

Something squeezes in my chest, and I tear my gaze away. I haven't slept next to a woman in a long, long time. Whatever's happening below my belt is just a physical response. It's natural. It doesn't mean anything.

I throw the pain pills down my throat and take a big gulp of water, then reach for the crutches. Simone doesn't wake as I lift myself up and head downstairs. The smell of bacon wafts toward me, and I find Eli in the kitchen, humming to himself. Having Sean and Alina here isn't my idea of fun, but I could definitely get used to Eli's cooking.

He nods to the table and I sit down, accepting a cup of coffee with a grateful grunt.

"How's the ankle?"

"Broken."

Eli returns to the kitchen, coming back a moment later with a plate of bacon, eggs, and perfectly golden toast. He pauses for a moment, tilting his head. "Thank you for letting me stay at the cabin."

I pause, then nod. Right, Simone set it up for him. There's been so much going on, I haven't been able to keep track of everything. "No problem, Eli. You got everything you need?"

"I do. The cabin is well stocked. Looks lived-in." His eyes

meet mine, and the meaning is clear: *I know you've been living there.*

Great. Wonderful. Fantastic.

I nod, reaching for a piece of bacon. "It sure is. My man-cave."

He stares at me for a moment longer and backs away when my uncle appears.

Sean lands in the chair across from me and doesn't even look at Eli as the older man serves him his coffee and breakfast. He must be used to being waited on hand and foot. "I like it here," Sean announces.

"Oh?" I scoop some scrambled eggs onto my fork.

"This town has grown a lot since I grew up here. It feels like coming home."

"Uh-huh," I answer, unable to form actual words. Where is he going with this?

"Alina and I have decided to stay."

Oh. *Oh.*

My fork stays suspended halfway to my mouth as I gape at him across the table. "You want to stay?"

He nods. "Alina and I will rent somewhere to get out of your hair. You and Simone seem happy together, we don't want to intrude. Perhaps Eli could remain at the cabin?"

Eli's eyes dart toward me, and I ignore the gaze. I find myself nodding, agreeing, even though my mind hasn't caught up. Staying? They're...staying?

My uncle continues. "I think I could open a shop here. We've been looking for new locations, and Heart's Cove is growing. People love the outdoors, and there aren't any specialized sporting goods stores for thirty miles."

My fork makes it to my mouth and I chew slowly, trying to digest this new information. He wants to stay. He wants to set up a store, which means he'll be staying for a long while. Weeks, months, even. Maybe...forever.

He thinks Simone and I are happy and...together.

Oh, shit. Oh, no.

As if she could sense my thoughts, Simone appears in the kitchen. She smiles at Eli, plucking a piece of bacon from the plate beside him and saying something that makes him laugh. She waves him away when he tries to pour her coffee for her and opens the refrigerator to show him something.

My uncle is talking, but I don't hear it. I'm just watching Simone in the kitchen, sleep lining her eyes, smiling at my uncle's butler like he's an old friend. And Eli's smiling back. He never smiles at me like that, like I'm a favorite nephew of his.

Simone pats his arm and fixes herself a plate before coming to sit to my left. She's facing the big windows that look out on the ocean and lets out a long sigh. "I don't think I could ever get sick of that view."

"You won't have to," my uncle says, the meaning of his words clear. He thinks Simone and I will get married. He thinks the trust will be available to me. "I was just telling Wesley that I can see you two are happy here together."

Her eyebrows arch as she looks at my uncle, then at me. "We are."

My uncle continues, oblivious to the panic starting to flare in Simone's eyes. "I think Heart's Cove would be a great location for one of my stores. It's growing, has a bustling tourist economy, and there aren't any similar stores in the area."

Simone puts her cup of coffee down and turns to look at him. "You want to open a store here?"

Sean nods. "If you don't mind us in your hair for a little while longer, you'll have a staff discount for life." He flashes a smile at Simone, who tries to smile back, but ends up just baring her teeth at him.

"You're staying?"

Sean nods.

"That's wonderful," she repeats, her voice mechanical. "Isn't that wonderful, Wes?" Her eyes bore into mine, the sleepiness in her face burned away by anger.

"Morning!" a sing-song voice calls out. Alina sways her hips as she crosses the kitchen into the living room, not sparing Eli a glance. She leans over and plants a kiss on my uncle's cheek, giving Simone and me a view of her breasts in her low-cut top, then heads around the table toward me. She puts a hand on my cheek, concern lining her eyes. "How are you, Wes? Sean and I were so worried yesterday."

I pull my face away and shrug. "I'm fine. Sean was telling me about your new plan."

Alina sits in the chair across from Simone, smiling sweetly. "Isn't it great? Heart's Cove is such a cute town. I can't wait to get to know more of the locals. If every day is as entertaining as yesterday, I don't think I'll ever want to leave."

Simone forces a laugh, crunching down on a strip of bacon. "That's Heart's Cove for you."

. . .

BREAKFAST IS a tense affair that ends with Simone shooing Eli out of the kitchen and taking her aggression out on innocent pans that definitely don't need to be scrubbed so hard.

I wait for my uncle and Alina to walk out the back door toward a forest trail while Eli retreats to the cabin, and lean against the kitchen counter. Simone's shoulders are tense. She doesn't look at me. "Are you okay?"

"Oh, I'm fine," she responds in a way that says she definitely isn't. "I'm swell. Just wonderful. You're injured, my friend's kid is blackmailing me, and now I need to pretend to be your girlfriend for an indeterminate amount of time. We can't stage a breakup because he'll be back here like a vulture, and I can't pretend to be your girlfriend without the whole town knowing we're either dating or faking it." The pan bangs against the sink, and Simone grunts. "You know, my life was great a week ago. Simple. I was broke, but I was my own person. I was independent. Sure, my marketing business barely made enough to live on and I put all my savings into the café, but I was moving forward. I wasn't tied down. Now I've waded into an absolute mess of my own making. Figures. That's very on-brand for me."

Hopping across the kitchen on one leg, I put a hand on her lower back. "Hey."

She flinches away from me, and the movement makes something deep in my chest sting. Shaking her head, she shifts her body to increase the distance between us. A growing chasm. "Stop, Wesley. Just stop. Stop cuddling me and touching me and acting like you care. This is getting out of control."

I do care. The words stay stuck in my throat, and I back away, bracing myself beside the sink so I can see Simone's face.

She drops the scoured pan into a sink full of soapy water and lets out a sigh, lifting her eyes to mine. "I need to go check on Clancy and Allie. It's past seven."

"Is that sentence supposed to make sense to me?"

Simone just shakes her head. "Never mind. I need to borrow your truck again."

"Sure."

She fishes the pan out of the water, dries it, puts it away, and throws me a pained look. "We need to talk about this when I get back. Are we going to continue this...thing...the whole time your uncle and his girlfriend are here?"

My chest squeezes and I shrug a shoulder. "I don't know."

She nods without saying anything, turns, and walks away.

Grabbing my crutches, I hobble to the couch and flop down into it. My ankle is throbbing and I can't think straight. There's a lump in my throat that just won't go away and a tightness in my chest that I haven't felt before.

The longer I pretend to be with Simone, the more real it feels. A week would have been fine. More than a week? Trouble. There's no other word for it. Nothing but trouble.

TWELVE
SIMONE

THE GIRLS AREN'T at my apartment. I look at the neatly
made bed and the two washed glasses beside the sink and let out
a long sigh. At least they cleaned up after themselves. They're
not bad kids. If Fiona gets mad at me for this, I'll deal with it
when it happens. I don't regret going to pick them up—I'd do it
again in a heartbeat.

Dropping my purse on the kitchen table, I sink down onto
the couch and close my eyes. When I open them, my Birkin is
staring back at me. I hadn't even noticed I'd grabbed it on my
way out. Maybe it's the bag's fault. I've hauled it around all
these years while things have gone wrong left, right, and center.
I should burn it or get Dorothy to stuff it with sage and crystals,
or something. An offering to whatever curse has been following
me around.

I'm starting to sound like Candice.

Sighing, I rub my temples. Wesley's family is staying in

town. We'll need to interact with townspeople while we're pretending to be a couple. There's no doubt in my mind that this charade will explode in my face.

What else is new?

A knock on the door makes me lift my head. I trudge toward the sound and open the door to see Dorothy on the other side. A woman in her seventies with a love of animal-print clothing, Dorothy is like the town's favorite aunt. Today's outfit is a bright pink-and-green leopard-print top with loose, wide-leg white trousers. It works. She looks quirky and glamorous.

"May I?" She gestures behind me.

I step aside and groan in appreciation when she hands me an iced coffee. "You're an angel."

We move to the couch and sit down. Dorothy tells me about new guests at the hotel that have been causing issues for three days, then finally waves her hand and runs an assessing eye over my face. "You look stressed, Simone. What's going on?"

I open my mouth and close it again. What can I say? I settle on a shrug. "Long day yesterday."

"How's work?"

Nonexistent. "I'm looking for more clients. You know how it is to run a business—feast or famine." And if you're me, mostly famine.

"Well, you know Marge and I have been very happy with your services. This is usually a slow season for us, but it's been a steady stream of guests for weeks now. Your copywriting and social media strategies have been very effective."

I let my lips slide into a smile. At least something's going right. "I'm happy to hear it."

Dorothy sips her coffee, looking around my apartment. "You came in with Wesley yesterday." Her eyes meet mine, shrewd and curious. "With his family."

"I, uh..." I clear my throat. "I did."

The older woman hums, crossing her ankles over each other as she leans back. I've only lived in Heart's Cove for a few months, but Dorothy and I have grown close. We're both insane, probably, and no one else understands our particular brand of crazy.

But Dorothy doesn't look crazy right now. Her eyes twinkle as she glances at me again, her painted red lips curving into a smile. "You wouldn't happen to know who that man was, would you?"

I frown. A man... My eyebrows jump up. "Eli?"

"Was that his name?" Her eyes are all innocence, but Dorothy won't be winning an Oscar any time soon. She knew damn well what Eli's name was, I'm sure of it. She probably found out through whatever network of Heart's Cove spies she employs.

"He works for Wes's uncle Sean." I take a sip of coffee to hide my smile.

"Does he, now," Dorothy muses, running her nail along the edge of her coffee cup. She clears her throat. "And is he... married?"

I've spoken to Eli a few times. When he first got settled in the cottage, I went to make sure he was doing okay and interrupted him video-calling his daughter and new baby granddaughter, but when I asked, he spoke of his wife in the past tense. "I think he was," I say slowly. "I got the sense his wife passed away. I'm not sure when or how."

"How sad." Dorothy's face doesn't look sad, though. She turns to look me in the eyes. "Would you... Do you think you could introduce us?"

My lips curve. "I'll see what I can do."

"Good girl." Dorothy pats my knee, the gesture tender. "But do me a favor, will you?"

I arch my brows, waiting.

"Don't tell the she-devil I asked."

"Agnes?"

Dorothy grunts in acknowledgement. "She has a history of scaring away my lovers. I'd rather this...Eli...get a chance to know me before she roars and sends him running."

"I thought Agnes and Mr. Cheswick were together," I muse.

"They are. Or at least, they're as close as anyone could ever get to that hag."

I hide my grin as I sip my iced coffee, but can't quite stop myself from chuckling as I slump down on the sofa, kicking my legs up to rest on the coffee table.

The two of us talk about everything and nothing until Dorothy glances at me with a curious smile. "So, you and Wes, huh? I knew there was something there when the two of you walked into the hotel the other day. He doesn't look at anyone the way he looks at you."

Ha. Right. The Heart's Cove rumor mill is in full swing. So there were two reasons for her to come here and ply me with coffee—her own romance, and her need to know what's going on with mine.

My face is a neutral mask. "I think you're mistaken, Dor. Wes and I are just friends."

"Of course you are." She pats my leg. "Life is short, honey. Screw the daylights out of him while you have a chance." She winks, pulls herself off the couch, and tells me she has to leave.

When I close the door behind her, I let out a long sigh and look around my little apartment.

I'm forty-four years old, divorced, I live by myself, I'm a flailing business owner on the verge of going broke, and I have a fake boyfriend. My life is a mess.

I might as well head back to Wesley's place and face the music. His uncle is staying, and we need to figure out how long this charade will last—but at least there's a silver lining. If Dorothy and Eli get together, not everything will be a loss.

WES IS SITTING on the back porch when I get back, book in hand, sun gleaming off his bronze skin. He's shirtless, which is annoyingly distracting, and nibbling his bottom lip in a way that makes me want to fall on the ground and spread my legs.

"Hey."

He glances up, that lush bottom lip falling from between his teeth. Ugh. "Hi. Did you get everything figured out at your place?"

"Sure did. Where's the dynamic duo?"

"They've gone to scope out the sporting goods and outdoor stores in the area."

"So they're really thinking of staying and setting up a new location, huh?"

Wes lets out a long sigh. "I have a feeling there's more to it than that, but yeah. It appears so."

I sink into a chair next to him and look out at the ocean. This property really is gorgeous. The balcony juts out, a short cliff below us making it seem like we're floating above the ocean. The sound of the waves crashing on the rocks below is soothing, and if I turn my brain off for just a moment, I can feel my muscles slowly unwind.

Then Wesley speaks. "So...we should talk."

I swivel my head to look at him and catch him staring right at me. Green eyes search mine from under thick lashes, something like concern swirling within them. He's ridiculously handsome. This would be a lot easier if my body didn't see him and blare, *All systems go!*

"Can you not do that?"

Wes frowns. "Do what?"

I wave my hands in his general direction. "That."

"I'm literally just sitting here, Simone."

"Exactly. It's distracting."

He stares at me for a moment longer, then lets out a sigh and shakes his head. "While you were out, I did some thinking."

"Did you survive?"

"Huh?" He meets my gaze again.

"Well, I know thinking is very strenuous for you. Just wondering if you made it through."

A growl rumbles through his throat. "I'm trying to talk to you about something serious."

And I'm trying not to have a nervous breakdown.

"Right. Sorry. Go ahead." I cast my gaze out to the ocean,

hoping it'll help me focus. I can still feel him though, sitting inches away from me. Shirtless. Looking good enough to lick. Or suck. Or bite. Last night, it felt good to fall asleep in his arms. Too good.

I had a dream that he and I... Never mind. Not important.

"I know we agreed on this...arrangement...for one week, but with my uncle and Alina staying in town, I have a proposition."

"I love it when men proposition me."

"Simone." A snarl rattles just behind the sound of my name. It turns me on, because I've officially lost my mind.

I say nothing in response. It's safer that way.

"I'll keep paying you," Wesley finally says.

I turn to stare at him. "You'll pay me to pretend to be your girlfriend for an indefinite amount of time?"

"I'll pay you five grand per month they're here, plus whatever expenses you might incur. If they're here past the end of January, we'll stage a breakup." He winces at the words, but I don't want to read into that right now.

Instead, I just stare at him. "This is insane."

"You should feel right at home, then."

I roll my eyes. "Ha-ha."

A grin teases at the corner of his lips. I look away before I catch sight of the dimple.

"Five grand a month, plus the five grand for this week. I'll throw in another grand for the last week of November. Think about it, Simone. You could make sixteen grand by the end of January. Five this week, one next, and ten for each December and January."

"Thank you for the math lesson, Professor." I brave another

glance at him and catch him clenching his jaw, fire sparking in his eyes. Oops. Maybe I'm taking this too far. I need to rein in the sass.

Sixteen thousand dollars for what, ten weeks of girlfriend duties? That's a lot of money, and truth be told—I haven't minded being Wesley's fake girlfriend. That money could last me a few months the way I'm living now. I could take my time to find new clients and get settled in Heart's Cove. I could even take five grand and buy myself a little car so I don't have to walk or borrow other people's vehicles. Sixteen thousand dollars would solve a lot of my more urgent problems. It would give me space to breathe.

Between using my cash to invest in the café, moving to a new town, and starting the marketing business from scratch here, I'm more than broke. I'm dead-ass broke. Don't have two pennies to rub together. Wesley's offering me a way out. All I have to do is spend all my days and nights with him and pretend to be madly in love with him. Easy.

"Simone?"

"What about other people? My friends? Am I supposed to lie to them, too? I can hide here for a week, but two or three months is too long. People will notice. Hell, people already noticed me driving around in your truck. This morning, Dorothy told me to screw the daylights out of you!"

Wes's eyebrows jump up, his eyes flashing as his gaze falls to my mouth. He catches himself and looks away. "It's up to you. We can tell them the truth or we can pretend in front of them, too."

I worry the edge of my shirt, running my fingers over the

hem and back again. If I tell Fiona, Jen, and Candice about this, they'll know what I did for the café lease. That will cause questions I don't feel like answering, like, *Why would you agree to that? What were you thinking? Are you sleeping together? Why not?*

The more people know we're faking this, the greater the chance that someone will slip up and tell Sean and Alina, and the whole thing will be a waste. It's easier if no one knows. Once we have our fake breakup, I can brush it off as a casual relationship. No questions, no fuss, no strings attached.

"We'll pretend," I finally answer. "We'll pretend in front of everyone."

Wes nods. "Okay."

The door opening behind us makes us both turn our heads. Alina's beautiful face appears in the opening, her eyes glued to Wes's chest. An ugly feeling creeps through my chest as her eyes flick to me for the briefest moment then back to Wes, the want clearly written in her eyes.

Yes, yes. It's a nice chest. We all know it.

"Can I help you with anything?" My tone is short. Harsh. I sound like a possessive girlfriend.

Alina ignores me. "How are you feeling, Wes?"

"Same as I did a couple hours ago. Fine."

"I bought you some chocolates. We passed a beautiful little chocolatier in the next town over. I remembered you love chocolate-almond bark, so I got you a big bag." She dangles the clear plastic bag, her manicured fingers sliding along the green ribbon along the bag's closure. The movement is almost... sensual.

Well aren't you just great, Alina. Did you buy your own boyfriend anything, or just Wes?

I take a deep breath. He's not actually my boyfriend. I'm not actually jealous. I'm just high-strung and going through a lot of stress. I just need a day or two to get used to this new...thing. Money will help. Everything will be fine. Alina can sleep with Wes for all I care. Maybe that can be the cause of our fake breakup.

But as I stand up and excuse myself, my stomach balls itself up into a tight fist. The thought of Wes sleeping with his ex-fiancée makes me want to vomit. The thought of him sleeping with *anyone* makes me want to be sick. Pretending or not, I hate the thought of him with someone else.

So, basically, I'm screwed.

I've entered into this stupid arrangement because I have no other options, but my feelings are a mess and my hormones are a constant, deafening marching band stomping through my veins. I want to sleep with Wes and rip his head off and also make sure Alina never touches or looks at him.

I nod to Eli and Sean, who are hovering around the refrigerator, and escape upstairs. I collapse onto the bed and scrub my face.

Wonderful. What else can go wrong with my life? Next thing, Nate will materialize and ask me why I haven't returned any of his calls after we slept together, thinking he still has a claim on my life. Or maybe Fiona will find out about Clancy's party and our friendship will be irreparably damaged. Or maybe another flood will ruin our new café, and I'll lose the last of the money I had to invest in anything.

But yeah, my forties are going great. Just fucking dandy.

THIRTEEN

WESLEY

IT TAKES us all a few days to settle into a new routine. By the time Sean and Alina are here for five days, I'm just about getting used to waking up with Simone in my bed. Those little booty shorts aren't getting any longer, though, and my body seems to think it's a good idea to wake me up with a raging boner every morning.

My arms are sore from the crutches, but all in all, I'm getting used to using them. The doctor said four to six weeks before I can put weight on it, though, and in the meantime, I feel useless.

On the morning of the sixth day of my uncle's visit, Simone wakes up next to me and stretches her arms above her head, yawning as she arches her back. My gaze snags on her T-shirt and the way it clings to her breasts. I should look away. I should really, really look away. No, not down to her legs. *Away*.

There. The ceiling. That's better.

"Yesterday, Candice asked me if you wanted to come to Thanksgiving at her place," Simone says, her voice still thick with sleep. "She said Eli, Sean, and Alina should come too. I think she feels guilty about the whole broken ankle thing. Blames herself for opening Four Cups and causing the injury." She rolls onto her side, tucking her hands under her head. Her eyes flash, an arch tugging at her brow. "I told her not to worry, you were the moron who went stomping on a rotten roof, but she insisted."

"Stomping, huh."

"I think she'll be offended if you don't come."

"You realize how it'll look for the five of us to show up together."

"We're supposed to be in love. It would be weird if we *didn't* spend Thanksgiving together."

"True," I say, chewing the word.

Simone sighs. "Plus, Dorothy and Margaret will be there too, and..." Simone bites her lip. Heat lashes across my body. She gives me a coy smile that does nothing to temper the flames. "I think Dor might have an...ulterior motive."

I arch my brows in question.

She grins. "She's interested in Eli."

"Eli? My uncle's driver, Eli?"

Simone nods, grinning.

"You're okay with everyone thinking we're dating?"

"Wasn't this the point of this whole thing?"

I nod, turning back to the ceiling. She's right. It was the point of this whole thing, but going to a Thanksgiving dinner together makes it seem so much more...real. The past five days have been fairly isolated at the house, with no prying eyes and no pointed questions.

Her hand slides onto my forearm, drawing my gaze. "Are you okay? Should we pull the plug on this whole thing?" Blue eyes widen slightly as she searches my face, making me feel more naked and exposed than if I were wearing nothing at all. When she looks at me like that, I feel like she can see down to my soul.

My own gaze betrays me. It drops to her lips—like it always seems to do when I can't stop myself in time—and I watch her lips part, tongue sliding out to moisten that pink rosebud mouth. This woman is fucking killing me. I'm lying in bed next to her, talking about going to a Thanksgiving dinner with all our family and friends, and I can't even reach over and run my fingers over her cheek. I can't kiss her, or touch her, or do anything but lie here and crave her.

"Wes?" Her brows draw together. She props her head on her elbow, waiting for me to say something.

My hand moves of its own will, and I don't have the discipline to stop it. The pads of my fingertips brush her jaw, my thumb coming to rest on her chin.

She gasps ever so slightly, staring at me, her pulse thrumming beneath my fingertips.

The sky is blue today for the first time in over a week. Dust motes twirl in shafts of sunlight that stream through the window, the light carving a diagonal line across the bed. I run my thumb over Simone's skin, the edge of it nudging the bottom of her mouth.

I want to kiss her so bad it hurts. It hurts everywhere. I can't think of anything except that mouth.

How did I get here? How did this happen?

My fingers slide toward the nape of her neck, and Simone's eyes flutter closed. She leans toward me. An inch. Then two. Three.

I can't take this anymore. I need to taste her mouth. The sassy, difficult mouth that's been driving me crazy for weeks. The mouth I've stared at whenever I have a chance. The lips that haunt my dreams.

There are reasons I shouldn't, but I can't quite think of them right now. Something about complicating an already messy situation. Distance is good, but I don't exactly remember why.

The only thing in my world right now are those lips. They part as Simone opens her eyes. My heart thumps. Something falls away from Simone's gaze. Her guardedness dissolves, and I see something new. Lust. Pure, white-hot desire rages in her gaze, finally laid bare for me to see.

She wants me.

All those times my mind jumped to sex when she walked in the room, was she thinking the same? Her hand moves toward my forearm and she moves her head slowly, so slowly toward my palm. I brush my thumb over her lips and let out a sharp breath when she parts them for me, taking the tip of my thumb in her warm, wet mouth. My God.

Then someone knocks on the door, and we jerk apart. My uncle's voice calls through the door. "A man is here to see you, Wes. Said his name is Grant. It's about the café roof. He's needs the final word on which contractor you want to use."

"Be right out," I call out, my voice thick.

Simone says nothing. She just swings her legs over the edge of the bed and sits there for a few moments, her back to me, sucking in ragged breaths. Then she stands, tugging her shirt down, and disappears out the door toward the bathroom.

Well, okay then.

I scrub my face and let out a sigh. What the hell just happened?

We were both there. We both wanted it. We were about to make a huge mistake. If we sleep together, that's the end of the simplicity. It crosses a line that we can't un-cross. Sex always complicates things, and this situation would be no different. We can't sleep together. I look at my thumb, still feeling her lips around the tip of it. Holy fucking shit.

I need to get up. The boot keeping my ankle secure lands on the floor, and I wince as a jolt of pain knocks the lust from my veins. The desire is still there, but I can almost think now. I need to get out of this room before Simone comes back. I pull on some sweatpants and a shirt, grab my crutches, and head downstairs.

GRANT HAS NARROWED down the roofing contractors to two companies, and it takes us only a few minutes to agree on which one to choose. After my accident, we decided it was best to hire professionals. Grant hasn't been up there since the day I fell through.

We sit around the dining room table with the quotes in front of us, coffees in hand. My uncle and Alina are in the living room cuddling on the couch. For once, it doesn't bother me to see them together. It's weird to see it, but it doesn't sting. Alina can date whoever she wants, and if my uncle thinks he can make her loyal, then good luck to him. Maybe he can provide for her the way she needs. Keep her in designer clothes and expensive shoes.

Simone's steps are light as she walks down the stairs. Our eyes meet as soon as she turns the corner. Her hair is twisted up on top of her head with a few red tendrils framing her face. She's wearing a black turtleneck and tan, pleated pants. Every inch of her is covered, but for some sick reason it turns me on. All that clothing only makes me want to peel it off, revealing her skin inch by inch. Did she think clothes would make me want her less? Did she think if she covered her body up, we'd forget what just happened?

"Morning," Alina calls out in a sing-song voice.

Simone startles, head turning toward the two of them on the couch as if she hadn't even noticed they were there. "Hi. Good morning." Her gaze swings back to us. "Grant." She nods in greeting. Nothing for me.

"Hey, Simone." Grant's gaze flicks to me, a grin threatening to spread over his lips. "You guys coming to Candice's tonight?"

"Of course." She smiles at him, dutifully avoiding looking at me. "As long as Eli, Sean, and Alina want to come." She turns to them. "We've been invited to Thanksgiving dinner at our friend Candice's place."

Alina beams. "Thank you. That's so kind."

"It sure is." Simone smiles, and for the first time since she mentioned Thanksgiving dinner to me, I see a hint of trepidation in her face.

WE ARRIVE at Candice's place in the late afternoon. Candice and Allie live in a four-bedroom house near Cove Boulevard. It's a two-story home with an open-plan living room, dining room, and kitchen on the ground level, and all the bedrooms upstairs. She has a massive table set up dominating most of the space, with a mix of chairs that people have obviously brought from multiple houses. Candice greets us with a wide smile, then hugs every single person who walks through the door. She's a short woman who loves yoga, meditation, and public displays of affection. I give her an awkward one-armed hug around my crutches and let her guide me to a place on the sofa.

I can see Jen and Fallon in the kitchen, their backs to each other. Jen looks angry about something, glaring at Fallon every two seconds. He's completely oblivious. Allie and Clancy are sitting in the corner on the floor, their heads close together. A short woman with the same bright eyes as Candice is introduced as Candice's youngest sister, Iliana, in town for the holiday, and Rudy, of all people, shouts out from the refrigerator to offer us a drink.

My uncle, Eli, and Alina are introduced to everyone, and they take their seats and accept a drink from Candice. Fiona and Grant come in from outside carrying bags of ice. They smile at me and nod to my uncle and Alina.

Simone has done her best to ignore me without seeming like she's ignoring me. We agree that this morning was a mistake, then. Doesn't make it any easier to forget the feel of her skin beneath my fingertips, or how violently my body reacted to her slightest move.

She drifts away from me, heading toward the kitchen. I watch the way the light plays off her alabaster skin. How she leans a hip on the counter and sips a glass of wine, laughing at something Candice says. Fallon flexes his bicep for some reason as Jen rolls her eyes. Simone reaches over to squeeze it, pretending to need both hands. Everyone laughs. I frown.

The doorbell rings, and Dorothy and Margaret's voices float down the hallway. Eli sits up straighter, his gaze peering toward the front door.

Margaret comes through first, carrying a dish wrapped in foil and a bag full of clinking wine bottles. Candice leads her to the kitchen, and Dorothy's gaze lands on Eli. Is she...blushing?

Eli stands in a graceful movement, catching Dor's hand to lay a kiss on her fingers. My eyebrows jump. "You look beautiful tonight, Dorothy," he says in a voice I've never heard from him before.

Dorothy pulls her hand away and preens, then gestures toward the kitchen. "Wine?"

Eli inclines his head. "Please."

Simone's face splits into a smile at the sight of them, the first I've seen from her since this morning. The setting sun is catching her hair just right, gilding her fiery hair as she beams. Gorgeous. Rudy notices, too, sliding up beside her to say something in her ear to make her laugh. She swats his arm, and I realize I wish that were me standing next to her.

"I didn't think I'd ever see you like this," my uncle says,

taking a seat next to me. He tips his bottle of beer into his mouth, glancing over at Simone.

I jerk my eyes away to stare out the window instead. "Like what?"

"In love. Even when you were with Alina, you didn't look at her like you look at Simone."

A lump forms in my throat. I'm not looking at Simone in any special way. I'm definitely not in love with her. She's just... It's just the way the light catches her sometimes. It's striking.

Things this morning got out of hand, and I'm still trying to regain my footing, that's all—but I can't exactly tell him that.

"Yeah," I finally croak. My eloquence knows no bounds.

"I appreciate you hosting Alina and me. I was worried about how you'd react."

Yet you still decided to show up without a hint of warning. "You're family."

"Still, Alina told me how things ended between you two. She told me how much you were struggling with the failure of your business venture, and she always felt guilty about how things were left."

"Funny that she wouldn't tell me that herself." I can't quite keep the bitterness from my voice. Alina dropped me the minute things started looking like they wouldn't end up with us as multimillionaires and attached herself to a sure bet in my uncle. That doesn't scream guilt and remorse to me. That screams cunning and manipulation and a desire to be taken care of.

"Cut her some slack, Wes."

"Why are you telling me this?"

My uncle clears his throat. "Well, I...I asked her to marry me yesterday, when we went out for dinner. I'm hoping we can all move on...together."

Wind whistles past my ears, and I don't hear another word. They're getting married. They're getting *married*. I don't know why I care, but I do. I could deal with her being the girlfriend. I could almost deal with her living in my house for a couple of months.

But for her to become *family*? What, so technically she'll be my aunt?

I'm not okay with this. I don't care how much they think they care about each other. My uncle couldn't have chosen literally any other woman? He couldn't have found some other younger woman who wanted a comfortable life? He had to choose *her*?

The world turns red. He's speaking, but I don't hear a word.

I've been a fucking fool. I thought pretending to be with Simone would let me stay in my parents' house in peace for the next eighteen months, but I didn't expect it would give him a free pass to marry my ex-fiancée. Those things aren't related, I know. But, but, but...

My neck creaks as I swivel my head, as if every muscle in my body has turned to stone. I stare at the man beside me, unable to move or speak or think.

"Dinner!" Candice calls out. "Let's sit down and eat, folks."

Simone appears by my side, the scent of citrus and lavender clearing some crimson fog from my vision. Her blue eyes search mine as my uncle makes his way to the table, her hand cool as she puts it on my shoulder. "Are you okay?"

"My uncle and Alina are engaged."

She lets out a long breath and squeezes my shoulder. The touch is comforting. I don't want her to pull away. "Let's just get through this dinner, okay?"

She helps me up and lets me lean on her as I get my crutches in place, her hand hovering near my lower back as we make our way to the table. Happy fucking Thanksgiving, everyone.

FOURTEEN
CANDICE

IT WAS important to me to get everyone together for this meal. I haven't had a dinner party at my house for a long time. Since before Paul died. Setting up the table, getting Jen and Fallon over to cook with me, greeting people at the door, and seeing everyone talking and laughing—it feeds my soul.

I smile at the people around the table. So many of them are new friends, but it feels like we've known each other forever. Fiona's sitting to my left, with Grant on the other side of her. Allie's across from me, beside Clancy of course. To my right, Wesley's uncle and his partner, then Eli, his head angled toward Dorothy.

My sister Iliana, the free spirit of the Viceroy clan, has breezed in for the weekend on her way to Europe. She's currently leaning against Margaret and laughing about something, Probably some romantic, compelling story about her travels.

Directly across from me, Rudy winks. Agnes and Mr. Cheswick decided to go on an impromptu weekend away to Vegas, and I couldn't bear the thought of him spending the holiday alone. Okay, fine. We've also had a bit of a flirtation going, and it...intrigues me. I've never been with a younger man. I met Paul in college and thought we'd be together forever. He died eighteen months ago, and it feels like a blink of the eye since he was sitting at this table with us.

Glancing at Rudy, I give the handsome, blond man a shy smile. He grins back, and my heart jumps. It feels too soon, but maybe...maybe flirting is healthy.

"Let's eat," I say, raising my glass. "Happy Thanksgiving, everyone."

A chorus of "Happy Thanksgivings" answers back, and everyone digs in. Jen and Fallon are masters, and their help was invaluable for this meal. They did a better job of cooking than I would, to be honest, and it let me organize everything else, even if there was incessant bickering between them. As I stare around the table, a weight lifts off my shoulders and I can't keep the smile off my face.

"So, you've been staying at Wes's, huh. Have you been enjoying the forest view?" Fiona grins at Simone, wiggling her eyebrows. "Forest view" sounds different when Fiona says it like that. "It's a bit more luxurious than your old apartment."

"I think my apartment is getting lonely without me."

Jen helps herself to another scoop of mashed potatoes. "Not if Clancy and Allie keep crashing there."

Simone, Fiona, and I freeze at once. Jen doesn't notice. The three of us glance at each other, then at Jen, then back at each other. Simone's face is red, her eyes full of panic.

Conversation dies around the table as the tension ratchets higher. I'm the first to speak. "What are you talking about, Jen?"

"Last weekend. Sunday morning." She jerks her head at Clancy and Allie. "They were at Simone's."

I turn to Allie, who's very, very focused on cutting her turkey into bite-sized pieces. "Allie?"

She looks up, cherubic innocence written on her face. "Yes?"

"Were you at Simone's on Saturday night?"

Clancy shifts in her seat.

Simone stares at her, a silent command written in her eyes that Clancy is doing her best to ignore.

So much for a wonderful family meal. The only sound is the clink of utensils on plates, chewing, and the collective speeding heartbeat of half a dozen people caught in a lie.

I put my fork down and intertwine my fingers under my chin, leveling my daughter with a stare. "Explain."

Allie ducks her head, and Clancy does the same. Fiona and Grant look angry enough to have steam curling out of their nostrils.

Simone looks at the two girls, leans back in her chair, and crosses her arms. "You didn't tell your parents about the party."

"What party?" Grant's voice is a rough growl.

"I'd also like to know," I say through clenched teeth. "Last I heard, Allie was at your place for a sleepover last Saturday night."

"That's funny," Fiona cuts in, "because we were told the girls were at your place."

As one, Fiona, Grant, and I lean back in our chairs and stare at the girls. They squirm. Good.

"Allie." My Mom Voice is cranked up to full power.

"Maybe Simone can explain what the girls were doing at *her* place." Fiona's words are cold as ice.

Simone closes her eyes for a long moment and shakes her head. "They promised they'd tell you."

"First of all, tell us *what*, exactly? And second of all, you trusted two fifteen-year-olds to come clean about something they obviously did wrong?" Fiona snorts, shaking her head.

Simone shrugs. "I mean...yes?"

Grant leans forward. "What. Happened."

This is just great. *Hey everyone, come over for Thanksgiving! You can have a front-row seat for some primo family drama. And bring your extended family, too! Hey, how about your butler as well! I'll invite the town gossips to make sure everyone in Heart's Cove knows by nightfall, and I'll do it in front of the first man I've felt an ounce of sexual attraction for in over a year.*

I steal a glance at Eli, Sean, and Alina, who are just watching the drama unfold, sipping wine and saying nothing. Fallon's eating like he doesn't have a care in the world, eyes firmly stuck on his plate. Jen has a completely neutral expression on her face, scooping mashed potatoes into her mouth like it's her job. Wes looks like he has thunderclouds brewing on his brow, which makes no sense at all. He's not involved in this. I don't have the energy to look at Dorothy and Margaret. The embarrassment is too much.

This is not what I wanted when I invited everyone over. I wanted a nice meal, where we could come together and celebrate the success of Four Cups together. I wanted to show my appreciation to Wes for letting us lease his space, and my appreciation to Dorothy and Margaret for letting me set up my yoga studio in one of the hotel's spare reception rooms. I wanted this to be a time that we could laugh and drink and celebrate new beginnings.

Instead, my teenager and her best friend are facing an inquisition. I don't know whether to be mad at them, at Simone, at Jen, or at myself. I should have known something was up with Allie last weekend. She came home way too early for it to be a sleepover at Clancy's house.

Clancy takes a deep breath and straightens up. She meets her father's gaze head-on. "There was a party."

"I said you couldn't go," Grant replies.

"I know, but that wasn't fair. I went. I didn't drink, Dad. Not a drop. I didn't *want* to drink."

"But you went when I specifically told you that you weren't allowed."

"Why, though? Why couldn't I go? You never gave me a reason."

"After what happened at your birthday party, you're really asking me that? All the work we've done with the therapist talking about trust and responsibility and communication? Did none of that matter to you?"

"Da-ad." She stretches the word to two syllables. "I just... I wanted to go."

Grant looks like he's ready to explode. I need to cut in.

"What happened?" I look at Simone, thinking she might release this mounting tension.

Simone takes a deep breath. "Clancy called me."

"Why you?" Fiona snaps.

"Maybe because she knew you'd react like this."

Wrong thing to say, Simone. I want to drop my head in my hands and groan, but all I do is sit still.

Simone glances at the girls. "They called me around midnight. They told me they got a ride to the party but got stranded when their designated driver started drinking, so they called me to pick them up. I was going to bring them home, but they begged me not to. I told them they could stay at my place on the condition that they told you everything in the morning, which they obviously didn't."

"And you didn't think to follow up?" Fiona asks.

"I've had other things on my mind, Fi."

"Like what? Your new boyfriend?" She snorts. "Really? Is that really more important than my *kid*?"

I clear my throat. "Maybe we should shelve this discussion for now. We can have a nice meal and deal with this later." I look at Allie, making sure to sink a lot of menace in my gaze. She knows she's in trouble.

"Fine," Grant says through clenched teeth.

"Great," Simone replies.

Fiona says nothing.

My sister takes a big gulp of wine, eyes sparkling across the table.

Utensils clink on plates until Eli finally clears his throat.

"That's a beautiful brooch, Dorothy. Where on earth did you find it?"

"Oh, this old thing?" Dorothy smiles, her fingers brushing the brooch almost sensually. "One of my many treasures, Eli. I'm like a magpie. I love shiny things."

"It's gorgeous. Just like its owner."

I glance at Rudy, who arches a brow and nods, impressed. He looks like he wants to take notes as Dorothy's face flushes pink, a delicate laugh falling from her lips.

From then on, conversation is stilted, but eventually starts up again. Sean and Alina tell us about their plans for a new sporting goods store, and Sean does a good job talking about himself until everyone nearly recovers from the earlier drama.

Once the plates are cleared, Fiona and Grant make their excuses, grab Clancy, and head for the door. Simone, Wes, and Wes's family aren't far behind. Allie gets sent to her room with a few stern words.

"Well. That was awkward." Jen shudders, putting the last of the dishes in the dishwasher. "I wouldn't have said anything if I'd known that would happen."

"It's not your fault."

"I know. I still wouldn't have said anything, though."

Fallon dries the roasting pan, puts it away, and snaps the lid on a plastic container full of leftovers before sliding it into the fridge. "The conversation was a disaster, but the food was good." His lips curl at the corners and he wraps me in a big bear hug. "You can't win 'em all."

He moves to hug Jen, but she just glares. Her gaze swings to me, pinched lips and all. "You want us to leave so you can go ground Allie for the rest of her life?"

I snort. "Sure."

I close the door behind them and turn to see Rudy sliding his jacket over his shoulders. His blue eyes are soft, lush blond hair curling around his ears and neck. He pushes a rogue strand off his forehead and winks at me. "I had a great time, even with all the dramatic revelations."

"You have to promise not to tell your grandmother what happened."

"I'll leave that for Dorothy to do." He grins as he buttons his jacket, then leans toward me. For a terrifying moment I think he's going to kiss me, and panic rips through my body. But his lips just brush my cheek as he squeezes my arm, then he gives me a quick nod before disappearing through the door.

I lean against the wall, letting out a long sigh. It's too soon. I can't handle whatever's going on with Rudy. It's way too soon.

"He's hot," my sister says behind me. I turn to see a wine glass dangling from her fingers. "You should definitely go there."

I shake my head. "I have to go deal with Allie."

"I'll be here with a bucket of wine for when you're done."

I squeeze Iliana's arm and take a deep breath. With frown lines marring my forehead, I trudge up the stairs to talk to my daughter. Times like these, I wish Paul were here. He would've known how to save the dinner and how to make Allie under-stand that what she did was wrong. My husband was always better at talking to her, at understanding her.

But he died, and it's my job to pick up the pieces. I stand in front of my daughter's bedroom door and take a deep breath before knocking and listening to her quiet voice telling me to come in.

FIFTEEN

FIONA

IT'S ALMOST TOO cold out to sit on the back porch, but I know I need to give Grant and Clancy some space. When we walked into the house, he asked me if he could handle this on his own and I was all too happy to let him. He and Clancy sat down in the front living room, too far away for me to hear anything.

I hope he's not too harsh with her. Grant and Clancy have been going to counseling together and he thought they'd been making progress. Her lying about this party must feel like a betrayal. Still, the girl needs unconditional love from us. She grew up in an unstable household with a mother who wasn't always there for her. I hope Grant can see that.

I boil the kettle and make myself a mug of tea, then wrap a big blanket around myself and settle into one of the Adirondack chairs at the back of the big farmhouse. This is my nightly ritual since the first day I came to this house.

I've been in Heart's Cove seven or eight months now, but it feels like so much longer. As soon as I sit down and hold my steaming mug between my fingers, looking out on the lawn, the ocean, the trees lining Grant's property, I feel the tension in my body unwind.

I'm not mad at Simone. I was angry at dinner, but that feeling has faded as quickly as it appeared. Clancy obviously felt she could trust Simone to come help her in the middle of the night, and Simone was a good enough friend and decent enough person to go pick up two little girls who aren't even her responsibility. Simone did the right thing.

Guilt worms through my stomach as I let the sound of the crickets and distant waves soothe me. I was rude to my best friend. I snapped at her—on Thanksgiving, no less—and gave her no opportunity to explain herself. Of course I would have liked if she told me about picking Clancy and Allie up, but she trusted the girls to come clean to us. She actually wanted to give Clancy a chance to step up and be responsible for herself.

The French doors open and Grant slips through like a silent shadow, his own mug steaming with a hot cup of tea. He sits beside me in the second Adirondack chair, stretching his long legs as he releases a sigh.

"How did it go?" I ask after a pause.

He shrugs a broad shoulder and shakes his head. "I sent her to bed. Took her phone and said she was grounded for the foreseeable future. She wouldn't speak to me, so I said we'd try again tomorrow when we've both had a chance to think and sleep on it."

His hand is warm when I slide my fingers over it, curling them around his broad palm. "She's a good kid, Grant."

"She lied to me."

"Kids will do things we don't like. Clancy, especially, is probably used to having no boundaries whatsoever. Who knows how her mother disciplined her, if at all? We knew there would be an adjustment period to her living under our roof."

Our roof. This relationship is new, but it warms every bit of my heart to say those words. It feels...like we've been a team since the very beginning.

Grant leans his head back in the chair, staring out across the ocean. Under my blanket, I can already feel the chill of the night, but Grant seems unbothered. He sips his tea and ruminates, his mind far, far away from me.

I need to bring him back.

Taking both our cups, I set them on the ground and slide into his lap. I hook my arms around his neck and lean my forehead against his, inhaling the scent of him as the night grows darker around us. "You're doing really well, Grant. There will be hiccups, and the important thing is how we react to them. Clancy obviously didn't feel comfortable calling either of us when she was in trouble, which is something we should address."

"Why would she call Simone? Why wouldn't Simone *tell* us?"

My head nestles into the crook between his shoulder and his neck. I close my eyes, nuzzling into him. "If you were a kid in Heart's Cove and you did something you knew was wrong, would you call your parents, or someone like Dorothy?"

"My parents."

"Really? What if Dorothy was like an aunt to you? What if she treated you like a grown-up and listened when you spoke? What if your own parents were a little overprotective and a little too quick to anger?"

"You think I'm wrong to be mad." His voice rumbles in his chest, barely contained emotion. But his fingers find my waist and start drawing small circles on my skin.

I shake my head. "You're completely justified in being mad. I'm just saying, maybe we need to handle Clancy differently. We only know the broad strokes of her childhood. She's as mature as a teenager can be, and she craves independence. Maybe we need to give it to her."

"She lied, Fiona. How am I supposed to give her more freedom if she does shit like this? I specifically told her she couldn't go to this party and she still did it. I don't want her to go anywhere near Simone if she's going to hide things from us, too."

Sitting up, I run my fingers over Grant's temples. My strong, sensitive man. He was a rock in the middle of the ocean for so long. All alone, weathering the waves that battered him year after year. Now he's got not only me to think about, but Clancy, too.

"Grant," I say softly. "I've known Simone for the better part of twenty-seven years. Let me talk to her. She dropped everything and went to pick up Allie and Clancy in the middle of the night. She trusted them to speak to us and gave Clancy an opportunity to own up to her mistake. She thought she was doing the right thing. Of course I wish she'd told me, I wish she'd followed up with me, but that's not the issue here. Please don't blame her for this."

There's one thing I don't tell Grant—in almost three decades, Simone has told me everything about her love life. If she went on a date with a new man, I got a play-by-play. If she started seeing someone, she'd show me pictures and ask for my opinion. She wouldn't always tell me all the gritty details of her sex life, and if a relationship became more serious, she'd grow more private, but she'd *tell* me.

She didn't tell me about Wesley. One day everything was normal, and the next she was bringing flowers and candles and new sheets to his house. Then she shows up at Thanksgiving dinner with him and his family. It's too quick. Too serious, too fast. Something's going on with them—something odd. I don't want Simone to drift away from me because of this thing with Clancy.

Finally, *finally*, Grant meets my gaze. His grey eyes are dark, full of pain. He lets out a long breath and tightens his hold on my waist. "I don't know how to handle all this. I don't know how to be a dad or how to be a good partner to you. I feel like I'm screwing everything up."

My lips curl into a smile. "You're not."

His shoulders seem to relax, then, and he closes his eyes. I press my lips to his and wait for his mouth to open, for him to let me in. He kisses me softly, tenderly, sending heat rolling through my body as my toes curl in my slippers.

"Let's go to bed." His voice takes on a sharper edge. "I need you right now, Fiona."

Heat washes over me as my need for him grows in response. I nod, pressing my lips to his. "I'm here."

SIXTEEN

WESLEY

I DON'T KNOW if it's the turkey, the pain meds, or the high-emotion dinner, but as soon as I got home, I collapsed onto the couch. Simone sat beside me for a while, then got up and mumbled something about going for a walk.

I wanted to go with her, but crutches in the forest at night is never a good idea.

We met when she came stumbling out of the forest after sundown, lost and alone. I know she likes walking at night, and this place is as safe as any, but I still wish I could be there with her. That kind of protectiveness is odd for me, but I'm too tired to think about it. Too tired to brush it aside. So I just sit here and think of her. Worry about her.

Now, I'm drifting in and out of sleep in front of the television, unsure how much time has passed. Fifteen minutes? An hour? Two?

Sean is snoring in the armchair to my left, and Alina is

nowhere to be seen. Probably in bed. My crutches are leaning against the arm of the sofa, and the trip from here to my room upstairs seems like an impossible task. I could just fall asleep here...

With an almost inhuman effort, I sit up and rub my eyes with the heels of my hands. If I sleep on the couch, I'll be sore as all hell tomorrow. Bed will be nicer. I need to get upstairs. Simone will climb in, then, and I'll be able to put my arms around her and fall asleep.

My crutches clatter against each other, but Sean doesn't wake up. I swing my way to the steps, then slide both crutches under one arm and use my other hand to hold the bannister. Then it's one step at a time, all the way up to the second floor.

Everything aches. My ankle is throbbing. My armpit is sore. I need sleep.

There was a time when I could stay up late and wake up early, go for a run, do a workout, and feel like a million bucks. These days, not so much. A broken ankle is kicking the shit out of me. Where I used to be able to shake off a hangover with a hot shower and a greasy breakfast, now three or four beers has me in bed the entire next day.

I'm getting older.

Gritting my teeth, I make it up the last three steps and finally stop on the second floor landing. I'm sucking air, a thin sheen of sweat covering me from head to toe. Fitting my crutches under my arms, I start down the hallway—and stop.

A thin strip of light is shining from under my parents' bedroom door.

I stare at the yellow light spilling onto the hallway carpet, frowning. The light is on. That means someone's in there. Who the hell would go in my parents' room?

Hobbling over to the door, I turn the knob. The door opens on silent hinges, and I find my ex-fiancée standing in my parents' old closet, looking at my mother's clothes.

What the actual fuck?

"Alina?" My voice is a rasp. A growl.

She turns, eyes wide. "Wes! Hi."

"What are you doing?" I take a step inside the room. My chest tightens. The smell in here... It still smells like them. A book my mother was reading is still sitting on her side of the bed, bookmark sticking out where she left it. All their clothes are in the closet, Mom's jewelry collecting dust on top of the vanity. It's all still here, just like it was when they were alive. Emotion balls in my throat, and I shift my gaze to Alina.

She hangs one of my mother's dresses back in the closet and brushes her palms down her sides. "I'm sorry, Wes. I just came up here to..."

"To what?"

She arches her brows, giving me a puppy-dog look that used to work so well on me. "I was curious."

"You were curious about my dead parents?"

"Sean told me this was a three-bedroom house, and I'd never been up here."

"So you thought you could just waltz in and make yourself at home?" Ice crackles in my voice. My whole body grows colder by the second. "Is this because you think you're going to get this place? I wasn't good enough to provide for you, but you'll still snatch my inheritance out from under me?"

This isn't hot rage. It's not anger that makes my blood boil while fire flares in my eyes.

No, this is cold, black fury.

My ex-fiancée—who broke up with me when I was at my lowest, when it became obvious I wouldn't make her a candidate for a *Real Housewives* show, who turned around and latched onto my rich uncle—is desecrating the one space in this house that I said was off-limits. She just made her way up the stairs and into the last space that belongs to my parents without care or respect for anything I asked.

How did I date this woman for so long? How did I consider *marrying* her?

She's selfish, egotistical, manipulative, and cruel. I must have been blind, out of my damn mind.

"Get out." I hobble over one more step to give her space to leave.

"Wes, please." She walks toward me. "I didn't mean to make you mad."

"Leave." My voice is like a whip lashing toward her. I want to hurt her. I want my words to sting, because she has no right to be here. No right to glide her way back into my life and make me feel this way.

"I loved your parents—"

"Oh, fuck off. You thought my parents had no ambition. You sneered at their café, at their life. I don't owe you anything. I welcomed you into my home out of respect for my uncle. I fielded your questions about this house and tolerated you sniffing around every corner because... I don't know why. Because I'm a fucking chump, I guess. Because even after you ripped my heart out of my chest, I still can't manage to tell you to leave me the fuck alone."

Alina's eyes grow wide, but I'm too far gone to care.

I point a crutch at the door. "Get the fuck out of this room. You didn't love my parents. You didn't love me. You probably don't love my uncle. If I catch you or Sean in here again, I won't hesitate to throw you out. Oh, and congratu-fucking-lations on the engagement, Alina. I'm glad you finally found someone with a big enough bank account to suit your needs."

Wide-eyed, Alina looks at me like she doesn't know the man in front of her. Hell, maybe she doesn't. Maybe I've changed.

I fucking hope so.

She straightens her spine and lifts her chin, then puts an extra sway in her hips as she walks away.

I knock the door closed with a crutch and sink down onto the floor, leaning my head against the edge of the bed. Anger leaks out of me as I deflate.

Exhaustion settles over me like a blanket, and all I can do is sit here and ache.

A WHILE LATER—I don't know how long—the doorknob turns. I watch it, eyes narrowing, and wait for it to open. Fiery red hair appears in the doorway and I let out a sigh. Simone stands in the opening, and when I say nothing, she slips inside and closes the door.

She takes a seat beside me, smelling of fresh air on a cold evening. She leans her head back and crosses one ankle over the other, the heat of her arm soaking into mine.

The last shard of ice melts in my heart, and I let out a sigh. "How was your walk?"

"It was nice. I feel better."

"Good."

Instead of answering, Simone moves her hand and places it on top of my thigh. Warm, comforting, familiar. Her touch feels too good to be real. Another bit of tension dissolves inside me.

"I found Alina in here and snapped at her."

"She told me."

"She did?"

"Mm," Simone answers. "I came in the door and it took her about three seconds to appear in the foyer with her arms crossed and a holier-than-thou look on her face. She said you were, quote, 'extremely rude' to her when she was here, and 'must be feeling unwell due to the ankle and the stress of the day,' but don't worry"—Simone grins, tilting her head toward me—"she forgives you."

I snort.

"I said that was very magnanimous of her. You know, I don't think that woman understands sarcasm. She just gave me a self-satisfied nod and went to her room."

My next snort sounds almost like a chuckle. I shake my head. "I can't believe I almost married her."

"Was she always like this?"

"Arrogant, needy, manipulative?" I ask.

"Mm."

"Probably. I don't even know anymore." I let out a long sigh and shake my head. "I shouldn't have gotten mad at her. Seeing her in this room...it felt...sacrilegious. Like she was desecrating the memory of my parents."

Simone's hand tightens on my thigh, her thumb making small circles over my pants.

I turn to look at her, pinching my lips together. "That sounds ridiculous, I know."

"It doesn't."

"I haven't been in this room for months. With the café leased to you four, this room is all I have of them." My voice cracks, and Simone's brows draw together. She lifts her hand to my face, letting her fingers skate over my cheek. I close my eyes, leaning into her touch. It feels too good to resist right now. I don't want to push her away. Having her here, beside me in this room, it doesn't feel like a sacrilege. It feels *good.*

"When my parents died," she says, "it took me a full year to sort through their house. Thank goodness they'd paid the mortgage, because if I'd had to get rid of the house right away, I think it would've broken me." Her fingers drift to my temple and down to my jaw. I keep my eyes closed as she speaks. "You grow up thinking your parents are invincible, and then you get older and logically, you know they'll pass away. Death is inevitable. In your head you know it's going to happen, but it's still a horrible shock when it does. It's so...final."

"I wasn't ready," I admit.

"None of us are. You don't need to explain why you don't want anyone in this space, Wes. And you don't need to feel guilty about throwing us out of it. You grieve the way you want to grieve, okay?"

I open my eyes to see her staring at me, her pale blue irises almost silver in the moonlight. Her hand is still on my cheek, thumb sliding over my stubble.

The need to be honest with Simone builds up inside me, a pressure that needs release. This whole situation—the will, the trust, my failed business, my parents' deaths, the fake relationship with Simone—it's worn me down to nothing. The words come before I can stop them.

"I lied to them," I whisper.

Simone frowns. "To your parents?"

Nodding, I swallow past the ball of emotion in my throat. "They thought my business was going well. I told them I had investors, which was true, but I didn't tell them the investors had pulled out. Three years before they died, my venture officially died. I was over three hundred grand in debt, Alina had left me, and I was nearly out on the street. I worked three jobs. At a bank during the day, rideshare driving in the evenings, stocking shelves at night. Paid off all but sixty grand of the debt when they died."

My throat is so tight it's hard to speak, but I need to get the words out. I need to tell Simone about my greatest shame, if only to say it out loud. I think a part of me wants to tell *her*, too, because I don't want to hide who I am from her. All the ugly parts of me.

"My parents worked their whole lives to build their wealth. They never had high-paying jobs, but they were savers. They invested. They built this house over years, slowly expanding and upgrading it while they ran the café. I didn't think they had as much as they did. I didn't know I'd be inheriting anything, let alone a couple of million. They'd bought and sold a couple properties in the area and made a lot of money, reinvested it. They were clever. When my father died, he told me they were leaving it all to me. They were so proud of what I'd done, how hard I'd worked, what I'd made of myself. He said I reminded him of himself, of his industriousness. Part of the will was a gift that I inherited when they died, and the rest—the money, the house, the café, the land—it's in a trust. My father told me marrying my mother was the greatest joy of his life, and he wanted me to find someone to share my life with. He said he knew Alina wasn't the one, but he was confident there was someone out there for me, I just needed to open my heart and allow that person to come. So my parents put a condition on the trust—I have to be married by the time I'm forty-five to access anything in it." I suck in a breath, focusing on the slow, steady movement of her fingers over my temple. "I didn't have the guts to tell them I was a failure. I was up to my eyeballs in debt, and after they passed, I had to use their hard-earned gift to pay off *my* debts. It made me feel sick. The thought of then inheriting all the rest of it... I don't deserve any of it. I turn forty-five in eighteen months, and I just figured I'd spend that time saying goodbye. None of this should be mine, anyway."

It takes all my effort to meet Simone's gaze. I expect to see pity, or a hint of judgement. Instead, I see softness.

She combs her fingers through my hair in a way that sends tingles down my spine. Her touch is like magic. "Wes, you deserve it all," she finally says. "Even if your venture flopped, you crawled out of the hole and didn't give up. You paid over *two hundred grand* in debt with your own hard work. Using sixty thousand dollars of your inheritance to finish it off should be something that makes you proud, not ashamed."

"I failed."

"You *survived*. You kept fighting."

"I shouldn't have used their money to fix my mistakes. I don't deserve the rest of what they earned."

She's quiet for a beat. "Am I right in assuming everything in the trust would go to your uncle if it doesn't go to you?"

I shake my head. "It'll get chopped up. I'll get part of it, he'll get some, various charities will get the rest. The land will be donated to Heart's Cove to be turned into a nature reserve, apart from a half-acre around the house and lodge. That goes to Sean."

Simone's eyes glitter like two aquamarine jewels. Somehow, my hand has slid onto her thigh. Her fingers are still running over my scalp, her other hand moving to my chest. The only time we've ever been this close is at night, when our bodies wrap themselves around each other while we sleep despite all our efforts to stay apart.

"Your parents would be prouder of your efforts to get yourself out of that hole and start over than they would be if your very first attempt at a business was a roaring success. Resilience is admirable, Wes, and you have truckloads of it."

Maybe it's the way Simone's looking at me. Maybe it's the breathiness of her voice when she finishes that sentence. Maybe it's just the fact that all I've been dreaming about is her lips, and hearing her say something like that about me mends some small ache in my heart.

Whatever it is, her words sink in. A rush of heat floods my body, and I can't take it anymore. I can't take having this beautiful woman by my side every day and not being able to crush my lips to hers. I can't take the dreams and thoughts and fantasies of claiming her body without being able to touch her. I need her like I need air. I need to taste her lips. I need to feel her skin against mine, her arms around my neck. I need to be able to run my hands over her body—otherwise I'll go insane.

It's more than lust. This need crawls up from somewhere deeper inside me. Some broken part of me that wants a woman like Simone to look at me like she needs me, too.

"Simone," I rasp.

"Yes?" A breathy whisper, barely audible.

"I want to kiss you."

We've drifted closer, almost nose to nose. Her hand is on the side of my face, her other fingers curling into my shirt. My own hand is sinking into her hip, dragging her closer.

She tilts her head a fraction of an inch, her chin dipping in a nod. It's all the permission I need. I close the distance between us and kiss her.

Simone's lips taste like candy. She parts them for me and I swipe my tongue over hers, groaning when I finally, *finally* get to taste her. Touching her feels like starlight dancing over my skin. Her mouth is the sun, the moon, the sky. My entire universe shrinks until all that exists is me and her and our lips.

I'm hungry for her. Starved. My hand moves to her cheek, tangling into her hair, pulling her closer so I can taste her more, more, more. When she claws at my shirt, fingernails scraping against my collarbone, I groan against her mouth.

Fuck fake. Forget about this being a business arrangement, about keeping my distance. Maybe tomorrow I'll care about any of that. All I want right now...is her.

I'M KISSING WESLEY BYRON. I'm *kissing* Wesley Byron.

In some distant part of my brain, I realize this is a bad idea. It muddies already murky waters. But I cave to the desire coursing through my body and ignore logic, reason, and responsibility.

And damn, it feels good.

My body arches into him as we sit on the floor, his hand curled into the hair at the nape of my neck. It's possessive, the way he holds me. Like he's dreamed of exactly how he'd want to kiss me, and he's finally getting to do it. My own hands have ended up twisted in his hair, his shirt. His lips drop to my jaw and he groans—oh, that *sound*—as his tongue slides over the skin of my neck. When he pulls my head back and leaves a trail of kisses down my throat, I have to gulp down air in short gasps.

After a week of absolute hell, when everything went sideways and every decision I made seemed to be the wrong one, this feels so right. As my fingers rip open the top few buttons of his shirt and my hands finally skate over those broad expanses of muscle, I sigh against Wesley's cheek.

"I've been waiting so long for this," Wes growls, his lips near my collarbone. "You have no idea, Simone."

"I have *some* idea." My chuckle is breathy.

The way his mouth moves over my skin makes my mind spiral. His lips move back up my neck as he inhales me, groaning as his teeth scrape over my earlobe. Fire jolts down my spine, pooling between my legs. My thighs are so hot I can feel every pulse of my heart. Every stitch of clothing on my skin.

Swinging my leg over to straddle him, I land on his lap with my forearms resting on Wes's shoulders. He leans his head back against the bed, eyes hooded and dangerous, hands sliding around my waist to rest on my lower back. A languid smile teases his lips, those damn dimples making me wish our clothes would dissolve into thin air.

Wes's fingers draw slow circles over the skin on my back. "When you came crashing through the forest that first day—"

"Crashing?"

His grin widens, eyes sparking. God, that expression on his face makes me want to melt. Like he's got me right where he wants me. Like I'm just a little rabbit trapped in his paws, and now he can slow down and play with me. I stop myself from grinding my hips against him, even though all I want to do is roll my hips until I feel how much he wants me, too.

"I thought you were crazy," Wes finally says. One hand moves from my back to my chest, his broad palm lying flat on my breastbone. His fingers tease the neckline of my shirt, and then it's his turn to pop my buttons open. One, then the next, then the next.

When my shirt lays open, his eyes drop to my chest. Hunger sparks in his gaze, and I've never felt sexier. He stares at me like I'm the most beautiful woman he's ever seen. His fingers move slowly, as if he wants to commit every line of my body to memory.

"You walked up to me and demanded I drive you home," he growls. "All fire and attitude. No fear." Fingertips slide down my bra strap and trace its outline over my breasts.

Heat curls in my gut as my back arches toward him before I can stop myself, as if my body needs more. Demands more.

The day I met Wesley, I was lost in the forest and I came upon some shirtless, tattooed Adonis chopping wood beside his cabin. I thought it was some sort of fever dream served up by my pesky hormones. It wasn't. He really was shirtless, chopping wood, looking like he wanted to chop *me*.

"I was afraid," I admit, my voice breathy. "It was dark and I was lost and you had an axe."

His fingers move lower, to the space between my breasts. My pulse hammers so hard I'm sure he can hear it, but Wes doesn't move any faster. His fingers trace the other side of my bra, teasing the skin on my breast as he lets out a long sigh.

"Do you remember—you explained to me what a conversation was? You said, 'It's called a conversation, Wesley. I say something, then you respond with something related, then we do it again a few times. It's actually considered quite normal among humans.'" His hand moves higher again, and I miss the warmth of his fingers on my breasts. He traces my bra strap up to my shoulder and pauses.

My lips twitch. "You seemed confused."

"You pissed me the hell off. I wanted to throw you out and tell you to walk home. I told myself I was glad I didn't have to deal with you any longer, because I could barely stand being in the cab of the truck beside you for the ten minutes it took to drive you back."

"Is that right?" My grin widens, and then I see something in Wes's eyes that makes me pause.

Feral hunger lines his face as his eyes rise up to mine. The hand that was on my back moves to my other shoulder. He hooks his hands over my shirt and under my bra straps, then tugs. My shirt and bra slide down, pinning my arms to my sides. Oh. Oh, wow.

He drops his gaze to my breasts, releasing a breath that says a thousand things. It says he's been waiting for this, wanting this, imagining this.

When he speaks again, his voice is nothing but a gravelly rasp. "I told myself I never wanted to see you again, then went home and jerked off to the thought of you." His right hand palms my left breast. "I came so hard thinking of bending you over and fucking that attitude out of you, Simone. You woke something up inside me that I haven't been able to ignore."

Breath catches in my throat. My nipples peak as heat floods my body from head to toe. With my arms stuck to my sides by way too many layers of clothing, my legs straddling Wes's lap, and his hands painting fire over my skin, I'm not sure I need him to bend me over and fuck me. I might just come apart right here, like this.

And when he rolls my nipple between his thumb and forefinger, a jolt of pleasure rocks me. I gasp, arching, and let myself grind my hips against him. Wesley moans at the movement, dropping his lips to my breast. God, his mouth feels good. I close my eyes and lean back, loving the way he touches me. Tastes me. Bites me. His hands are possessive as they hold me in place, one muscled arm hooking around my body to keep me pinned right where he wants me, my clothing twisted around my arms so I can't move. Not that I want to.

How the hell did we get here? A couple of hours ago, I was at a disastrous Thanksgiving dinner. I was waiting for the next bad thing to happen because I knew my life was just one big train wreck. Best friend angry with me, bank account dangerously low, and fake boyfriend having a mental breakdown over his uncle's engagement.

Now I'm straddling the hottest man I've ever seen, feeling his tongue slide over my pebbled nipple as he groans like he's tasting the sweetest nectar.

There was a time when I worried that I was getting older, that I was past my prime, that life was passing me by. It was around the time I turned forty. I'd been divorced for four years at that point and had no prospects, a fledgling business and a couple side jobs, and my love life consisted of a string of first dates. Logically, I knew it wasn't over, but then I'd look in the mirror and pluck out half a dozen grey hairs and more than a few wiry black ones from my chin. I'd find new wrinkles around my eyes, deeper laugh lines around my mouth. It felt like I'd wasted my chance at a happy, successful life.

But in this moment, with Wes's hands and mouth claiming me, I know I was wrong. I haven't wasted any chances. My body is healthy and it still works, damn it. I'm a woman who wants sex and passion and a man who makes me feel like I'm going to come with nothing but a swipe of his tongue across my skin. I'm smart and driven and I'm a survivor. A fighter. Every time life knocks me down, I'll get back up again. Over and over and over again—because I want moments like this. Moments that make me feel *alive*.

"You woke me up, Simone," Wesley whispers, sliding his hand up to the nape of my neck. He crushes his lips to mine, then pulls back. "I was asleep, and you woke me up."

My heart flips in my chest. It squeezes and releases and does its best to jump through my ribcage. I let out a trembling breath, not knowing what to say.

I could tell Wes I feel the same way. That I've been crawling through the past decade of my life, feeling like the weight of the world keeps me from standing up. He jerked me to my feet and showed me what it feels like to run again. To feel the wind in my hair and be *free*.

There are too many words though, too many feelings. Whatever's happening between Wes and me is so new, so fragile. If I say all those things, will he pull back? Will it ruin our arrangement? Will he retreat into himself again and leave me out in the cold?

Instead of speaking, I just angle my mouth against his. We

kiss, panting, and palm at each other like two teenagers in heat. My body is on fire, and all I want is Wes, Wes, Wes.

Then an elephant starts stomping up the stairs, and I freeze. A meaty fist bangs on the door, and Sean's voice calls out behind me.

"Wes! You made Alina cry, you childish piece of shit. Are you in there?"

I freeze, a bucket of ice water launched over my body. I'm stuck somewhere between blind lust and fear of being caught with my breasts flying free.

"Give me a second," Wes calls out, tugging my clothing back onto my shoulders before moving to his own half-removed shirt. We fumble with our clothes and I stand. Wes struggles to lift himself onto the bed, wincing as his injured limb drags across the floor. By the time he's sitting on the edge of the bed, a thin sheen of sweat covers his forehead and temples, but I don't think it's from our little make-out session. It's from pain.

I'd forgotten he was injured. I was so caught up in my own lust that I forgot his ankle was in pieces. Cursing myself, I nod to Wes and head to the door. Sean's angry face greets me on the other side. He startles when he sees me, then drops his shoulders and looks past me. "You made my fiancée upset, boy. I thought I could leave it, but she's still crying."

Wes combs his hand through his hair as he releases a long sigh, shrugging. "I'm sorry. I saw her in here and I freaked out. I'll talk to her in the morning."

Sean's lips pinch and he stares Wes down for a few moments, then turns on his heels and walks back down the stairs.

I release a breath and close my eyes, the last of the heat escaping my veins. Picking up Wes's crutches from the floor, I help him to his feet and open the door for him, leading him back to our room.

We don't say anything until we're behind another closed door. The moment is over. I don't regret it, but I can tell we won't be continuing where we left off tonight. Maybe not ever. There's tension in Wes's face, his shoulders, his posture.

Fucking Sean. He had to refer to Alina as his fiancée just then, too. Another ill-concealed barb to remind Wesley of his past. Maybe a jab at me, too. A reminder of all the complicated relationships that existed long before I was in the picture.

A reminder that maybe all I am to Wes is a way for him to get his parents' trust money, a way for him to keep this house.

What was I thinking, kissing him? Straddling him? Letting him rip my clothes off? Lust fogged up my brain and I couldn't think straight. Now what, I'm supposed to go back to being Wes's fake girlfriend for a few grand a month? Does sex negate that arrangement? *Stupid, stupid, stupid!* I shouldn't have given in to these urges.

I reach for my sleep clothes and avoid Wes's eyes until he drops his crutch and hops over to me, catching my hand. When I lift my gaze up to meet his, I see softness in his eyes.

He reaches up to tuck a strand of hair behind my ear. "I don't regret kissing you, Simone."

Oh. Right. I bite my lip and nod. "Me neither."

"I think we should take things slow. Things are... complicated."

"Yeah."

"And"—he moves closer, his breath warming my cheek—"I want my ankle to be healed before we take things further. I want to be able to do all the things I've imagined. Anything less than that isn't enough."

My heart skips a beat. His ankle won't be able to take his weight for another five weeks. I close my eyes and lean into him, nodding. "Let's go to bed, then."

Wes's eyes sparkle. He brushes his lips over mine, the movement soft, tender. That kiss—barely a touch—tells me more than the passion we shared earlier. It says he's telling the truth. He doesn't regret this, and he wants to take it further.

Maybe this fake relationship isn't so fake after all.

EIGHTEEN
SIMONE

I'M up before anyone else, as the sun is just painting the sky in pastel pinks to chase the night away. Throwing a glance at Wes's sleeping figure, I shrug on a pair of sweatpants, a hoodie, and some thick socks. When I get downstairs, I pull on my shoes and duck out the door.

My feet take me down to the coast, where the steep shoreline falls down ten feet to collapse into the ocean. Walking along the edge, the scent of salt-laden air and lush forest fills my lungs. A smile tugs at my lips at the thought of what happened last night.

At least something went right, finally—but now it's time to put on my big-girl pants and face my best friend. Fiona always wakes up early, and I'd like to catch her before she leaves for the café. My feet carry me along the coast until I see a familiar pier jutting into the ocean.

No one's in the water, unsurprisingly. It's freezing out. I turn up the dirt path, pass the outdoor shower, and make my way up and over the grassy knoll toward the house. The lights are on in the kitchen, and I see Fiona look up from the sink when I approach. She lifts a soapy hand to wave, and moments later she's at the back door.

It opens a sliver as Fiona uses her hip to prop it open as she dries her hands on a kitchen towel. "Hey."

"I come in peace," I say, palms up.

Fiona's lips tilt into a grin. "Coffee?"

"I wouldn't say no."

I watch her move around the kitchen like she's lived here her whole life. There's a new fruit bowl on the butcher's block island, and a stack of papers that looks like Clancy's homework. When we first arrived in Heart's Cove, Fiona and I ended up staying with Grant. This place felt like home the moment we walked in, but it's even more apparent now. It's warmer than it was a few months ago. More lived-in.

People might call it a woman's touch, but I think it's just the physical manifestation of love. The growing love between Grant, Fiona, and Clancy is so obvious in all the little touches around the kitchen and living room, in the sense of comfort and peace in here.

Fiona hums to herself as she pours me a mug, then nods to the French doors. "Let's talk outside. I can turn on the outdoor heater if it's too chilly."

I follow her out and take a seat in one of the porch chairs, watching her roll over an electric heater and set it between us.

We sip our coffee in silence for a few moments until I finally take a deep breath and speak.

"I'm sorry I didn't tell you about Clancy."

Fiona smiles at me, no animosity lining her face. "Thanks. Forgiven."

"Just like that?"

"By the time I got home last night, I wasn't mad anymore."

A breath leaves my lungs, relief flooding me. I hadn't realized how worried I was about Fiona being angry with me. Between last night's kiss—well, more than a kiss—with Wesley and today's conversation with Fiona, I might actually be catching a break.

"You made me think," Fiona continues, wrapping her fingers around her mug, "about the way we've been dealing with Clancy. I think she turned to you because you treat her like an adult—or at least more so than Grant and I do."

"I'm not sure that's a good thing." I snort, shaking my head. "She didn't exactly follow through with telling you two about the party."

"No, but she went there and didn't drink. She called a grown-up to come pick her up instead of getting in the car with someone who was drunk. She stuck by Allie's side. She made a lot of good decisions, apart from lying to us about going to the party. It made me think that maybe we need to give her a bit more freedom. I spoke to Grant about it last night, and I think he saw where I was coming from. If we give her more responsibility, she'll step up. If we keep treating her like a child, she'll rebel."

"Is Grant mad at Clancy?"

"Yeah."

"Mm." I take a sip, letting the hot coffee warm me. "Is he mad at me?"

Fiona pauses for a beat. "Yeah. But he'll come around."

"I'm sorry."

"Don't be." She reaches over and pats my arm. "What about you? How are you feeling? That wasn't exactly a perfect Thanksgiving."

I huff a laugh. "Nope, it wasn't."

Fiona stares out at the ocean for a few moments before speaking. "What... What's going on with you and Wes? You never even told me you were attracted to him, let alone dating him, but Clancy told me Alina thinks you've been together a while, and the way you were acting last night..." She frowns. "First it's just a project you're helping him with, and now you're staying at his place and hosting his family?"

I bite my lip. How much should I tell her? If I tell her about the fake girlfriend thing, I risk the whole town knowing. But if I don't, I'm no better than her teenage kid. Lying and hiding what's going on.

Fiona's my best friend. We came to this town together. We've been through divorces and breakups and grieved each other's parents together. She was by my side when I had my miscarriage and cheered me on when I started dating after the divorce. If I start lying to her now, it's tarnishing all those decades of friendship. The past two weeks have been awful, and it's because I've been making decisions I wouldn't normally make.

Last night, I didn't hold back when I kissed Wes. I was true to myself. This morning, I looked for Fiona because I wanted to be honest with her, too.

I can't stop now.

Turning to my best friend, I catch her studying my face. She tilts her head, the edges of her dark hair brushing her shoulders. "Fi, you can't tell anyone about this."

Her eyes glimmer. "About what?"

"I mean it. Not Grant, definitely not Clancy, and no way can you tell Dorothy or Margaret."

A smile tugs at Fiona's lips. "Cross my heart."

"I'm serious."

"I'll take it to my grave."

As she brings her cup of coffee to her lips and stares at me over the edge, I almost lose my nerve. I shouldn't tell her. Once I tell her, I'm putting it out in the open. I agreed to have a fake relationship with a guy. I'm faking this whole thing—and I might be falling for him while I'm doing it. What kind of person does that make me?

But Fiona just sits there, waiting for me to speak. The waves crash in the distance, and the electric heater whirrs between us.

With a deep breath, I begin. "When I asked Wesley to lease us his parents' café space, he asked me for something in exchange."

Fiona's eyes widen. "Simone! Did you tell him you'd have sex with him for the lease?"

"No!" A laugh bubbles up. "No, God no. I swear."

Fiona lets out a breath and leans back. "I almost just smacked you."

"Violence is never the answer."

"Says the woman who burned her ex-husband's clothing in a barrel."

"Since when is burning an inanimate object considered violence?"

Fiona purses her lips, but I know that look on her face. She's trying to hide a smile. Her brows arch. "You were saying?"

"Well, see, Wes's uncle was coming to town, and Wes knew he'd be expecting luxury, so he hired me to be the maid."

Fiona snorts, and I throw her a death glare. She waves her hand for me to continue.

"So the uncle shows up with his new girlfriend, Alina, who happens to be Wes's ex-fiancée."

Fiona's eyes widen. "No."

"Yep."

"Wow." She blinks and shakes her head. "That's...wow."

"I know, right? Anyway, I think Wes panicked. I happened to be standing next to him, and when he saw his ex, he just put his arm around me and pulled me close, then introduced me as his girlfriend."

"He..." Fiona's lips twitch as a little laugh escapes her. She glances at me, lips pinched together so hard her cheeks are starting to bulge. Another little giggle, then, "I would pay good money to see your face when he did that." She doubles over and lets her laughter overtake her.

"Laugh it up, Fiona," I drawl. "I'm sittin' over here with a mess on my hands, but by all means, keep laughing."

Between snorts, she manages to say, "I will. Don't worry, I will." And laughs some more.

After a few seconds, I can't hold back any longer and join her. The laughter feels like a release. Like all the stress of the week just leaving my body, like old times with a good friend.

Wiping her eyes, Fiona shakes her head and finally looks at me again. "You're pretending to be in love with each other...out of spite?"

I bite my lip. There's the whole trust and inheritance thing, but that's not my secret to spill. "Essentially, yeah."

Fiona stares at me for a second, blinking. "That's the most ridiculous thing I've ever heard. And you agreed?"

"What choice did I have? We needed a lease, and he just grabbed me! If I pushed him off and denied I was his girlfriend, he could have turned around and pulled the lease."

"We could have given him more money. You know, negotiated something normal."

I shake my head. "He wouldn't have wanted money."

"So now..." She frowns. "You're still pretending? Why didn't you tell me?"

"It was only supposed to be for a week. I thought I could get away with it. I guess I was embarrassed. I haven't been on more than first dates except for that one guy two years ago who lasted two weeks."

"The sleep-talker?"

"Mm-hm. I thought it would be simpler to do the week and tell no one. But then his uncle decided to stay."

Fiona blows out a breath, leaning back in her chair. "Wow. At least it wouldn't be hard to pretend. Wes is hot."

"Well...yeah. That's the problem." I bite my lip. "We...kind of kissed last night."

"In private?" Her eyes widen, gleaming.

God, it feels good to talk to her. I've kept this secret for so long, from the moment Wes and I made this stupid bargain till now. Telling Fiona the truth feels like lifting a weight off my shoulders. All my energy is flowing freely now, no longer blocked by the lies and half-truths. I feel like myself again.

I smile at her, nodding. "Yeah. It was a bit more than a kiss. It was a full-on make-out session."

She giggles. "Simone. This is such a bad idea."

"I know." I groan, closing my eyes. "It's going to blow up in my face and I'll have no one to blame but myself."

Fiona grins, a purely evil expression. "And I get a front-row seat."

She doesn't react when I roll my eyes and shoot her a sideways glare. She just laughs harder. Soon I'm giggling with her, feeling the tension in my heart unwind a bit more.

This is us. This is our friendship. Open, honest, fun, supportive.

"I'm glad you told me," Fiona finally says once we're done giggling like two schoolgirls. "I knew something was up when I saw those flowers and pillows in Wes's truck. I thought you were pulling away from me because I started dating Grant."

"What? No."

Fiona shrugs. "We came here together, then I found Grant. Then Clancy showed up and I got all wrapped up in this new life. I figured you might feel like I left you behind, and that's why you weren't talking to me. You didn't feel comfortable being around me when I have all this"—she waves a hand in a small circle—"going on."

Sighing, I shake my head. "I'm *happy* for you, Fi. I was embarrassed that the only way I can get a date is by getting a guy to fake it with me."

"Maybe he's not faking it." She nods to the forest, where Wes is hobbling through the trees, swinging on his crutches along a dirt path.

I jump up and rush toward him.

His cheeks are red and sweat makes his hair stick to his forehead, but he grins when I approach.

"What the hell are you doing here?" I glance at the thick forest. "Did you crutch the whole way here?"

"There's a path that goes straight through between the properties. I knew you'd want to talk to Fiona after last night, and I took a guess that you'd be here. It's not that far."

He knows me well enough to know where I'd be. He came looking for me. Something collapses in my chest, but I'm not ready to fully admit it.

Instead, I cross my arms. "Wes."

"Fine. My arms are sore. Happy?"

"How did you plan on getting back?"

He shrugs a big shoulder. "Same way I came."

Through the forest. On crutches. Alone. Even though it's ridiculous, there's something about seeing him here that warms my chest. I hide it with a glare. "Come sit down, you big oaf. What are you even doing here?"

"I got up and you were gone." His voice sounds almost... reproachful. He shrugs. "Plus, I thought you might need some moral support."

Fiona stands up and ushers us inside, where Wesley collapses onto a couch with a groan.

I plant my hands on my hips and stare at him. "You know there's this invention called the telephone? We even have pocket versions now, so you don't have to go traipsing through the forest looking for people. You can just call them to check where they are and if they need moral support."

"But then you wouldn't call me names and pretend to be mad."

"Who says I'm pretending?" I arch a brow. When the only response Wes gives me is one of his panty-melting smirks, I spin on my heels to see Fiona grinning at me from ear to ear.

Who says I'm pretending, indeed.

WHEN GRANT DROPS WESLEY and me back home—well, at Wes's house, but doesn't it feel like home?—there's a touch of awkwardness between us. I need to get to town to check on the café and start looking for new clients, and Wes needs to...do whatever it is he needs to do.

The kiss we shared blazes inside me, still hot and alive. We make our way to the kitchen, and I find myself sliding a hand over Wes's side. He's so solid. Muscular. Warm.

But he flinches away, eyes flicking toward Sean and Alina's room. "Simone." He closes his eyes, inhaling. "Last night..."

Oh, God. Blood rushes to my cheeks, flushing all the way down to my neck and chest. I read everything all wrong. He doesn't want this at all. He said he didn't regret it, but he made no move to touch me again. We're still just pretending. He doesn't want me at all. Last night was a mistake.

"I meant it when I said I want to take things slow." His eyes, emerald green in the early morning light, look earnest. "I just want to make sure we're not getting confused here. We've been spending a lot of time together, and sleeping in the same bed, and... I don't want you to get hurt."

My face turns to stone, if only to hide the hurricane raging inside me. He doesn't want *me* to get hurt? What a fucking hero. He's pulling away and making me feel like a fool, and then giving me nice words to soothe the sting. How can he come hobbling through the woods to find me because I left before he woke up, then turn around and flinch away when I touch him?

This is why I don't do more than first dates. I get too excited. I fall too far, too fast. I end up doing things like crawling back to my ex-husband after eight years apart just to get laid.

Not that I'd do that now. The thought of it repulses me.

Still...it's telling. I crave intimacy so much that I'm willing to debase myself for it. Wes is no different. I should listen to what he's telling me—really listen.

He doesn't want this.

But before I can turn away, Wes's hand reaches for my cheek. His touch is soft, calluses rough on my cheek, and his thumb teases my bottom lip. Then, he dips down and lays a kiss on my lips. It's quick, but it rips through me like lightning. I part my lips and Wes hesitates, pulling back, then lets out a sigh and deepens his kiss. It's like he's trying to resist, trying to pull away, but he can't help himself.

"All right, lovebirds," Sean's voice says from the living room.

"We get it. You're in love." He guffaws, gliding past us and angling for the coffee pot.

Wes and I fall apart. His eyes are warm, but I can't quite return the stare because I know exactly what's going to happen. He doesn't know what he wants, and he's going to play hot and cold with me—and I'll be the fool who falls for it.

I'VE NEVER TAKEN things slow with a woman. Not like this. Not sleeping in the same bed as her and not being able to touch her. Not kissing her whenever I can't resist anymore, only to tear myself away from the want and the need roaring in my blood.

But I'm taking things slow with Simone.

There's a constant tug of war inside me that only gets worse as the days go on. I want... I want *her*. But a voice in my heart tells me to hang back. Every time Alina walks into the room, I remember how easy it was for her to leave me. I remember how it felt to be reduced to nothing by the woman I loved because I couldn't provide for her. I couldn't pay for all the things she wanted, and she decided it wasn't worth it. *I* wasn't worth it.

Simone doesn't make me feel that way, but...but...

She kissed me right after I told her about the trust. In the moment, it felt natural. Our kiss was like a dam breaking, pressure rushing out of me as I did the things I'd been dreaming of doing to her, to her body...

But that *voice*. That voice in my head just won't shut up. The one that says it'll happen again. Simone found out about the money I stand to inherit if I marry someone, and she kissed me not two minutes later. What if she's playing me as hard as Alina was? What if these feelings bubbling up inside me are going to blow up in my face?

So, I keep my distance. I make excuses about my ankle, about wanting to be able to make love to her the way she deserves—but that's not all there is. I need...time. I need to figure out if this is real, or if I'm just making the same mistakes all over again.

Taking things slow, day by day, hour by hour...it makes me notice things about her. Appreciate them.

She once told me that my smile made me look more attractive. "From Broody McBrooderson to sex on a stick." As the days wear on, I find myself cataloguing her smiles, too. There's the slight tug at the corners of her lips when she says something snarky. She won't quite bring herself to laugh at her own jokes, but I can tell she enjoys them all the same.

Then, there's the polite veneer of a smile. Lips closed, eyes blank. My least favorite of her smiles.

There's the happy, peaceful smile that she sometimes graces me with first thing in the morning, when sleep hasn't quite cleared from her face. That smile never fails to stab me in the heart.

But my favorite smile of Simone's is one of full-blown delight. The first time I saw it was when I agreed to lease her the café. That day, it was tinged with relief and a hint of desperation. The next time I saw it on her face was when the trees cleared and she saw my parents' house for the first time. That smile isn't contained. It's wildfire brimming in her body, untamable.

I saw it again that day I stumbled out of the woods, after she was done berating me and calling me a bumbling idiot oaf of a man. When we were settled inside Fiona's house, Grant and Clancy shuffled into the kitchen, looked at the two of us, then at Fiona, and back at us. Simone glanced at me then, and her smile was pure sunshine.

Simone has this incredible ability to make me *feel*. So, as the days turn into weeks and the weather turns colder, I find myself hoping my uncle never leaves. He and Alina look for a temporary place to stay, but they haven't found anything to their taste. They stay in that room on the ground floor, and Simone stays in my bed.

Fine by me.

When he goes, Simone will move back to her place, and my life will turn dull and grey again. I won't feel the heat and energy that Simone gives me with nothing more than a smile or a touch.

Maybe there's something else between us, but I'll have to wait to find out. I can feel Simone's frustration mounting, though. Ever since we kissed, there have been questions in her gaze. Once or twice her hands have wandered, but I always catch them and press her knuckles to my lips.

"I don't want to take it slow," she says to me one night, breathless, when we're alone in our room.

Me neither.

There's a constant need inside me to claim her. To wrap my arms around her and drag her closer...but I hold myself back.

Nothing in my life has ever gone right. Nothing has fallen into my lap the way Simone did. It's too good to be true. A part of me doesn't believe...doesn't believe that I deserve it. That I deserve *her*.

Two weeks after our disastrous Thanksgiving dinner, my uncle confirms he's opening a store in Heart's Cove. He's found a space for the store and his corporate team has started doing research on competition in the area, and he sees a good business opportunity. He's going for it.

If he'd told me that a few weeks ago, dread would have seeped into my heart and I would've had to force a smile onto my lips. I would have wondered if it was some power play, some way to get the money in my parents' trust, an intimidation tactic. Maybe it is, but when he tells me, I find a smile already there.

"That's great," I say. "Heart's Cove is going to grow in the next few years."

"That's what I think," Sean says, smoothing his meaty hands over his hair. It gleams silver in the lamplight of the living room as my uncle meets my gaze. "Alina and I will be out of your way soon. We're going to her family's place for the holidays, leaving on Monday. When we get back, we should have a place of our own sorted out."

My face turns blank as my fingers and toes grow cold. I jerk my chin down, hoping I don't look as uncoordinated as I feel. He's leaving, which means Simone and I...

We'll have to decide what this means. What we want.

"I wanted to say thank you for hosting us. I can see you and Simone have made a home here. I"—he clears his throat—"I'm hoping to do the same with Alina."

I'm not sure when, but some time over the past couple of weeks, the sting of my uncle and Alina's relationship has faded. When he says her name, I feel nothing. No jealousy, no hurt, not even any sense of familial duty to be happy for him. I'm just...blank. And it feels *good*.

A part of me still thinks my uncle is opening a shop to keep an eye on me. To see if this thing between Simone and me is real, to see if that trust money will end up in my hands or broken up and partially in his.

Then a thought pops into my head, and I can't quite keep the tension out of my voice. "You're moving to Heart's Cove?"

Sean laughs, shaking his head. "God, no. We'll get a vacation home here, somewhere close to the ocean. It's too small for us. Alina likes the city." My uncle stands, dropping a hand on my shoulder, and shuffles toward his bedroom.

I sit in the living room for a few more minutes, until my hands find my crutches and I heave myself up. The muscles in my shoulders have strengthened over the past few weeks, and they no longer ache so much after a long day on the crutches. My ankle, too, doesn't pound with every heartbeat. Times like now, in the late evening, it gets sore, but it's manageable.

The front door opens, and Simone appears in the opening. Silhouetted in the night, she looks like a fiery, wild angel. She gives me one of her smiles—dazzling, bright, blinding. I respond with one of my own, and Simone kicks her shoes off before looping an arm through mine, crutch and all.

"Fiona's hosting Christmas dinner. She called Candice and Jen, and we're having a do-over. Your uncle, Alina, and Eli are invited, of course."

"They're leaving on Monday to spend the holidays with Alina's family. I'll have to check what Eli's doing. He might want to stay." I grin.

She smiles back, then my words sink in. My uncle is leaving... Understanding flits across Simone's face, then some other emotion I can't read. Her body goes still, the only movement a slow swipe of her tongue over her bottom lip. Slowly, she lifts her eyes to meet my gaze. "Do you... Would you like to come to Fiona's anyway? I know Thanksgiving wasn't much fun, but I promise Fiona knows how to throw a party, and I don't have any skeletons in my closet that will ruin another meal."

My heart stutters. I should say no, shouldn't I? Whatever's going on is complicated enough already. The words bubble up inside me. A thousand and one questions for Simone about her and us and what the hell this *thing* between us is.

None of them come, though. I find myself nodding. "Sounds good."

Simone's arm tightens around mine, and she gives me a new kind of smile. Warm, soft, and almost shy. It pierces through me like a spear. Then, as if catching herself, she shakes her head. "Let's get you to bed, sugartits. That ankle must be killing you by now."

So she noticed it hurts more in the evenings. She cares.

I follow her up the steps and let her help me onto the bed,

then watch her duck out of the room to go brush her teeth and get ready for sleep. Mundane routine isn't something I've ever cherished. I never thought I could have something so comfortable with a woman...but I have it with Simone.

SEAN AND ALINA leave a few days later, on Monday morning. Eli drives them to the airport in the rented car, having decided to stay here a few days before heading to see his daughter in Vermont. Simone grins at him, and we both know he'll be spending his days off at the Heart's Cove Hotel with a certain animal-print-wearing lady. Simone and I wave them away on the front porch. We stand there, unmoving, until the noise of the engine fades and all that remains is calm, winter-cooled silence.

"That's that, then." Simone looks at me, a question glimmering in her eyes.

"That's that," I repeat. "They'll be back in three weeks."

"Oh." She shifts her weight from foot to foot, opens her mouth and clicks it shut again.

I clear my throat. This awkwardness...is it my fault? Is it because I told her I wanted to take things slow? I gulp and blurt out the first thing that comes to mind. "I guess you'll enjoy sleeping in your own bed, huh."

Simone freezes, looks at me, and as if it takes all her effort, gives me a slow nod. "Yeah. I will."

"I mean," I stammer, "I figured you'd prefer to sleep at home. You always complain about me hogging the blankets, and with my uncle gone, I thought you'd want to go back."

"Of course." Simone looks at me, her face still frozen in that unreadable mask. "I guess I'll grab my things."

My joints lock up. I can't move. She thinks I want her to leave. She thinks I said that to kick her out.

"You can stay if you want," I add, but it sounds like an afterthought. It sounds like I'm throwing her a lifeline out of pity. "I mean it."

She shrugs, a casual gesture—but doesn't meet my gaze. "Two weeks in our own beds isn't a bad idea." A tight smile. "Won't take me long to pack my things up."

Pain flashes across my chest, my throat clogged with emotion. Words don't come, so I don't try to speak. I just gesture to the door and follow her inside, then sink into the couch while Simone heads upstairs. Distantly, I hear her moving around. I hear the clink of metal hangers against each other in the closet. A zipper. The bathroom door opening and closing again. Plastic knocking while she puts things in a bag.

I never thought packing made such noise. I never thought each of those sounds would make me wince with some invisible pain.

As I sit there, listening to Simone gathering her things, I realize I don't want her to leave. I don't want this to be fake, or a business arrangement, or some sort of half-baked plan to get my uncle off my back. I want her to *stay*. Tomorrow, I want to wake up with her by my side and see that first smile on her lips.

I'm falling for Simone. The truth of that thought blazes through me, bright and impossible to ignore.

But...does she feel the same way about me? Can I move past my demons and accept another woman into my life, especially when she knows everything that hangs in the balance? That trust money is like a weight around my neck. It makes me doubt her. Makes me think I've just attracted the same kind of woman all over again.

Then Simone's foot appears on the top step, then lower, and lower, until she's standing on the ground floor with her little suitcase propped up beside her. She glances at me, then over at the kitchen.

I stare back. "Simone, I meant it. You can stay if you want to."

"Do *you* want me to stay?" Each word is measured, weighted, slow.

Yes. God, yes. "I don't want to force you to do anything. I...I like having you around."

Her eyes dim. "Let me know if you need anything from me for your ankle. I'll be happy to help." The doorbell rings, and Simone gives me a sad smile. I haven't seen that one before. She jerks her thumb toward the entrance. "I asked Fiona to drive me to town."

She disappears for a few moments, then comes back with Fiona in tow.

Fiona's wearing a black beanie, almost the same color as her hair. Her cheeks and nose are rosy with fresh air, and she gives me a small wave. "Hey, Wes. Simone said you'd come to Christmas dinner?"

My tongue feels heavy, but I manage a nod. "Yeah."

"Good. She'll text you the details. See you in a few days!" Fiona smiles and gestures for Simone's bag.

Simone shakes her head and hauls it up herself, then

glances at me once more. "Call me if you need anything, okay?" She sounds sincere, and I thank her, but I already know I won't.

I'll spend these days alone, just like I used to spend my days before she came crashing through the forest. Relying on no one but myself, protected from the hurt and the pain that someone like her can inflict upon me.

It's better that way.

TWENTY

SIMONE

"YOU'RE RUNNING AWAY." Fiona shoots me a meaningful stare from the driver's seat. When I ignore it, she huffs. "Did you hear me?"

"I'm not running away from anything. And don't use your mom voice on me, Fiona."

Fiona snorts, turning off Wesley's driveway and onto the road that will lead us to Cove Boulevard and back...not *home*, exactly, but to my apartment.

"I saw his face, Simone. He didn't want you to leave."

"It's complicated."

"You're running away."

Frustration rumbles in my chest, but how can I put it into words? A couple of weeks ago, I was sure things with me and Wesley would progress. But every time I've tried to get close, he's backed away. He gave me some excuse about taking it slow and wanting to make love to me properly when his ankle was healed, to which I say, *Horseshit.* Does he think his injured ankle would stop me from orgasming? Does he think I'd be unable to climb on top of him and ride him? Are his hands broken? His mouth? His tongue? Did his cock suddenly malfunction because his foot is in a cast? Last time I checked, ankles weren't necessary for good sex.

No—I can read between the lines. Even when I told him about Christmas dinner, I saw him hesitate. Whatever happened in that room, with that kiss...he doesn't feel the same way I do.

But, coward that I am, I haven't been able to speak to him about it. I've just clung to the hope that one day he'll wake up beside me, tug me closer, and give me what I've been craving.

I'm not opposed to taking it slow. I can respect that, of course. But with Wes, it doesn't feel like it's sex itself that's holding him back. Every time I touch him, he flinches away. It's like it's *me* that makes him react that way, even if he says he wants to take things further.

What is it about me that's so repulsive? Am I too old for him? Too washed up? Too snarky?

I asked him directly if he wanted to stay, and the only thing he could come up with was, "I like having you around." Like I'm a pet. Is that really someone I want to sleep with? Am I so starved for intimacy that *that's* what I'm willing to accept?

"What's the big growl about?" Fiona turns onto Cove Boulevard. "You sound like you're about to punch through my car window."

Twisting my lips into a pinched grin, I shake my head. "Just pondering why-oh-why I continue to try to date when I know for a fact that men are useless lumps of meat without two brain cells to rub together."

"That bad, huh?" She parks the car outside my building, turning to look at me.

"I just... I thought we were going somewhere. We kissed, it was hot, and I thought something was happening. Then he played this whole hot-and-cold thing, and then as soon as his uncle left town he basically told me to go sleep in my own bed."

Fiona chews her lip. "Maybe he's scared."

"Of his big bad feelings for me?" I scoff.

"Well...yeah."

"I doubt it."

"Cut the guy some slack. You guys had this weird arrangement and he wasn't expecting to actually like you."

"You're really good at this pep-talk thing, you know. Please, tell me more about how unlikeable I am."

Fiona's smile fights its way onto her face. "If snark were fuel, you'd have enough of it to power an entire fleet of vehicles. That's what people see when they meet you. Irreverent, incorrigible, totally unexpected. But now, he's seen your squishy insides and he knows there's more than meets the eye. It took him by surprise."

"No, see, that's the problem. He *hasn't* seen my squishy insides."

Fiona bursts out laughing, swatting at my arm. "You're disgusting."

"Sex is not disgusting. I'm a woman, Fiona. I have needs. Just because you've got your sexy hunk of a man ready to attend to your every desire doesn't mean I've been so lucky."

Fiona lets out a sigh. "At least Wes is better than Nate. Wouldn't you rather a guy who plays hard to get over one who pesters you all the time and pounces when you're vulnerable?"

I wrinkle my nose. A few months ago, before I decided to move to Heart's Cove, Nate did exactly that. He could sense I was lonely and took me out, wined and dined me, and I ended up in bed with him. Old habits and all that.

"You know what? No." I pop my seatbelt out of its latch. "I don't want hard-to-get *or* pestering. I refuse to believe those are my only options where men are concerned. I want a man who is mature enough to tell me what the hell he's feeling, listens to me when I tell him what I want, and enjoys going down on me often and enthusiastically. Simple! I don't ask for much. But does this mythical creature exist?" I spin to stare at my best friend, needing a willing audience for the rant currently building inside me.

She doesn't oblige. Instead, Fiona just grins. "I'll see you tomorrow."

"Yeah, yeah," I grumble as I slip out of the car. I wave at my best friend and make my way upstairs, collapse in bed, and groan.

THE MORNING GREETS me with a grey drizzle. I throw on whatever clothes are closest and make my way across the street with my laptop under my arm.

Sven jerks his head at me in greeting. "The usual?"

"Hot latte today, please. Too cold for iced coffee."

"I thought there was no such thing as too cold for iced

coffee?" He flashes a smile at me and I swear—I freaking *swear* —I'm not attracted to him, but it still makes my stomach tighten in that particular way. My body has official gone off the rails. I'm no longer in control of this locomotive, and heaven help the next man who tries to hit on me. It ain't gonna be pretty.

I need to get laid. Desperately. Sven isn't even my type! Way, *way* too young. Being attracted to twenty-five-year-olds with big holes in their ears and half their heads shaved is not what I wanted for my life right now.

Plonking myself down on a chair in the back corner of the café, I start going through emails and trawling through online freelancing forums for my next gig—which, by the way, is also not what I wanted for my life right now. Then my phone dings. My bank is alerting me of a large deposit.

Wes's December payment just came through.

Sven drops my steaming-hot latte on the table and gives me another dazzling smile, but I barely even see it. My mouth tastes like acid and I lean back in my chair, staring at the phone screen. I should be happy about this money, but all I can think about is how I'd rather be waking up in Wes's bed than looking at a slightly higher bank account balance.

Ugh.

The cafe door opens, bringing with it a blast of cold, damp air. I'm ready to present the new customer with my very best scowl when it melts right off my face. Wes has the door propped open with one shoulder, moving his crutches over the small ledge at the threshold. His eyes meet mine immediately, then move to Sven as the barista rushes to grab the door. Wes nods in thanks, then hobbles directly over to me.

Wonderful. Fantastic. Just what I wanted for my morning.

I sip my coffee, licking the milk froth off my top lip. Wes's gaze snags on the movement, and I take back what I said before about Sven. That was a tiny little speck of a shadow of what I feel when Wes looks at me like that. Wes's eyes on my lips make my body feel like I've just dropped into a bonfire. I squeeze my thighs together as my heart skips, my cheeks flaming so hot I wish someone else would open that door.

He props his crutches on the wall and sinks down in the chair opposite mine. "Hey."

"Hi. I got your money."

A curt nod. A deep inhale. "I'm sorry about yesterday." His green eyes lift to mine. "I wanted you to stay. Not just because I like having you around, but because I like *you*."

I gape. It takes me a few minutes to recover, and I snap my mouth shut. Then I blink a couple of times and remember I'm supposed to answer. "Oh."

Real smooth, Simone.

Wes looks down at my coffee, then over to Sven. He doesn't even have to say anything; the barista just gives him a thumbs-up and starts making a coffee. Wes looks back at me. "I don't know what we're supposed to do."

My brain still isn't working. "About what?"

"About...us."

"Us," I repeat.

Spots of red appear on the apples of his cheeks. He takes a deep breath. "I like you, Simone. A lot more than I thought I would."

"How flattering." First Fiona, now him? Can't a woman get

a break around here? Just someone to give me a compliment that's an *actual* compliment for once? Not, *Hey, I thought you'd be horrible but it turns out you're not that bad!*

Wes combs his hand through his hair and blows out a breath. "I didn't mean it like that. I just mean…I like you. I'd like to…see where this goes. But with my uncle in town we had to pretend about so many things, and I don't know what's real and what's not anymore. And…" His face twists.

"You don't know if your feelings for me are real?" I arch a brow.

"They are." He meets my gaze. "It's just…a lot. My last real relationship ended six years ago. It was Alina. I don't know what I'm supposed to do, and I don't want to make the same mistakes I made back then."

Cool air washes over me. *Honesty.* That's what he's giving me. An honest conversation about his feelings—exactly what I asked for last night. Swallowing down another mouthful of coffee, I nod. "Okay. I understand now."

"So when I say I want to take it slow, it's not because of you, Simone. It's because I have no fucking idea what to do with… this." He moves his pointer finger between us. "I'm sorry if I hurt you."

"Apology accepted." My shoulders relax, and I let my lips slide into a smile. "Basically, you want to wait until the business portion of our arrangement is concluded. Once your uncle leaves, we can…start over. See where this goes."

Wes lets out a huge sigh and nods, relieved. "Yes."

"I can do that." I tilt my head. "For the record, my last relationship ended eight years ago. You're not a freak."

"Or maybe we're both messed up."

"Highly probable."

His lips curl, both dimples visible. Damn this man and damn his dimples. He's too handsome for his own good. He nods to my laptop. "Working?"

"One day I'll make enough to afford an office space." I grin.

He smiles as Sven drops his coffee off at the table, and finally looks around the coffee shop. "Is Grant here? He told me the roof repairs were finished. I was supposed to meet him here at eight."

"Ah. So you weren't here to profess your undying sort-of-maybe-probably-like for me at all." I pop a brow.

Wes laughs. He *laughs*. That sound shakes something loose in my heart, and I know I'd wait as long as he needs me to. Nothing else I've felt in the past decade, the past two decades, even comes close. Shrugging a big, strong shoulder, he smiles at me. "If you weren't here, I was going to go across the road and bang on your door until you let me explain myself."

My chest warms at that, and I can't even blame the hormones for it. I can't blame anything except the fact that I might be falling for this man—and falling hard.

TWENTY-ONE
FIONA

ON CHRISTMAS DAY, Candice arrives early with armloads of food, decorations, drinks, and all kinds of other supplies for the party. She hauls them into the kitchen and onto the island, blowing a strand of hair away from her face.

"Extras from Thanksgiving."

"Hopefully today goes a bit more smoothly." I glance across the kitchen to where Clancy is peeling potatoes. "No secrets to reveal today, kiddo?"

"I'm not a kid," she grumbles, then flashes me a smile over her shoulder. She's doing that more often these days—smiling—and it makes my entire soul tingle with happiness. Our relationship is brand new, but this kid has already wormed her way into my heart. Even when she takes off and goes to parties and defies our rules.

Grant strides into the kitchen holding bits of wood that apparently will extend the dining room table to seat all the guests. "She'd better not have any secrets. What did the counselor say?"

"Honesty and communication, Dad." Clancy salutes him with the potato peeler.

A curly blond head bobs into the kitchen. Allie smiles when she sees Clancy, immediately sliding over to her friend and showing her something on her cell phone. Both girls start giggling, Allie's face turning bright red. Probably a boy.

Candice glances at me, letting out a sigh, and uncorks a wine bottle. "Allie, make yourself useful and help Grant with the table. When you're done, you can go to the car and grab the presents."

Within minutes, there's a hum in the kitchen. I love having people over at the house. I love hosting parties and dinners, and I love knowing that there are so many people we care about in this town. I'm not expecting Simone and Jen until later, but someone still knocks on the door.

Grant ducks down the hallway and reappears with Agnes, her grandson Rudy, and Mr. Cheswick—a silver-haired older gentleman who has been a furniture maker longer than I've been alive—trailing behind him. Agnes has a Santa hat on. It has little LED lights flashing around the rim and a ridiculously large pompom. I repeat: Agnes the she-devil *has a Santa hat on.*

"Oh! Agnes." I move to the sink to wash my hands.

Agnes thrusts a wrapped, book-shaped present toward me, and another toward Candice. "For you two. A thank you for all the work you've done with Four Cups. It's added a lot to the town. I'll leave Jen and Simone's under the tree. I assume they'll be here later?"

I've never seen a surlier Santa Claus, but I just smile at her and accept the present. "Thank you, Agnes. You're too kind."

"She's an angel," Mr. Cheswick croons. His gnarled fingers curl over Agnes's, and her face softens ever so slightly.

I asked Dorothy about the two of them once, and she said they've been courting each other for the better part of a decade. All I know is Agnes is a lot nicer when Mr. Cheswick is in the room.

I nod at the old man. His silver-white hair is neatly cropped, and he's wearing a vest over a shirt and a bright-red bowtie with snowflakes on it. "You're looking very dapper, Mr. Cheswick. Did you get a haircut?"

"No, I got them all cut." His eyes sparkle, and I can't help but laugh. Clancy just rolls her eyes, but there's a hint of a smile on her face.

When I look at Candice to see her reaction, there's an odd gleam in her eye. Rudy and she are gazing at each other, both slightly blushing, both not wanting to look away. She's fiddling with the strings of her apron, and Rudy's doing his best to take on a casual pose as he combs his fingers through his hair. Huh. I remember a time when Candice told me to pursue Rudy—when she said a younger man might be exactly what I needed. Maybe she wasn't talking about me at all.

My attention is pulled away when Grant pulls a present from a cupboard and gives it to Agnes and Mr. Cheswick. He's spent hours carving a picture frame for them, and even found a photo where the two of them are actually smiling. It must be the only photo in existence where Agnes isn't scowling. Don't ask me where he got it—I have no idea.

When they open it, I see Agnes smile in my presence for the first time since I arrived in Heart's Cove. She looks almost... friendly. Grant sees me notice and winks. After a few more minutes, Agnes, Rudy, and Mr. Cheswick leave, and Grant slides his hands over my back. He places a soft kiss on the crook of my neck, tightening his hold on my waist. "This is very different from the last ten or so Christmases I've had."

"Same here." I spin in his arms and lay a soft kiss on his lips, my heart full of happiness. "Let's hope we have many more like it."

The sound of a loud engine pulls me away from Grant's arms, and I head to the front of the house to see Wesley arriving on a riding lawnmower, his crutches tied across his back like two very bulky spears. I open the front door as he cuts the engine.

"That's quite an entrance."

He grins at me. "My truck has a manual transmission. Can't drive it with this ankle."

A voice calls out from the driveway, "A couple of days without me and you're already falling apart, Wes." Simone appears around the corner carrying a big bag over her shoulder, filled with presents and food, I assume. "Couldn't you just call me to give you a lift?"

"I don't see you driving a car," he shoots back. "And I'd hardly call this falling apart. More like being resourceful."

Simone's face splits into a smile. Wow. I haven't seen her smile like that in ages. Her gaze shifts to me, and she seems to remember I'm standing here. Her face rearranges itself into a more neutral expression, but I know the truth—she's got it bad, and Wes is no better. They'll either get over themselves and admit they want to be with each other, or this will end in tears.

I know, because I just went through this a couple of months ago.

"Bickering like an old married couple already?" I grin. "Come inside, lovebirds. We've got booze and food and central heating."

Simone pointedly ignores my jabs, choosing instead to help Wes off the mower. They exchange a long glance, and yet another one of my friends ends up blushing all the way to the tips of her ears. I head inside to give them a bit of privacy.

I'M FULL OF FOOD, wine, and I've laughed so much my cheeks will ache for hours. By the time people start making moves to leave Fiona and Grant's house, my heart is overflowing. Wes's eyes meet mine from across the room, his eyelids drooping.

"You need a designated driver?" I ask.

"Are you offering?"

"I wouldn't want anything to happen to you. The forest is dangerous at night."

"I'm not sure you're any more alert or sober than I am." Wes smiles easily, arching his eyebrows at me. I haven't seen him scowl all evening, and I wonder if he needed an evening like this as much as I did.

Within minutes, I'm loading Wes and his crutches up on the riding mower and planting my hands on my hips. "How is this going to work?"

Wes pats his lap. "More than enough room for you here."

I laugh, only to see Fiona appearing in the doorway. "Should I be worried right now?"

Grant walks up behind her and slings an arm over her shoulders. "We better not have to unwrap you two from a tree later on."

"This thing tops out at four miles per hour," Wes replies. "I think we're safe."

"Brave words." I laugh, waving to Grant and Fiona as they close the door. Then, with a nibble on my bottom lip, I climb on top of Wes's lap. His arms wrap around me, and I put my hands on the steering wheel. "Let's go."

Wes leans forward and turns the mower on, his breath brushing against my ear. I resist the urge to arch my back against him.

The engine roars, sounding too loud in the quiet night. I laugh, maybe a little bit drunk off wine and happiness, and start driving the mower down the winding driveway. We bounce and rumble, and all of a sudden I become all too aware of the parts of me that are touching parts of Wes. My legs against his. His arms wrapped around my waist. My back touching his front.

And these damn *vibrations*. I grip the steering wheel, a smile curling my lips.

He leans forward, resting his chin on my shoulder. We don't speak, but my heart still flips in my chest.

I like this. I *want* this. I want to be able to go home with him after a nice evening and wake up next to him in the morning. I want intimacy.

When we arrive at Wes's house, in all its woodland fairytale glory, I cut the engine but make no move to get up. Neither of us moves. Wes's arms stay wrapped around me, his heart thumping against my back so hard I wonder if he's thinking the same thing I am—that it would be so, so easy to stumble inside together and take this relationship all the way.

I spin on his lap, sitting sideways across his thighs, and hook an arm across his shoulders. One of his arms is across my back, curling around my waist. The other is resting over my lap, its weight hot on my thighs. His arms feel safe and warm and so, so comfortable. I don't want to leave.

Even when the chill of the air makes my breath puff, I don't move. His eyes look dark, the color of pine trees at night. And his lips...

Wes leans in and kisses me. His mouth is warm, soft, needy. With his grip tightening on my waist and my lap, I lean against his chest and part my lips, needing more of him. Needing his tongue to claim me, his mouth to take me. Every day since our first kiss, I've been wanting this. I've replayed what we did over and over again, but it's nothing compared to the real thing.

The hand Wes had on my lap lifts to my cheek, his touch gentle. Reverent. "Simone," he growls like my name was ripped from his throat.

"Yeah?" I nip his ear, his neck.

"I want you so bad."

Electricity trips down my spine. He holds me tight and I know that I could die happy in his arms, hearing him rasp those kinds of things in my ear. Knowing what he told me a couple of days ago, though, I pull back and look in his eyes. "But?"

"Maybe I've been an idiot to push you away."

I arch an eyebrow. "Maybe?"

A dark chuckle slips through his lips, the sound making my gut tighten with anticipation. "Fine. I wanted to take things slow because it felt like too much, too fast. I didn't know if I liked you because we'd been thrown together, but these few days without you..." He leans his forehead against mine. "I missed you."

My poor, fragile heart. It doesn't stand a chance.

I've always been this way. I love easily and quickly. No matter how much snark I dish out, it's all just to hide how easily I let myself fall.

When I met Nate, he swept me off my feet. He spoiled me, flattered me, made me feel like a princess. Then the years wore on, and we realized we didn't have much in common at all. I was bored. I started my online marketing business, thinking Nate would understand. I wanted him to see me as a contributor. As a *person*. As someone worthy of his respect, not just a wife with a little side business to keep me busy—but I never had his respect. I fell for the lifestyle and the safety and the routine, and I fell for the idea of who I wanted Nate to be. Not who he was. We didn't build a strong partnership; we just fell into marriage because it's what we were supposed to do.

It ended, and neither of us was devastated. It was hard to leave him, of course. There was heartache—but we both bounced back. We both moved on—well, mostly. We stayed civil, and we still sometimes circle around each other wondering if maybe there was something between us all along.

There isn't. I know that now with a certainty that reaches

deep into my soul. My ex-husband and I will never be what the other needs, and that's okay.

Now, as I sit astride Wes's lap and look in his forest-green eyes, I wonder if I'm being the same fool I was all those years ago. Is he just some strong, sexy man that makes me feel wanted? Is it the *idea* of him that I like, or the actual man? Am I looking for security and intimacy, and he happens to be the first guy who might be able to provide it? Am I just sick to death of being alone?

In short—am I making the same mistakes all over again, or do Wes and I actually have something special? With how things started between us, I'm just not sure. It's been so fast. So confusing.

But right now, under the moonlight in the silence of the woods, it feels real. It feels special. It feels like it could be the start of a real partnership between adults who know what they want.

His breath skates over my cheek as my eyelids flutter closed. "I missed you too, Wes."

"Stay here tonight." It's barely a whisper, but it clangs through me.

I open my eyes again to see him staring at me, hopeful. All I can do is nod.

BETWEEN CRUTCHES, stairs, doors, and a lot of grunting, it takes a few giggling minutes for the two of us to make it upstairs. As soon as I enter the bedroom, I let out a sigh. I turn to see Wes standing by the door, watching me. He makes his way to the bed and sits down, laying his crutches on the floor by his feet. Then, his fingers start working to unbutton his shirt.

"Here," I say, closing the distance between us, "let me help."

His hands drop to his sides and I work on the buttons. I can feel his gaze on me, hot and hungry, but I keep my attention on the buttons. One by one, they pop open. I pull his shirt from his pants and push it off his shoulders, letting my fingers run over his skin. Warm, hard muscle. Wes lifts his arms and I pull off his undershirt, revealing a broad expanse of chest.

My fingertips graze his tattoo, the way the whorls and curves paint over his side and pectoral muscle, breath hitching in my throat. Finally, I find the courage to lift my eyes to meet his gaze. In his eyes, I see dark, feral hunger. Need.

Lust crashes into me, but I try to rein it in. My hands tremble as I take his clothes and lay them across a nearby chair, then walk back to him and let my hands drift down his chest to his belt.

Wes's breathing speeds up when my fingers work the buckle open. "You first," he rasps, reaching for my dress. His hands slide over my hips and he turns me around, reaching up to the center of my back to tug down the long zipper. I hear him inhale, then his hands slide over my shoulder blades to push the fabric off my body. It pools at my feet as I turn.

Thank goodness I wore decent underthings today. Just a plain, nude bra and lacy boy shorts that don't leave panty lines, but judging by the feral growl in Wes's throat, he doesn't mind their simplicity.

Wes looks at me, eyes shining. Every woman should have a man look at her like that—like she's the most incredible being he's ever seen. My heart stutters, fire blazing through my core. His fingers slide over my hips, tugging me closer.

I climb on top of him, straddling his legs with mine. He exhales slowly, eyes hooded, letting his hands slide back toward my ass. With my forearms resting on his shoulders, I lean down and kiss him. I don't think I'll ever get sick of doing that—of melting every time my mouth connects with his. His lips are soft, and warm, yet demanding. He nips at my bottom lip, his hands squeezing my ass as he pulls me closer.

Breathless, I kiss him harder. I tug his hair, arch my back, grind against him.

"Simone," he rasps, the noise sending a thrill jumping down my spine. Heat pools in my stomach. Lower.

"Yeah?" I reach down between us and palm the hardness below his belt, exhaling as I feel him. All of him.

He groans. "I'm sorry."

I pull back. "For what?"

"For pushing you away these past weeks." His fingers dip below the waistband of my undies, hands sliding onto the bare skin of my ass.

I shiver at the touch, my lips finding his again.

When his hands slide up my spine to unclasp my bra—oh, his hands feel like heaven on my skin. The moment my bra is unclasped and thrown across the room, his mouth is on my breast. Splaying one hand on my back, he cups my breast and takes my peaked nipple between his lips. I arch against him, sighing. His teeth graze my breast, gently, gently, but it turns my body molten.

I tremble, tugging his hair, palming his shaft, feeling like I'll come apart with nothing more than his mouth on my breast. He moves to the other one, moaning, his thumb brushing over the wet, pebbled nipple he just left behind. With his other hand sliding down my back and pulling at my panties, I slide off him and let them fall to the ground.

He growls, animalistic, sliding his hands down my thighs. Then, before I can even yelp, Wes grabs my legs and pulls me on top of him. He falls back, his hands still gripping mine, pulling me higher on the bed. He's rough, hauling my body up so my knees land on either side of his face, my center close, so close to his mouth. I fall to my hands, looking down at the sight of his face between my thighs.

A whisper of breath over my most private parts sends my whole body trembling. Then Wes licks me once, closing his eyes. "Finally," he groans against my clit before sliding his tongue over it, gently, possessively, his hands gripping my thighs so all I can do is kneel on top of him and gasp. He devours me just like that, as I pant, grinding his face, feeling every part of my body slowly coming apart at his touch.

Moving his mouth lower, Wes slides that tongue—that wicked, beautiful tongue—down to my opening. I gasp when he thrusts it inside me, bucking against him. He holds me down, chuckling, his hands gripping me so tight I know they'll leave red marks. I don't care. My arms can't hold my weight and I fall to my forearms, my back arching, hips grinding, and I come apart.

Wes doesn't stop until I stop bucking, until my body is limp, until I push back and roll off him, both of us lying sideways across the bed. His smile is pure male arrogance as his hand slides up my thigh and over my hip. "I've been wanting to do that for a long time. You taste like heaven, Simone."

All I can do is blow out a breath, closing my eyes for a moment. The bed dips as he sits up, and I crack an eyelid to see him standing on one foot as he unbuckles his belt. His gaze meets mine, fire flickering in his eyes.

I curl an arm behind my head and watch him push his pants down, a slit I hadn't noticed in one pant leg letting him remove the pants over the grey air cast on his foot. His considerable length springs free as he pushes his boxers to the floor, hopping on one foot to take them off.

"Is your ankle sore?" It's been nearly six weeks now, so he should be almost ready to put weight on it, but I don't want to hurt him.

Wes shrugs. "Don't worry about my ankle. It's fine." He sits on the bed again, pulling himself up to the pillows and patting the space beside him. "Come here."

"I don't want to hurt you," I say, glancing at the cast.

His hand curls around his shaft, and a new wave of heat spills into my veins. Seeing that broad hand wrapped around his cock makes everything inside me burn up. He moves his hand up and down once, twice, and before I know it, I'm crawling toward him. *Crawling.* His eyes turn wicked as he watches me swing my leg across his body, straddling him once more.

"There are so many ways I want to fuck you, Simone," he growls. "As soon as this cast is off, I'll take my time showing you every single one."

My body is already craving him again. The ache, the emptiness inside me almost hurts. "Condom?"

He shifts to the side table, finding a condom in the top drawer. I watch him slide it over his cock, every glorious inch of it. My breaths are barely more than gasps, my whole body bathed in fire. I hadn't realized just how much I wanted him. How much I needed him.

But now...

As I shift my hips on top of him, reaching between us to grip him with one hand as my other hand sweeps over his broad, muscular chest, I realize that I've been waiting for this since the first day I stumbled on him in the forest. I've dreamed of him. I've thought of him with my vibrator, my fingers, my shower head between my legs. I've imagined all the ways I want to make him come. I've pictured his cock in my mouth, his tongue all over me, his body caging mine in every position imaginable.

Being on top of him like this, while he watches me through hooded lids like I'm a goddess, makes me feel so sexy and powerful and alive.

So, when I lower myself on top of him and gasp at the *feel* of him, I let a smile curl my lips. Better than I imagined, definitely.

Wes growls, his hands finding my waist, sliding up to my breasts, down to my ass, as if he's trying to memorize every bit of my body. I open my eyes and lean down to brush my lips against his, rolling my hips to take him deeper. He rewards me with another growl, with a tweak of my nipple with his fingers. Then, he slides his hand up to curl into my hair as he thrusts his tongue into my mouth and bucks his hips toward me.

I gasp, arching, and then everything becomes a blur of flesh and lips and lust. I forget about the cast, about being gentle. My hips grind and buck as he urges me on, his mouth open in a groan as I lean back, slamming myself on top of him.

I love the way he watches me move. How his eyes drift down my body to look at where we're joined. How his hands are soft, reverent, then claiming and rough.

Being with Wes…it's magic. It's better than any sex I've ever had, and he only has one fully functional leg. When his hand moves between us and his thumb finds my bud, it only takes me seconds to come apart on top of him. Like lightning striking my body, like every nerve ending screaming at once. Pleasure blows me apart and puts me back together again.

"That's it," Wes growls, his voice doing as much to make my pleasure crest as anything else. "Come on my cock."

Dirty words that only make me moan, grinding against him until I feel him tense, a guttural groan rumbling through his throat. Finding his own release, Wes wraps his arms around me and pulls me down on top of him. We're panting, sweaty, sated.

His fingers curl into my hair and he tilts my face back, kissing my lips so gently it makes my head spin. I whimper against his lips, then lay my head in the hollow of his shoulder, sighing.

"Merry Christmas." I can hear the grin in his voice. "Best. Present. Ever."

TWENTY-THREE
SIMONE

I WAKE up snuggled in Wes's arms. This time, instead of quietly slipping out of his hold, I burrow deeper into his arms.

A rumble goes through his chest as he wraps his arms around me and pulls me close, my back to his front. He nuzzles into the crook between my neck and my shoulder, his breath hot at my nape. His body is warm at my back as we fit together like we were made for each other.

"You smell like you," he mumbles in a sleepy voice, inhaling the scent of me deep into his lungs.

Warmth spreads through me, a smile curling my lips. "Is that a good thing?"

"It's a great thing."

His hand drifts down my stomach, then lower, and a line of red heat goes through me.

We don't get out of bed for a while.

. . .

THERE'S something different about having breakfast in a quiet house with no one but Wesley and me. When Eli would cook for us, or when Sean and Alina would be on just the other side of the wall, there was always...distance. Now, though, Wes hobbles behind me when I'm making coffee and wraps his arms around my waist. He smooths his hands down my hips, over my thighs, as if he can't resist touching me, can't stay away from me for long.

We enjoy the weak winter sun as it streams through the living room windows, sipping our coffees. I prop one foot on Wes's thigh as if I, too, need some point of connection to him. He keeps his palm over my ankle, his thumb making slow circles over my skin.

Yes, I could get used to this.

We spend the day together, lazy, enjoying the warmth of the house while the weather stays cool outside. I haven't had holidays like this in a long while. Days where I just feel peaceful, where there's no hidden feeling deep in my heart that I'm missing something in my life.

The next day is much the same. I do a run into town to get some groceries and fresh clothes, but I end up back at Wes's place. Food, sex, laughter, and lots of cuddling.

By the time the new year comes along, I've spent hardly a moment away from Wes. I've done a bit of work, but mostly I've just enjoyed how it feels to have somewhere that seems like home. When I met Wes last summer, I never would have imagined that six or so months later, he'd be my New Year's kiss. Now, though, when we ring in the New Year from the comfort of his sofa, looking at each other as the countdown on the television strikes midnight, I couldn't imagine anything different.

How could it be less than two months since this little bargain started? I've been waiting, stumbling through the dark looking for him for decades, and now that I've found him, my entire past shrinks to nothing. Life is perfect with him in it.

IN THE FIRST week of January his cast comes off, and I grin as he takes his first wobbly steps. A predatory gleam shines in his eyes, and I know he's thinking of all the things we'll be able to do now that he has the full use of his body.

We barely make it through the front door when we get back from the doctor's office. Our shoes and coats fall from our bodies one by one, leaving a trail behind us. Then Wes cages me against the living room wall at the foot of the stairs. He inhales the scent of me, his nose running up my neck as a groan rumbles through his chest. I close my eyes and sigh, my whole body tightening when he takes my hands and pins them by my head.

I never thought sex could be like this. So...intense. With rough movements, Wes pushes my pants down before pressing his body against mine. I fumble with the fly of his pants, reaching in to feel him. Feeling like I'll die if I don't.

Then he's hooking my leg around his waist and fucking me up against the wall. Feral, wild, with no sounds but our gasps and grunts and moans.

When we fall apart, I cling to the bannister of the stairs and let out a sigh. "You know, I doubted it before, but maybe healthy ankles are necessary for sex."

He grins. "I'm only getting started."

AS THE WEEKS GO BY, I pick up a couple clients for my online marketing business, and even convince Agnes to let me set up some social media pages for her. She was impressed with my idea to set up a display in the café, and even though I'm friendly with the twins she can't stand, I seem to have entered her good graces.

Slightly terrifying to work with her, but I'll take any client I can get.

Things are...good. Really good.

Wes has a new project he's been working on—some sort of building in town that he wants to fix up. He says it used to be his mother's favorite space, but he won't tell me where it is or what he's doing. "It's a surprise," he promises, and even though it kills me not to pester him with questions, I do my best to refrain. There's always a grin on his face whenever he talks about it, and if I happen to catch him coming home from it, he's always dusty and dirty and sweaty, as if he's been doing physical work. The gleam in his eyes warms my heart.

Maybe Wes needed something like that. A project. A way to honor his parents instead of avoiding the memory of them.

It's nearly February by the time Sean and Alina come back. Eli, who left in mid-January to go work with them again, seems almost relieved to be back in Heart's Cove. He asks to stay at the cabin, and both Wes and I are more than happy to let him.

When Sean and Alina move into a rented place on the edge of town, I don't dread their arrival. Wes and I are good. We don't have to fake it anymore. What's happening between us is *real*. When we meet up with Sean and Alina for dinner on one of their first evenings in town, the meal is actually pleasant. The dynamic has changed—there's less tension. Less falseness.

The meal we eat is *delicious*. I haven't had food from a high-end restaurant like this in...years. I don't regret giving up that lifestyle when I divorced Nate, but I'm not too proud to say I do miss some of the nicer things that life had to offer. Wes gives me a funny look as I order a bottle of wine for the table, arching his brow when I go through the whole rigamarole of tasting it before the waiter pours. It's like he's surprised I'm comfortable in a place like this, when I'm usually the queen of casual.

But, hey—if Sean and Alina offer me a delicious meal and all I have to do is endure their presence, who am I to refuse?

It helps that Wes is beside me. He's a calming presence at my side, the warmth of his body always present. His uncle tells us about the research his team has put into the new store location, and—call me crazy—I actually think a sporting goods store will be a great addition to Heart's Cove.

When we finish our food and sit at the table with the last few sips of our wine, Sean's eyes flick between the two of us. "You two seem very cozy." He swirls his glass of wine a couple of times. "Even more so than when we left."

Wes shifts in his seat. "We had nice holidays together."

"That's great," Alina cuts in, curving her lips into a smile that doesn't reach her eyes.

Sean clears his throat. "Well, if that's the case, maybe we should talk about things."

I frown. Talk about things? I glance at Wes, whose face has flushed pink.

Sean takes a sip of wine before setting the glass down, its stem looking comically slender in his big hands. "If the trust will be released to you, Wes, I'd like to offer you a business proposition."

Wes stiffens beside me. "Simone and I aren't married."

Oh. *Oh.* I'd almost forgotten about that—about the trust and the inheritance and the multimillion-dollar payday hanging over Wes's head. Such a ridiculous condition on his parents' trust. Marriage should never be forced, and it certainly isn't necessary in order to be happy.

Sean waves his hand and looks me up and down as if he's searching for something—for what, I'm not sure. He returns his gaze to Wes before speaking. "If the trust doesn't go to you, I was going to use my portion of it to start the Heart's Cove location for my new store. But now that it seems you'll be inheriting it after all, I'd like to work with you. If you're willing to sell me some of your parents' land, I'll develop it—bed and breakfasts or an outdoor retreat, something that will feed customers to the store—and cut you into the deal."

"We're not married," Wes repeats through clenched teeth. A muscle feathers in his cheek. "I don't know what will happen to the trust money, to the land."

Alina snorts. "You'd be a fool not to get married when there's that much money on the line, Wes."

"You would know, wouldn't you?" he snaps.

I sit very, very still, my eyes on my glass of wine.

Alina tilts her head ever so slightly, her face a mask of calm. "Maybe this type of attitude is the reason your app failed to take off the way you wanted, Wes. You don't have what it takes to make it in business."

The subtext of her words is painfully clear. *This is why I left you*, she's saying. She might as well have a billboard attached to her forehead with the words painted on it.

I gulp, putting a hand on Wes's arm. "We're not talking about marriage right now," I say. "Whatever Wes wants to do about the land and money, that's his business."

He throws me a glance that has relief and softness written all over it, then hardens his expression to face his uncle. "I don't want to talk about this tonight."

"Regardless of what you want to talk about, Wes, you understand that you'll have to make a decision soon." He turns to me. "You both will."

"Especially if you want more bags like that one." Alina flicks her eyes to the Birkin hanging off the back of my chair.

Yes, I wore it to dinner—but this time, it wasn't in some vain attempt to fit in. This bag has actually become my everyday bag at some point over the past couple of months. Yes, I realize it's ridiculous to wear a bag worth that much around town. I know I'm probably ruining the resale value. But...why not enjoy it? It's mine, after all. It doesn't have to be a symbol of my failed marriage or a token of the lifestyle I gave up. It's just a bag. A nice one, at that. It matches my eyes.

I touch the blue leather and shrug. "One is enough."

"That's what they all say," Wes's uncle replies with a snort before draining his glass.

Wes seethes next to me, his whole body vibrating.

I clear my throat and stand up. "Thank you for a wonderful evening. I need to be up early tomorrow. Wesley?" I extend my hand toward him and he nods, then follows me toward the exit.

Cool air rushes over us as soon as we step outside, the night clear and crisp. Wes tilts his head up to the sky and lets out a long sigh. "He'll be pestering me about that trust for the next year."

"Isn't it in his interest for you not to get the money?"

"I thought so, but if he thinks he can get me to agree to a business deal..." Wes's lips scrunch. "He probably thinks he can make more money off me if the land and inheritance stay within the family. If I don't get it, a huge portion of it gets donated."

"It all seems so..." I blow out a breath. "I don't know. So far removed from what your parents must have wanted."

Wes slides his arm around my shoulders and pulls me close. "I know."

I tilt my head to take in the hard planes of his face, the rough-hewn features that have always made my heart flip. This whole business about marriage...I don't know what to think about it. It's not what I want right now. Jumping into another marriage when I lost myself so thoroughly in my first one seems like a terrible idea.

But if Wes asked me, if he told me he wanted to get married to keep the house that he loves so much...I think I'd say yes.

That probably makes me a fool.

A part of me screams at the thought of giving up my hard-won independence. Sure, it would be nice to have someone by my side. To not scratch together a living from the dregs people offer me, to not have to hunt down clients for payment.

But the money I have is *mine*. I don't have Birkin bags lining my closet, but I can stand with my head held high about what I've accomplished in the past eight years. Giving that up to marry someone...I don't know if I'm ready for that.

"What's the deal with the purse," Wes finally says. "Is it expensive or something?"

I grip the handles a bit tighter. "Um. Yeah. It's a designer bag."

"And would you"—he clears his throat—"would you want more bags like it?"

I consider his words, what they mean. What he's asking. Letting out a long sigh, I shrug. "Sure, who wouldn't? It's pretty. But it doesn't mean anything to me. Not the way it used to."

Wes glances at me, assessing. "What did it used to mean to you?"

I blow out a breath. "It was...a symbol of what I used to have, I think. Of what I gave up. The cost of my independence."

His arm tightens across my shoulders as we walk through town, our breaths misting with every exhale. "And what is it now, if it's not a symbol?"

"Now, it's a bag," I reply. "It's just a bag."

TWENTY-FOUR
WESLEY

WITH MY UNCLE and Alina's return to town, all my fears return with a vengeance. After weeks holed up at home with Simone without a care or a thought about the future, thinking about this inheritance feels...dirty.

I can't get married.

I don't *want* to get married just to pad my bank account.

I can't ask Simone to marry me for a thousand reasons. We just met, for one. We only just started taking things seriously. Sure, we get along, but that doesn't mean we want to spend the rest of our lives together.

Plus, the inheritance makes things...complicated. Logically, I know she's not faking her interest in me. She's not pretending to like me just to get that money. I know that. I tell myself that, and when my arms are around her and I see the light in her eyes, I believe it.

But when I'm alone with my thoughts, they circle like sharks.

She kissed me the moment after I told her about the trust, about the conditions. Our relationship deepened *after* I revealed that to her.

What if she's just like Alina?

The way she gripped that purse when I asked her about it... is that what she sees in me? Someone who will be able to provide designer bags and luxury for her? She seemed to enjoy that meal at a fancy restaurant. What if she really does value a wealthy lifestyle?

Still, our days continue much like they did before. With my uncle and Alina staying in their own place, and with Eli still using the cabin—although he insists on paying rent now, as if he intends to stay long-term—Simone and I stay in my parents' house together. It's starting to feel very much like home—especially with her in it.

But, but, but...

I can't let go of my past. Every time I see Alina, it reminds me of the hurt she caused me. The betrayal. The sting of her choosing my uncle and throwing it in my face.

Maybe this type of attitude is the reason your app failed to take off the way you wanted, Wes.

Her words from that night ring in my head. *I failed, I failed, I failed.* She left me because I failed. Because I couldn't provide. Because I didn't have that killer business instinct that seems to run through every other member of my family, parents included.

Simone doesn't bring up the inheritance, and I'm grateful for it. I watch the way she works, how doggedly she looks for clients and provides the best possible service she can. Half the town's businesses have hired her for various online marketing projects or to run their social media pages. Every time someone new hires her, she comes home flushed and excited, beaming with pride.

It really doesn't seem like she thinks about my money at all. She's more focused on her own work, her own achievements.

In February, with the cabin occupied and the rent money keeping me from having to dip into the last of the gift money my parents left me outside the trust, I end up walking to Grant's house one morning and asking him if he needs help. He does most of the odd jobs around town, having reinvented himself from a big-time lawyer to a humble carpenter over the past decade or so.

Watching the way he works, it makes me think that maybe I could enjoy it, too. I don't need Silicon Valley or a new app worth billions. The work I've done on my mother's old library space has been so rewarding I wonder if Grant has it all figured out. Making things with my hands...it could be exactly what I need.

I find Grant in his workshop, just off the main house. He has a carpenter's pencil behind his ear, wearing a stained plaid shirt and ripped jeans. He runs his hand through his thick dark hair and jerks his chin at me. "Wes. What can I do for you?"

I clear my throat, sliding my hands into my pockets as I take in the space. It smells like sawdust and glue and steel. I've never worked with my hands other than chopping wood and taking care of the cabin, the odd painting job. Even remodeling my mother's library has mostly been cleaning and a new coat of paint. I need to build desks and built-in cabinets, which is way beyond my skill level, but I'm determined to do it myself.

Looking at Grant to see him watching me, I shrug. "I was wondering if you needed any help. You seem to be busy around town, and...I might be looking for work."

His lips tilt into a smile. "You ever do any woodworking?"

"Beyond chopping logs for a fire? Nah."

He chuckles and reaches for a broom leaning against the wall. "Start with the basics, then, just like I did with Cheswick when I first got to Heart's Cove." He extends the broom toward me, a gleam in his eyes. "The place needs a sweep."

At another point in my life, I might have protested. I might have told him I wanted to learn about woodworking, not cleaning—but I take the broom and start sweeping.

Grant takes the pencil from his ear and marks a piece of wood. "I saw Dorothy walking through the woods this morning," he says casually. "Looked like she was coming from your grandfather's cabin."

I whirl, staring at him. "What?"

He chuckles. "Eli might be here to stay."

"Let's just hope Agnes doesn't try to run him out of town for daring to talk to Dorothy."

Grant laughs, a bright, happy sound I'd never heard until Fiona arrived in town. My own smile widens before I shake my head and turn back to my sweeping. Once the place is clean,

Grant gets me to help him cut some timber, shows me how to use the circular saw, gives me tips on safety and accuracy.

After a few hours, he shakes my hand. "What are you doing tomorrow? I'm building a deck for the Savoys over on Pinetree Drive. Could use the help."

I grin. "Sure. I'd like that."

We make a plan to meet and negotiate a base pay for me. I wander back along the coast, whistling, feeling lighter than I have in ages. When I spy the corner of my grandfather's cabin, I can't quite keep the smile off my face.

Hell, if Eli can find love in his sixties, why can't I do the same by the time I'm forty-five? Why am I convincing myself that this thing between Simone and me would never work? Why am I throwing out the idea of marriage, of my inheritance, just out of pride and stubbornness? My birthday is over a year away. Whatever's happening with Simone and me...we've got time to figure it out.

When I get home and shower the sawdust off my body, Simone still isn't home. When I text her, she responds with an emoji of a coffee cup. Then, a few seconds later, an emoji of an eggplant and a tongue sticking out, followed by a question mark.

I laugh. Yes, please.

My keys jingle as I toss them up in the air and catch them, heading to the truck to go pick her up. The sooner we can get this, ahem, eggplant party started, the better. I park across from the café and saunter inside, finding her in her usual seat. When she sees me enter, she closes her laptop and slides it into that blue bag she wears everywhere. Smiling as I approach, Simone stands and hooks her arms around my neck, a soft sigh escaping her lips as she touches her nose to mine.

"Hey."

"Hey, gorgeous."

Her cheeks turn pink, and I can't resist pressing my lips to hers. I kiss her slowly, gently, enjoying every second, every little noise and every tremble in her body.

"How was your day?" she asks, leaning back to look in my eyes. "You look...happy."

"Got a job working for Grant."

Her brows jump up. "Yeah?"

"Figured it was time for me to get off my ass."

"I mean, I wasn't going to say anything, but now that you mention it..."

I pinch her ass and relish her yelp, then jerk my head toward the truck. "Let's go home." My eyes drop to her pretty pink mouth, and by the flash in her eyes, I know she's thinking what I'm thinking—that it won't take long for our clothes to disappear when we get through the door.

I could marry this woman.

The thought hits me so hard it knocks the breath out of me. I twist a strand of her flame-colored hair around my finger and tuck it behind her ear, emotion clogging my throat.

Would it be so bad to end up together for...well, forever? Would it be that terrible to stay in Heart's Cove, to keep that house, to live here with all these people that have known me since I was a kid?

When I left Heart's Cove, I wanted to make something of myself. I wanted to be the businessman with the billion-dollar net worth. I wanted the sleek office in Silicon Valley. I wanted the glory.

But now...

I mean, look at Grant! He started a whole new business where he has a fraction of the notoriety and supposed clout of being a big-name lawyer, but he's happier than I've ever seen him. He took a chance in opening his life up to Fiona, and so far they seem to be thriving.

Why not me?

Simone completes me in a way I didn't know was possible. She doesn't judge. Doesn't ask anything of me. She pushes my buttons, sure, but she only ever nudges me toward becoming a better person. It's like when she asked me to come to Christmas dinner. Things between us were awkward, but she still knew I'd be spending the holiday alone—and as it was, that night ended up being the best night I've had in decades. Not just because we had sex, but because...because we were together.

The café door opens, carrying cold, sea-scented air through the café. Simone freezes, her eyes glued over my shoulder. Frowning, I follow her gaze and see a man enter. About my age, slightly shorter, with pale hair and a clean-shaven face.

He looks at the café counter, the art on the walls, the eclectic chairs, assessing. Then he sees Simone. Recognition flashes in his face—then his gaze slides to me. Wariness enters his expression along with a hint of territorial anger. Then a casual mask slams down on his features, and he stretches his lips in a roguish smile.

He's handsome. I'm not too much of a man to admit that.

Decent, strong body, and the easy grace of a man with confidence.

And he's looking at Simone like he wants her.

Fire blazes in my core, hot and bright and possessive. I turn, keeping my body between him and Simone, ready to stop this asshole from doing whatever it is he's planning.

But Simone lets out a soft sigh and puts her hand on my shoulder. She steps around me and crosses her arms. "Nate," she says, her voice flat. "What are you doing here?"

"After everything, that's how you talk to me?" He clicks his tongue, then slides his hazel eyes to me. "Who's your friend?"

Simone's shoulders tense as she gulps. Her eyes dart to mine, and something like resignation flashes in her gaze. "Wes, this is Nate, my ex-husband. Nate, Wes." She waves a hand between us.

I didn't get a label. I'm not her boyfriend, or her lover, or her friend. I'm just Wes.

Judging by the gleam in Nate's eyes, he noticed it too. "Is this my replacement?"

"Oh, please. Is there a reason you're here?"

"You haven't been answering my texts."

"So you came up here to ask me about it?" Simone's face hardens in a way that usually has my pulse kicking.

Nate takes a step forward, and I do the same. He pauses, a cruel grin on his lips. "So, he *is* my replacement." He looks me up and down, assessing. "You found someone else to take care of you, huh." His eyes flick to Simone. "Don't need me anymore as a backup?"

"You know what? Go haunt some other poor woman, Nate."

"A word to the wise," Nate says, facing me. "She has expensive tastes. I'd work that into whatever budget you currently have and make sure you plan for lots of designer clothes." He looks at the table, sees her purse, and snorts. "And bags."

Everything goes still as my heart slows. Ice forms in my veins, a dull ringing growing louder in my ears. My head swivels, looking at Simone, and I vaguely hear her dismissing her ex-husband. He says something back and turns.

I take in the tailored suit, the trendy haircut, the shiny shoes. He oozes wealth. *He's* her ex?

She has expensive taste.

My heart thumps, hearing still filled with a high-pitched noise. I flinch when Simone puts her hand on my arm, her brows lowered. "Are you okay?"

"Fine," I croak. "I'm fine."

In a daze, I walk to the truck and get in. Simone slides into the passenger seat and holds her purse on her lap. My eyes snag on it, on the blue leather, the gleaming buckles.

You found someone else to take care of you, huh.

The engine roars so loud I can't hear myself think. I can just hear Simone's ex-husband's words playing over and over in my head. I can see his sneer. The possessiveness he swaggered in with, followed by his contempt when he saw me. *Chump*, he seemed to say. *You're a chump.*

We drive home in silence, a long stretch of asphalt then a gravel road wending through the trees.

Is this my replacement?

I cut the engine, staring at the house that made Simone smile so brightly when she saw it. That smile... Was it just the joy of seeing the house, or was it something else? Was she seeing its value? Was she seeing me as someone she could latch onto?

Every interaction we've had, every moment—it's tainted.

I turn to look at Simone, who has concern written all over her features. "Are you sure you're okay?" she whispers. That concern—is it real, or is it just worry for her own future, her own stake in my inheritance?

Has she been playing me this whole fucking time?

TWENTY-FIVE

SIMONE

SOMETHING'S CHANGED. Wesley doesn't speak as we exit
his truck. I follow him into the house and watch him open the
refrigerator to pull out a beer. He cracks it open and takes a
glug, still not meeting my gaze.

My purse thuds softly as I put it down on a console table.
My coat whispering as I slide it off. Those are the only sounds
in the room apart from the hum of the refrigerator and the
distant creaking of the wind in the trees.

Wes takes another pull of his beer, and still, the silence
stretches. A shuttered, unreadable expression has masked his
features as he stares at me from across the room.

"Talk to me." I take a step toward him.

Tension stretches between us. The seconds drip by, oily and
thick, and I wait. Wait for the blow that will knock me down.

It only takes a few seconds for that blow to come. Wes's jaw
clenches, his teeth grinding so hard I can hear them across the

room. "Is *any* of this real?" Bitterness drips in his tone, his lips curled in an ugly snarl. I haven't seen this side of him before. I don't... I don't know how to react.

So, I freeze. "What?"

"This whole relationship. Us." He points the bottle of beer between us. "Did any of it mean anything to you?"

"What the hell are you talking about?"

I thought he'd be mad about my ex-husband showing up. I thought he'd maybe be irrationally jealous that I'd slept with Nate last summer, before we were ever together. But this—questioning if my feelings are real—it shocks me so thoroughly all I can do is gape.

"You kissed me mere minutes after I told you about the trust, about my inheritance. We got closer after my uncle left, when you had me to yourself. Have you been faking it this whole time? Has it all been some game to you?" he snarks, his words laced with poison.

They sting, and I finally dislodge the ball of emotion from my throat long enough to speak. "*Excuse me?*"

"Answer the question."

Thunder crackles in my veins at the *tone*. The sheer fucking *audacity* to question my intentions like this. I picked up the pieces of him in that bedroom and carried his pain with me. I didn't kiss him for his money, I kissed him because we'd been teasing and taunting each other for *weeks*.

But he thinks... He thinks...

I curl my hands into fists, nails biting into my palms. "Answering that question would give it too much credit."

"You never told me your husband was that wealthy. All you

said was that his family was difficult, that you understood those 'circles.' Is that the type of man you typically try to ensnare?"

"Ensnare?" My breaths are jagged. I can hardly keep up with the fucking *bullshit* coming out of his mouth. I stand there in the living room, right next to the spot where we had sex against the wall, staring at the man I've been falling in love with.

Ha! Love. I've been a fucking *fool*. I've been an idiot all over again, blinded by my lust or my own sheer stupidity. Once again, I looked at a man and saw what I wanted to see instead of what was actually in front of me. I thought Wes was different. I thought he was brave and strong and resilient, but...

I don't know him at all. This bitterness, the anger twisting his features...it scares me.

He lets out a snort and shakes his head, as if he can't believe me. As if *I'm* the one who's whirled around and changed my personality from one moment to the next. His eyes are black. "Simone, your ex-husband took one look at us and called you out. He said you were just trying to find some other dumb bastard to provide for you." His gaze flicks to my bag, arms spreading wide at his sides. "Another schmuck to buy you more of those bags that supposedly mean nothing to you." A scoff and a shake of the head. "I can't believe I actually bought that bull- shit when you've carried that bag around everywhere for weeks like it's a goddamn trophy."

Fire builds in my veins, so hot I feel like my skin will crumple and burn. The bag—he's mad about the fucking *bag?* He thinks me carrying it around was placing value on it? It was only when I *stopped* caring about that stupid sack of leather that I started actually using it. There are scuff marks on it now, stains. It's worth a fraction of what it was worth in pristine condition. Using that purse was a liberation, not some sad attempt at reviving my old, empty life. It was me proving to myself that I no longer needed a designer bag tucked away in my closet. Using that purse every day was proof that it *didn't* mean anything to me.

But Wes doesn't see it that way. He's looking at me like I'm a stranger. Like he can't believe he fell for it. If I try to explain anything about the stupid bag, it'll distract from the true problem here—that he thinks I'm after him for his money. He thinks I'm so shallow that I saw him and thought, *Provider. Safety net. Money.*

I take a deep, steadying breath. We can bridge this growing gap. He can come back to me, understand. He can see the truth in my eyes. "I'm not with you for your inheritance, Wes. I don't give a shit about the money. I've spent *years* building up my business, and it means more to me than being a kept woman. I tried that lifestyle with Nate, and I left it behind."

He crosses his arms. "I don't believe you."

"That's your fucking problem," I snap. Anger roars back to life inside me, and no amount of deep breaths is keeping it down.

The distance between us is too vast, and it's only growing larger. He stands behind the kitchen counter as I seethe in the living room, the walls closing in on me with every excruciating second.

"I thought I made my last mistake with women by dating Alina. She played me for a fool and left me when I was at my most vulnerable. I *promised myself* it wouldn't happen again."

"Let me get this straight." I steel myself, holding up my hands as I fill my lungs. "You think I heard your story about your parents' trust, decided I was going to be the one to get my grubby little paws on that money, and started working to seduce you? You think I hatched a master plan from the moment you told me you had a bit of money?"

Something like hesitation flashes across Wes's green eyes, but he clamps it down. "As soon as I saw your ex-husband, it made sense, Simone. You've told me countless times how broke you are. How much of a grind it is to start a new business." He shakes his head. "And that bag. How comfortable you were at that fancy restaurant we went to with my uncle. How you seemed to miss that kind of luxury. How your eyes just lit up when you saw this house..." His lips are a thin slash across his face, arms still crossed in a way that makes his biceps bulge even larger than usual.

He looks as immovable as a brick wall.

And he thinks all I want is his money.

Hurt zings through me, rattling across my bones as I grit my teeth against it. The fire inside me gutters, fading. Pain replaces it.

I thought... I thought we had something. I thought my life was finally starting to fall into place. I thought Wes might be the first man in decades who understood me. Who liked me for me.

But this person in front of me...he doesn't know me at all.

My shoulders drop, and I can't quite keep the venom from my voice when I say, "You're a weak, sad little man, Wes. You gave into your fears at the very first test without even questioning them. Without hesitating. Like you *wanted* things between us to fall apart, and you were just waiting for the right excuse." I suck in a trembling breath, my whole body so taut and brittle I might snap into pieces. "You believed two or three of my ex-husband's sentences over weeks and months of time with me. If you think I've been concocting some master plan to screw you out of your inheritance, you're sadly mistaken, and I hope you enjoy your lonely, pathetic little life."

Grabbing my twelve-thousand-dollar bag—the bag that might have been the nail in this relationship's coffin—I gather the scraps of my pride and straighten my spine. Steel pours into my veins as I hold my head up high, throwing on my jacket before heading out the door.

The door closes behind me, the soft clicking of the latch that sounds like thunder in the quiet woods. A heartbeat passes as I stand on the front porch, then I pull myself together and walk home.

I really need to get a new car.

MY APARTMENT IS STILL as a tomb. The musty, closed-in smell that smothers me reminds me I haven't been here in days. I drop my things on a table and head for the refrigerator, only to be greeted by some wilted lettuce and an impressive assortment of condiments.

Sighing, I close the fridge and slump down on the sofa. I don't even have the energy to light a candle to get rid of the stink.

I almost, *almost* regret what I said to Wes, but anger still buoys my sense of self-righteousness. I shouldn't have called him weak or sad or small. Name-calling isn't what I want to do. I'm better than that.

Still, when I think about all the things he said to me, all the accusations he leveled at me...I feel justified. I can't quite bring myself to feel sorry for what I said to him.

After everything, all it took was Nate appearing and making some very typically *Nate* comments for Wes to change his whole opinion of me. How long has he suspected that I've been after him for his inheritance? How long has he been faking it with me? How could he even think I was *capable* of that?

Fishing my phone out of my bag, I stare at the blank screen. Nope—he hasn't texted or called to apologize. I toss the phone aside and head back to the couch, wrapping a blanket around me as I flick on the television.

I watch some stupid reality show and switch my brain off. Whenever my thoughts start to drift toward Wes, I rein them in —mostly because I feel like such a damn idiot. Once again, I looked at a man and was blinded by the possibility of who he could be instead of who he is. Instead of Wes stepping up and defending me when Nate said those awful things to me, he kicked me in the knees and watched me crumple.

No, I'm not going to think about him. At least not tonight.

TWENTY-SIX
WESLEY

MY ANGER and betrayal carries me through most of the week. I ignore the pangs in my chest when I wake up alone in the morning. I ignore the niggle in my gut that tells me I might have made a mistake.

Wrapping myself in a cocoon of righteous indignation, I don't let myself think about what happened with Simone.

She was lying to me the whole time.

She never cared about me.

All she wanted was money.

None of it was real.

...Right?

FIDDLING WITH MY KEYS, I stand on my front porch next to Rudy. Handsome, charming Rudy, who's been flirting with me for months.

We went on a date. He asked me out a week ago and took me to a nice dinner. We had wine, we talked, we laughed.

It was nice.

"I had a really good time," he says, ducking his head to meet my eyes.

I smile, heart thundering. "So did I."

God, I suck at this. I haven't been on a date since I was nineteen. I know what's supposed to happen now, when I'm standing on my front porch with a handsome man and a belly full of wine.

But...

I don't have time to think, because before I can escape, it happens. Rudy's hand tugs mine as something heats in his eyes.

He hesitates, a shy-but-not smile on his lips. Flicking his gaze from my eyes to my lips, he angles his head and kisses me.

Ohmygod.

The first man I've kissed since Paul. The first date I've been on in decades. The first...*gah!* Feels like the first everything.

His lips touch mine. They're warm. Softer than Paul's were. He tastes like wine and he smells like cologne. He parts his lips and teases mine open, swiping his tongue into my mouth. It's intense. It's *really* intense. Too intense.

Pulling back, I shake my head. "I'm sorry." I stare at his chest. "I'm really sorry." My voice is nothing more than a whisper. All I can hear is my own heartbeat.

Rudy's hand squeezes mine. "Hey. Look at me."

Breath coming in short gasps, I squeeze my eyes shut, then force myself to open them and meet Rudy's gaze. His expression is soft, understanding. "I'm sorry, Rudy. It's too soon."

He nods, a sad smile tugging at his lips. "Okay."

"I'm really sorry." I arch my brows. "I thought I was ready, Rudy, I really did."

"Stop apologizing. You have nothing to be sorry for." He squeezes my hand, then leans over and brushes his lips over my cheek. "I had a good evening, and I hope you don't mind if I still stop by Four Cups for my daily fix."

Gosh, his smile is handsome. But it doesn't twist me up inside. Somehow, being with him makes me feel more alone than I was before. There's something wrong with me—there has to be.

I pull myself together and shake my head. "Of course I don't mind. I hope things won't be weird between us."

He grins and shakes his head. "Not weird for me. I wasn't lying when I said I had a good night, Candice." He nods, and a weight lifts off my shoulders. He really is a gorgeous man with a big heart. There's no animosity in his eyes when he winks at me, a smile tugging his full lips. Then I unlock my door and slip inside, peeking through the window to see him sauntering down my driveway. Rudy doesn't look back, and I let out a long breath, leaning against the door.

Maybe I'm broken. Maybe I'll never get over Paul's death, I'll never meet anyone who makes me feel the way my husband did. I met the love of my life when I was young, and I had twenty-two beautiful years with him. Isn't that something to be grateful for?

Still, my heart jags. Tonight *was* nice, and it made me realize I miss that. I miss being wanted. Needed in the way a man needs a woman.

But that man isn't Rudy.

As I shed my scarf and jacket, Allie pokes her head out from the mouth of the stairway. "How was your date?"

I give her a tight smile. "It was fine."

She takes another step, tucking a strand of curly blond hair behind her ear. My daughter recently discovered eyeliner and has been applying it often and excessively. Her piercing blue eyes stare out at me from the smokey makeup, a thousand questions in them.

"I'm not going to see him again," I tell her. "It was a nice evening, but..." I trail off, shrugging.

Allie closes the distance between us and wraps her arms

around me. "I miss Dad." Her voice is muffled against my chest, but her words hit me like a hammer.

As tears fill my eyes, I lay a kiss on her cheek. "Me too, honey." She's taller than me now, which is just another sign that time is marching on. Paul would have loved to see her grow up.

No.

I'm not going to break down. Not right now. Not when I just went on a date, when my daughter needs me to be strong.

Allie pulls away and wipes her eyes, smudging eyeliner across her face. "He would want you to date, you know. Dad would want you to be happy. And...I do too. You shouldn't worry about me, Mom. If you want to go out and date, don't think that it's going to bother me. I'm just crying because you look pretty and I wanted you to have fun, but I still miss Dad. I know it doesn't make sense."

My sweet, gorgeous daughter. She has as big a heart as my husband did. Even when the sight of me coming back from a date makes her miss her father, she still tells me she wants me to be happy. Allie may have a rebellious streak, but she's the best kid I could have asked for.

I run my fingers through her hair, then wipe away the smudges of eyeliner from her cheeks. "Thank you, baby. I appreciate that. And it makes sense. It makes complete sense."

She lets out a shuddering breath. "Why aren't you going to see him again?"

"I think I miss your father, too, Allie. All evening, all I could think about was Paul."

Allie leans her head against my shoulder. "People keep telling me it'll get easier, but it doesn't seem to."

A lump lodges itself in my throat. I pull away and squeeze my daughter's shoulder. "Come on. Let's go."

"Where?"

"To the café."

"Right now?" She frowns. "It's late."

"I know, but we don't have brownies and lemon tarts in the house."

A smile ghosts over Allie's lips, and then she laughs. "You sound like Dad."

"Maybe he rubbed off on me after all."

Allie giggles again and grabs her jacket before pulling on her boots. "That's not a bad thing."

"No it's not," I tell her. "Not at all."

WHEN WE GET to Four Cups, I'm surprised to see a light on inside. When I peer through the windows, I see Simone's red hair illuminated by the light of her laptop screen, her brows furrowed in a deep frown.

She looks up when Allie and I enter, brows arching high.

"We had an emergency that required immediate pastry ingestion," I explain.

Simone chuckles as Allie makes a beeline for the fridge.

I glance at my friend. "You want anything?"

"Give me one of those white-chocolate cranberry cookies," Simone replies. "I feel like I need a sugar hit, too. One of those days."

Allie preps the plates and food, then brings everything to Simone's table along with a pot of tea.

I grab the mugs while Simone puts her laptop away. "Working so late?" I ask as I slide my fork into an ooey-gooey brownie.

"New client. Deadline tomorrow," Simone replies, pouring the tea for everyone.

We eat in silence for a few moments until Allie pipes up. "What happened between you and Wes, Simone?"

Simone freezes, her eyes flicking to my daughter, then to me.

I nudge Allie. "It's not polite to pry, Allie."

"It's fine." Simone gives us a tight smile. "Things didn't work out, kiddo. Sometimes that happens."

"No wonder you two are friends," she grumbles between bites of lemon tart.

Simone flicks her gaze to me, and I reply with a wry smile. "My date with Rudy was a dud."

"Really?"

"It was fine, but he's not the man for me."

Simone sips her tea, thinking, then shakes her head. "It's amazing how men can promise you the world and underdeliver so spectacularly."

"So it's really over between you and Wes?" It's my turn to sip my tea, angling my head at my friend.

Simone lets out a long sigh and nods. "It's been a week since our fight, and he hasn't reached out. I'm not going to chase after him when he's the one who went all Jekyll and Hyde on me. I should just learn the lesson that the universe is trying to knock into my head. Stop making the same mistakes over and over again."

I grunt, finishing the last bite of my brownie, then stare mournfully at my chocolate-streaked plate. "I think I need another one."

Simone laughs. "Me too, girl."

Allie doesn't complain as she gets us all a second round. By the time we're done with our second desserts, I have a stomach ache, but somehow I feel lighter. Simone locks the café up behind us and gives us both a hug, and we go our separate ways.

I may not have a man in my life, but at least I have a daughter, friends, and a business I care about. That should be enough to be truly happy, shouldn't it?

TWENTY-EIGHT
WESLEY

IN THE SECOND week after Simone and I break up, Grant asks me what happened. He only does it once. I brush it off with enough bitterness that he doesn't bring it up again. We work together in near-silence most of the time, but I don't mind. Grant doesn't seem to, either.

Being outside and working with my hands helps. It tires me out, distracts me enough that when I get home, I barely have the energy to shower and eat before I fall asleep. Day after day, I work myself ragged to avoid the thoughts eddying in my mind.

I'm less alone than I was for the first few months I lived here after my parents' deaths. I have a job with Grant, Eli lives in my grandfather's cabin—but I feel infinitely lonelier. I hadn't realized how much Simone added to my life. How her presence lit everything up so thoroughly that the darkness inside me was hardly a sliver of what it is now.

Still, I don't let myself admit that I might have made a mistake.

She never cared about me. This was all about money. It's always been about money.

I failed to make money of my own and lost my fiancée. Then I lost my parents, crawled out of debt, but I don't deserve the money in the trust. I don't deserve what my parents worked for. Any woman who says I do must be trying to get a piece of it for herself.

Right?

I googled that bag Simone carried on her shoulder for months—it's worth thousands. Depending on the condition, anywhere from nine to twelve thousand, to be exact. It's not just a designer bag, it's a status symbol for the ultra-wealthy.

But I'm supposed to believe she never wanted anything from me? Please.

A few days later, I venture into town and see Simone at the café. She's sitting in her usual chair, sipping an iced coffee, tapping on her laptop keyboard. That blue bag is propped on the chair next to her.

When her eyes—same color as the bag, I realize—flick up to mine, her mouth tightens and her eyes drop back to the screen.

My chest constricts. Just a couple of weeks ago, I could have walked over to her and made her laugh. She would have graced me with one of her brilliant smiles.

Now, I get nothing from her.

I guess that's all I deserve.

The voice in the depths of my heart that screams I've made

a mistake gets louder. As the sun gilds Simone's hair, as fiery as her spirit, I wonder if that voice might be speaking the truth.

I'm a coward, though, because I just end up ordering a coffee and walking back out of the café, thinking—or maybe hoping—that I feel Simone's eyes on my back.

ANOTHER WEEK PASSES. Simone and I don't speak. It's... over. I know that, but it's still hard to accept it.

My uncle invites me to his new place for a drink, and on my way there I glance at the light spilling out of Simone's apartment window. She's cut me off so thoroughly, so completely, without so much as a word—but I know I deserve it. What I said to her...

Shaking my head, I grip the steering wheel a bit tighter and make my way to my uncle's place. He and Alina greet me at the door and invite me into their tastefully decorated, trendy, soulless home. It looks like they've plucked it out of *Architectural Digest* but forgot to put any of their own personality into it. Eli is nowhere to be seen, and when I ask, I find out he's handed in his resignation.

"After thirty years of working for me, he finally retired," my uncle says as he claps me on the back. "If you ask me, there's something that pushed him to do it. Or some*one*."

My smile is tight. I nod. "Dorothy."

Sean taps the side of his nose and shrugs. "We all have a weakness." He glances at Alina, who gives him a coy little blush and a giggle. His gaze shifts back to me. "What about Simone?

She's not around anymore. What happened?"

"Didn't work out," I grunt.

"That's a shame," Alina says, but her eyes gleam and I swear her lips seem to curl at the corners. As if she's happy that Simone and I broke up.

My uncle gives me another hard clap on the shoulder and snorts. "Women." As if that explains anything, or comes close to touching the way I feel about the whole situation with Simone.

We sit down for a drink and talk about my uncle's new store, which will be open within a year. Alina flits to his arm and back to the kitchen, playing the perfect host.

I feel...alone. So alone. When Simone was by my side, even when we were faking it, I had someone in my corner. She was so good at navigating these situations without looking like she was even trying. Without her, I feel lost. Adrift. Floating away without a tether.

"Well, what is it now, fourteen months?" My uncle swirls a tumbler of bourbon. "Fourteen months left until you turn forty-five?"

I grunt. "Fourteen months till your payday."

"Oh, come on now." Alina waves a hand. "We don't think of it that way." But she and my uncle exchange a glance, and I wonder what the hell I'm doing here. They're not sympathetic. They don't want what's best for me. Alina just wants to attach herself to a successful man, and my uncle is all too happy to play the provider. As long as I'm miserable and alone, they profit.

This whole situation is a clusterfuck. I can't trust Sean and Alina.

I thought I couldn't trust Simone, either, but is that true?

She walked away from me without looking back, and unless she's seriously conniving and manipulative, I think she means it. She never once spoke about my inheritance or made me think she even remembered it. She never spoke about marriage—if anything, it seems like she doesn't want to get married at all after trying it once before.

"So it's really, truly over between you and Simone, huh?" My uncle takes a sip of his drink, his eyes boring into me.

My gut twists. "Yeah. It's really over." I make a show of checking my watch. "I should go."

When I drive back down Cove Boulevard, Simone's lights are off.

THE NEXT DAY, I gather my courage and head to Four Cups again. I know I made a mistake. It took me weeks of brooding to realize it, but now I need to fix it. I need to tell her that I was an ass, and I'll get on my knees and beg if I have to.

Simone's in her usual seat, her brows drawn together as she works on something on her laptop.

I touch the chair across from her. "May I?"

She shrugs. "Sure." Icy tone, expressionless face.

Okay. So this isn't going to be easy. I probably deserve that.

With a deep breath, I sink into the seat. "I'm sorry," I start.

She looks at me, fingers still poised over her keyboard, then slowly lowers the screen.

Gulping, I look down at the table. There's a ring of moisture on the wood that I trace with my fingers. "I was an ass, Simone. I'm sorry I said those things to you."

"Thank you."

"My head was a mess with my uncle and Alina here, with the inheritance, and then your ex said things that spoke directly to my fears."

"I know." Her voice is quiet, but not exactly soft. Not friendly or warm.

I chance a look up at her eyes, and my hope withers and dies. There's nothing in her face—*nothing*—that makes me think she'll want to rekindle things with me.

"I was wondering," I say, clearing my throat, "if you'd want to come over for dinner tonight. I'll cook."

Simone holds my gaze for a long moment and finally exhales, her shoulders dropping. Dark smudges mar her under-eyes, and her hair looks even wilder than usual. As if she hasn't slept right in days. She looks in my eyes, then down at my lips, my shoulders, and finally drags her gaze back up to meet mine.

Then, like a slow push of a dagger to my heart, she shakes her head. "No, Wesley. I don't want to have dinner with you."

My breath staggers, and it takes all my discipline to keep from sinking in my seat. "Simone, I want you to know that I *know* I fucked up. I was out of line. It won't happen again."

Her eyes flicker, but her back remains straight as a rod. "You said things to me that I can't just forgive with a snap of my fingers. I've replayed our conversation in my head a thousand times over the past weeks, and every time I think about your words, your voice, your face...it makes me think I never knew you at all. A man worthy of my love wouldn't throw dirt in my face like that. He wouldn't accuse me of such awful things. I hoped you were the type of man I could love, but it was a fantasy."

"Simone—" My voice falters.

"I appreciate your apology," she continues, her voice so cold. So distant. "But I just can't... I can't be with you, Wes. I've worked too hard to be independent—to be my own woman—to throw it all away for the sake of a man who doesn't even see me for who I am."

"I see. I see now." There's an edge of desperation to my voice that I can't quite hide. I need her to understand.

She snorts gently, shaking her head. "You thought I concocted some scheme to get my hands on your trust money. You think I *cared* about your money in the first place. You didn't listen or absorb anything about the way I acted, the opinions I expressed. You ignored all the times I told you about my divorce and how hard I've worked to pull myself out of that dark hole— and how I wouldn't trade my new life for anything. I celebrated every success with you, every new client. It should have been obvious where my priorities lie. But none of that meant anything to you, Wes. You didn't listen or understand or believe. I spent eleven years of my life with a man who didn't see me as a person worthy of respect, who didn't support my ambitions, who didn't build me up to be better than I am on my own. Then I spent eight years building myself back up again. I accept your apology, and I appreciate it, but I'm not going to have dinner with you."

Simone holds my gaze for one heartbeat. Two. Three. Then she opens her laptop back again and glances at the screen.

I've been dismissed.

When I walk out into the springtime sunshine, with buds

forming on the trees and birds trilling all around, I almost wish it was grey and dreary again. My truck waits for me across the road, but I find myself heading to that little brown door beside the café.

This was supposed to be my surprise for Simone. It was supposed to be a present for her, to congratulate her on all her new clients, on her business's growing success.

The steps still creak, but the air no longer feels musty. It smells like fresh paint and cleaning supplies. I stand on the threshold at the top of the stairs, looking over the freshly reno-vated space, all the work I've poured in on evenings and week-ends when I'm not working with Grant. All the new skills I've learned, shoved into one little space.

Then my shoulders drop. She won't want this—not from me.

TWENTY-NINE
SIMONE

A HAND DROPS on my shoulder as I watch Wes walk away from me. Fiona's smile is tight and sympathetic, her eyes soft. "How are you holding up?"

"Oh, you know." I grimace. "Now I know how you felt when Grant left for New York City last year." *Except you got your happy ending.*

"Is it... Is it really over?" Fiona slides into the seat Wes just vacated, intertwining her fingers as she rests her elbows on the table. She drops her chin into her braided hands, arching her brows.

I nod. "Yeah."

After my fight with Wes, I ended up going to Fiona's for a cup of tea and a cry on her shoulder. That was, what, three weeks ago? Feels like a lifetime. Every day has lasted a year.

"He seems sorry," Fiona says, her eyes searching mine.

"Sorry isn't good enough. He accused me of plotting to steal his inheritance, Fiona. Me! Like I would want to get married to *anyone* again, for money or not. It made me feel like he didn't know me at all. Like he didn't *see* me."

Fiona hums. "Where did Nate go after he showed up here?"

"Damned if I know. I'm assuming the earth opened up and dropped him back down to the fiery pits of hell."

Fiona's lips tilt into a grin. "Why was he here, anyway? Did you tell him you moved to Heart's Cove?"

I lay my arms on the table and drop my forehead on top of them. Then, mumbling, I admit the one thing I haven't told her: "I had sex with him last year."

"*What?*"

"I know." I groan. "I know it was dumb."

"When you went and had lunch with him in L.A.?"

I nod, my forehead still resting on my arms. "I told him I was planning on moving here, and he asked me if he could come visit. I said yes, because I was post-orgasmic and my brain was malfunctioning. Then everything with Wes happened, and I just...forgot."

"Did he tell you he was coming?"

"I ignored three or four of his calls. And a few texts." I lift my head, cringing at the look on Fiona's face. She's wincing. "I had a moment of weakness, Fi. I won't sleep with him again. Not after his little display in here—and to be honest, after we had sex, I knew it would be the last time."

"Does Wes know?"

"It's none of his business. It's not like I was talking to Nate while he and I were together. It was before I even knew him. And it's over now."

Fiona snorts. "Well, I'm sure Nate got the message when he saw you with Wes."

"Why do I make such bad decisions, Fiona? What's wrong with me? You'd think by the time I'm halfway through my forties, I would have learned my lesson by now."

A deep sigh slips through my best friend's lips. She arches her eyebrows and shrugs. "Some lessons are just hard to learn, I guess."

"It was too good to be true, anyway. We couldn't both find hunky men to sweep us off our feet in this town."

"Simone..." Fiona bites her lip. "What if Wes just made a mistake? Like you did with Nate. He got burned by his ex-fiancée who happens to be in town, and like you told me before, makes all kinds of comments needling at his insecurities. What if it just all got to him?"

"You think I should give him another chance?"

"I don't know." She lets out a sigh and glances down, scraping her thumbnail over the corner of the table. "Like I said, some lessons are hard to learn. Maybe Wes learned this one with you."

"I'm not marrying him just so he can get his inheritance." I'd refuse out of spite. Just to prove to him that I don't care about the money. I'm petty like that.

Fiona rolls her eyes. "You don't have to marry him, Simone. But you've been sulking for weeks now. Maybe it's worth another shot."

"I'll think about it." I slide my laptop into my bag and let out a sigh. "It's just... I don't want to make the same mistakes all over again. How many chances did I give Nate? Even almost a decade after our divorce, I was still going back and trying again. Now I want to try again with Wes? How many times will I go back to him when he hurts me?"

"Wes isn't Nate," Fiona says. "He's a different man with different priorities."

I hum. I'm not so sure. "I'll think about it."

I THINK about it for a week, and still can't bring myself to go talk to Wes. My business is going well, the café is busy, and spring is in full bloom. Walking down that winding gravel road to Wes's house just seems...too difficult for me right now. I can't do it.

I still haven't bought a new car. I've been walking everywhere, which is great for my figure but not so good for convenience. I have enough money now, but using the money Wes gave me for anything feels like a slap in the face. I'd rather burn it.

Fiona's birthday is March 11, and we all gather at her place for a dinner party. Everyone is there and in good spirits—but it just reminds me of Christmas. Of what happened after. I leave early to walk home after giving Fiona a big hug and pause when I get to the end of the driveway. If I turn right, I could be at Wes's house in ten minutes. Left, and I'll be home in twenty.

The wind rustles through the trees, the air still chilled with the dregs of winter. I sigh and turn left.

. . .

THE NEXT DAY, I wake up to a text from Candice asking the three of us to meet her at Four Cups. Jen is already there when I walk across the street in my slippers and sweatpants, the two of them leaning against the counter with steaming mugs wrapped in their hands.

Candice's eyes twinkle when she sees me. "Morning, sunshine. Nice choice of footwear."

"I've given up," I proclaim, shaking my fuzzy slippers at her. "I'll claim I'm senile a couple of decades early."

"You've been a doddering old lady at heart since I met you nearly thirty years ago," Fiona says behind me, her cheeks rosy from the fresh air. She looks at Candice. "What was that cryptic text message about?"

"She has a surprise, apparently," Jen says, sipping her chai.

I frown. "A surprise?"

"Follow me!" Candice sing-songs, waving a hand as she leads us outside.

We stop in front of a gleaming red door right beside the café. I frown, glancing around. I never noticed this door before. "Was this always here?"

"New door," Candice explains. "Come on up." She flashes us a brilliant smile and shoots up the staircase. We trundle up behind her, my heart beating hard in my chest.

A surprise. Wes had a surprise for me, and he'd come home sweaty, covered in dust and paint. He said he was working on a project in town, but he wouldn't tell me what it was. Could this be...

No. It's not. Whatever Wes was working on, it wasn't anything for me—but we spill into the room above the café and my eyes grow wide.

Bright, light-filled space greets me, sunlight streaming in through new windows to the left. One wall is completely covered in shelves laden with well-loved books. Two desks line the far wall, one of them L-shaped and looking out on the street below. A little reading or conversation nook is in the corner by the farthest bookshelf, complete with a floor lamp and a cozy-looking throw.

There's wainscoting along the walls gleaming with fresh white paint. It's classic, comfortable, and stylish. My shoulders relax within moments of walking in.

I stand in the entrance, taking it all in. "What is this place?"

Fiona, who drifted to the kitchenette to look at the tea bags neatly displayed in little boxes, glances over her shoulder at Candice. "I'd also like to know."

"This, my friends, is where we can keep all the records for the café. Our new office."

"What..." My voice drifts away before I can form a sentence. I clear my throat. "Where did this come from? Did you do this? I thought this was an apartment. It wasn't part of the lease."

My heart thunders as I take in the space once more. The light, the comfort, the books. It's... It's somewhere I could see myself working.

Candice looks at me, biting her lip. "Wesley gave me the keys yesterday. He said he'd been working on it for a few months. His mother used to come here, apparently, and he said he'd like it to be occupied again. He told me the café's success made him realize that his parents would have loved us taking over, and this space should be ours to use, too."

I can't speak. Tears cloud my eyes, and I almost don't see Candice close the distance between us. My heart stutters when she puts her hand on my arm, her gaze finding mine. "I think..." She inhales, casting her gaze to our two other friends. "I think he meant for you to use this place for your business. I found a big wall decal with your logo on it rolled up behind one of the couches. He must have forgotten it there."

A sob escapes me, and I clap my hand over my mouth. Fiona's beside me in an instant, wrapping her arms around me. I feel another set of arms, then another. My friends hold me up as I fall apart, thinking of all those hours Wesley put into this place —for me.

He did this for me.

Even after we broke up, even after I told him in no uncertain terms that I wanted nothing to do with him, he still gave Candice the keys. And that desk—the fresh folders and colorful stationery. It's for me. I know it is. There's even a scented candle on the corner.

Wes built an office for me, and I've been stewing in my own bitterness for *weeks*, thinking he was a horrible person. I couldn't even see past my own anger to give him a chance.

"I don't even know why I'm crying," I say through my tears, my voice wobbly.

The girls pull back, Candice rubbing my back as Fiona

squeezes my arm. Jen drifts toward the bookcase as if that kind of intimacy makes her uncomfortable.

Fiona's smile is soft. "You're crying because he did this beautiful thing for you."

"He built me an office and then pretended he didn't." I look around the room, at the soft touches, the new furniture. The candles. He put scented candles on every horizontal surface. Oh my goodness, this man. He did this *for me*.

Wes didn't do this because he wanted to provide for me or make me feel spoiled—he did it because he saw me working at the café or at my apartment and he wanted to help me with my business. He remembered that I mentioned I would love to have an office one day, so he made one for me.

Wes is nothing like Nate. This proves it. Nate would have tried to buy me another purse. He would have dressed me in a gown and wined and dined me. He would have showered me with presents to prove his love. But Wes did *this*. He built me an office so I could continue working, so I could grow my business. *My* business. The one thing that gave me hope after the divorce, the independence that kept me trudging through the hardest years of my life.

Even when everything fell apart between us, he still gave it to me.

I wipe my cheeks with the heels of my hands and shake my head. "I have to go talk to him."

"Whoever bought all these books *loved* smut," Jen says, flicking through a paperback. She glances at the three of us. "Like—really loved it."

I giggle, snort, then giggle some more. With a sigh, I pull

away from my friends and straighten my shoulders. "I'm going to go talk to him."

"You want to borrow my car?" Fiona asks.

I shake my head. "The walk will help me clear my head. And hopefully hide the fact that I just burst into tears."

THIRTY
SIMONE

WES'S HOUSE appears through a gap in the trees. First, the apex of the roof covered in cedar shingles, then those gorgeous windows, and finally the big front porch shaded by tall trees. My breath hitches and I almost stumble on the gravel, then catch myself.

I can do this. Glancing down at myself, I groan. I should have at least changed. I'm not exactly dressed to win back a sexy man. Unless said sexy man is really into slippers and sweatpants.

I need to thank Wes for the office, and I need to tell him that...that I'm sorry, too. Our fight scared me in a way I didn't expect. It made me think I'd fallen for a man just like Nate— just as vindictive, just as arrogant, who saw me as a small, insignificant woman.

But Wes had his own shit to work through, and like Fiona

said, it couldn't have been easy with Alina in town, in his face and his ear, reminding him of all the bad choices he made.

Still, as I walk up the three steps onto his porch, it's hard to take a full breath. It reminds me of a day all those months ago when I walked up to the cabin door and knocked, hoping Wesley would be there and listen to me.

I hesitate, my finger near the doorbell, then pull myself together and press it. My heart thunders as I stand on the porch, waiting. What if he doesn't want to see me? What if I pushed him away one too many times? What if he doesn't actually want me at all?

I should go. He came to me, and I told him I wanted nothing to do with him. Coming here was a bad idea. I should turn around and go home and forget this ever happened.

But before I can move, the door opens and he's there. Shirtless, of course, in all his muscled glory. Because this conversation isn't going to be hard enough as it is. Stubble lines his jaw, his hair mussed from sleep. He looks absolutely delicious.

We stare at each other for a minute. An eternity.

I gulp. "Hi."

"Simone." The word seems to shock Wes out of his stupor and he shakes his head, clearing his throat. He steps aside to let me in, and I catch a hint of his scent as I enter. So intrinsically *Wes.* I missed that smell. My heart stutters as I kick off my slippers, stealing a glance at him as he closes the door behind me. He waves me forward, and I see a pan on the stove and a carton of eggs on the counter.

"Sorry to disturb your breakfast."

"You hungry? I'm no Eli, but I can make eggs."

I almost say no, then catch myself. He's offering me an olive branch. I give him a tentative smile. "Sure."

Leaning against the opposite counter, I watch the muscles in his back bunch and ripple as he cracks eggs into a hot pan one-handed. Hot. My heart thumps.

"I'm assuming Candice showed you the office space," Wes says without looking back at me.

I clear my throat as he cracks another egg. "Yeah. It's...it's gorgeous, Wes."

"It was my mother's space. She used to go there when she needed peace and quiet. She, the twins, and Agnes used to have a book club."

My heart stumbles. Oh my goodness. He wanted to give me his mother's old sanctuary. He converted *his mother's favorite space* into an office for me. My lip wobbles, and it's hard to get my breathing under control.

"Candice found a wall sticker behind one of the couches," I say. Wes freezes, his back still to me. The light plays on his hair —longer than the last time I saw him. "It had my logo on it."

"Did she, now," he says, cracking a third egg.

"Did you..." I inhale. "Was that the project you were working on before? The surprise?"

Silence stretches, punctuated only by the sizzling of the pan as Wes cracks a fourth egg into it. He stares at it for a moment then slowly turns, dragging his eyes up the length of my body to rest on my face. His gaze snags on my mouth, and I realize I'm biting my lip. When he finally reaches my eyes, he gives me a shrug. "You told me you wanted an office."

"Wes..." Pain shatters through my chest. I don't even know

why it hurts so much. Because I want him so bad, but I feel like...like there's too much between us.

The toaster pops, and Wes turns back around to start buttering the bread, then uses a flat spatula to transfer the eggs onto two plates. I use those moments to compose myself, to regain control over my rioting emotions.

"I'm sorry," I tell his back. "I'm sorry I pushed you away and I didn't listen to you when you came to apologize. I'm sorry I told you it wasn't enough. I was...scared. I still am. When you said those things to me, I felt so small. I felt like I was making all the same mistakes again, falling for a man who didn't see me for who I was, who didn't respect me. But..."

Wes turns around again. His eyes are full of devastation, guilt, and something I can't read. He swallows thickly, running a hand through his hair. We stand on opposite sides of the kitchen, leaning against our respective countertops, clutching onto them as if we both need something to help us stand.

"I'm sorry too, Simone." Wes's voice is full of gravel. He shakes his head. "I was a complete ass. I got scared of what I was feeling for you, of how easy it would be for you to shatter my heart all over again."

"We're both just big cowards."

He huffs, lifting those eyes of cut jade to meet mine. He hesitates, then slowly pushes himself off the counter and crosses the distance between us. He stops a foot away from me, that muscled, glorious chest close enough to touch. It's Wes who moves first, though. He lifts his hand and twirls a strand of my hair around his finger, then drops it, shaking his head.

"This past month has been the worst of my life, Simone."

He stares at my hair, my face, my chest. "I've missed you every second of every day. Everything in here reminds me of you. I would have moved back to the cabin if Eli wasn't in it just to try to get you out of my mind, but I would have thought of you there, too." He takes another step, sliding his hands over my hips. "I never should have said those things to you. It kills me to think that I hurt you, that I made you feel like you were anything less than perfect. I know it's no excuse, but I...I've spent the past year since my parents died coming to terms with the fact that I'd lose this house, the land, the money. I'd accepted it. I felt like I didn't deserve it, because I'd failed at so many things in my life."

He leans his forehead against mine, his eyes closed. "But you breezed into my life and made me laugh again. You made me see color. You showed me how to smile, how to live. I was drowning in my own guilt, my own self-loathing, and you swam down to grab my hand and pull me to the surface again. When I would wake up next to you, I felt like I could *breathe* for the first time in a decade. It scared the shit out of me."

His shoulders are warm and solid when I run my hands over them. I wrap my arms around his neck and twist my fingers into the silky strands of his hair. I let out a long sigh and pull back to look in his eyes. "Maybe we can...start over."

Fire skips over my skin as Wes's hands slide to my back, then down toward my ass. He pulls me close, hope sparking in his gaze. "Yeah?"

I nod.

When he tugs me even closer, my body pressed along the length of his, I let out a soft whimper. He nudges my nose with his, then drops his lips over mine. His kiss is soft, tentative, until I part my lips and let out a moan. I curl my fingers into the nape of his neck to deepen the kiss, needing...more. More of him. More of his lips, of his smell, his taste, his touch.

The leash he was keeping on himself snaps. His kiss turns hard, bruising, claiming. His hands sink into my flesh, pulling me close enough to feel how much he wants me. I moan against his lips, shuddering when his tongue brushes over mine. The kitchen counter presses against the small of my back, pinning me against his broad, strong body.

He pulls away, panting, sliding a hand over my cheek. "Forgive me, Simone. Tell me you forgive me for what I said to you."

The desperation in his voice almost undoes me. I grip his face in my hands and bring his lips to mine, kissing him softly. "Of course I forgive you. I'm in love with you, Wes."

He closes his eyes and lets out a shuddering sigh, as if my words just tore a weight off his shoulders. When he speaks, his voice is low. "I think I started falling for you the moment you explained to me how a conversation works," he admits. "It had been so long since someone spoke to me like that. Challenged me. Made me...want something." When he opens his eyes again, his hands still wrapped around my body, a smile teases at his lips. "And I knew I loved you when you told me you'd break my other ankle if I called you ma'am."

My cheeks flush as I giggle, shaking my head. "At least my sass is good for something. Makes broody men fall over themselves to win me over."

He traces a line up my neck with his lips. "I can think of a few ways to try to win you over."

"Mm?"

A soft kiss just below my ear makes my toes curl. "I'll start with my hands," he growls, sliding his palm under my sweatpants to run it along my thighs. Side note: sweatpants do have *one* advantage—easy access. I shiver, catching his lips in mine.

"Then I'll use my mouth," he says with a kiss.

"And then?"

A taunting male smirk is the only response I get before his hand moves to the front, dipping between my legs, and Wes indeed does win me over again, and again, and again, right there in the kitchen while our eggs get cold. The sweetest part, though, is when he tells me he loves me in a husky whisper, his lips brushing my ear. Then he says it again when he's deep inside me. Then a third time, when we've collapsed on the floor tangled in each other's arms, our heartbeats slowing after all that exertion.

"I love you, Simone," he says, wrapping an arm around my waist to pull me close. "I love you more than I can put into words. I'm in love with you. You make my life worth living."

Sighing, I sink into his words, his arms, and I smile.

EPILOGUE

SIMONE

WES and I lock ourselves in his house for a full week. We do nothing but sleep, have sex, eat, and repeat. It's fantastic.

On the eighth day, Wes curls his body around mine in bed and tugs me close, putting his lips near my ear. "Move in with me."

My heart does cartwheels. I inhale sharply, then turn my head toward him. Our lips brush and I shift away to meet his gaze. "You sure?"

"I've waited my whole life to feel this way, Simone. You sleep here all the time anyway. And I have more storage space for all your candles."

I laugh, happiness blooming inside me. With tears in my eyes, I give Wes a nod. "Okay. But don't propose. I don't care about the inheritance right now. I just want to enjoy this—us—and see where it goes."

He tightens his hold on me. "Deal."

I move in the next day. The landlord at my apartment grumbles, but agrees to start looking for another tenant so I can break my lease early. Then, using Wes's truck, I cart all my belongings (and candles) to his woodland fairy home nestled in the trees next to the ocean, and my soul lets out a long sigh.

I'm home. Finally, after all those years, I've moved into my dream house, I'm living with the sexiest man I've ever met, and my best friend lives a short walk away.

MY NEW OFFICE is the *best*. The L-shaped desk that overlooks Cove Boulevard becomes my new home, and allows me to take in-person meetings with clients. The girls agree to let me put the wall decal up, so my logo takes up the space behind my desk.

I'm a real business owner. A professional. Even though I started this business years ago, and it took grit and grinding to get here, I finally feel like I've made it. I have an office and a growing client base. I have my independence.

Wes is so supportive it makes me sick. Okay, that's a lie. It doesn't make me sick. It makes me happy. He's nothing like my ex-husband, in that he takes interest in what I do. He admires all the work I put in, and pride shines in his eyes whenever I tell him I've landed a new client. He's my biggest cheerleader, and I know he doesn't see me as an add-on to his life, but an integral part of it.

. . .

AS SPRING BLEEDS into summer and the annual Heart's Cove Fringe Festival comes around, I meet with Jen, Candice, and Fiona in Four Cups to set up our sidewalk tent for the week-long festival. It marks the one-year anniversary of my and Fiona's arrival in town.

"Feels like more than a year," Fiona says, her eyes on Clancy as the girl places chairs around outdoor tables.

"Thank goodness for geysers." I grin, nudging Fiona with my elbow.

Her cheeks flush as a smile tugs at her lips. Then strong hands slide over her hips, and Grant wraps himself around her. "You can say that again," he says in my best friend's ear.

I laugh, turning away to give them some privacy, and catch the sight of a tall, golden-brown-haired vision in faded jeans. With a plaid shirt opened to reveal a tight, white T-shirt, Wesley flashes a confident smile at me as he closes the distance between us.

His lips are on mine in an instant, and I find myself wrapped up in his arms. My favorite place in the world.

Then, things happen quickly. Music starts playing from our new speakers, and Clancy approaches with something clasped in her hands. Grant drops down on one knee, his eyes shining with emotion as he gazes at Fiona.

Fiona starts crying.

I start crying.

Jen and Candice, crowding in the café doorway, start crying.

"Fiona, I love you," Grant says, and Fiona starts sobbing. Hard. His smile widens. "You made my house a home. You gave me the family I never thought I'd have. My life is richer with you in it, and I can't imagine living without you. Make me the happiest man in the world and be my wife."

Clancy, with the same steel-blue eyes as her father, opens her hands to reveal a black velvet box. Grant plucks the box from his daughter's hands and smiles as Clancy leans down to kiss his cheek. She stands to the side, a smile spreading over her lips.

"A year and three weeks ago, I saw you across the street and knew you were the woman for me. All I could give you was an umbrella and an—*ahem*—preview of what else I could offer you."

"Dad!" Clancy exclaims, her cheeks flushing red. She rolls her eyes and I laugh, remembering that first life drawing class where Fiona and I giggled like schoolgirls about what, exactly, Grant had on display.

Grant laughs as Fiona lets out an exasperated sigh, then flips the velvet box open to reveal a beautiful emerald-cut engagement ring with a delicate white gold band.

Wes slides his arm over my shoulders and tugs me close, leaning his cheek against my temple as we watch Grant slide the diamond ring onto Fiona's finger.

She wraps her arms around Grant, tears streaming down her face, nodding her head like a maniac as she laughs and cries and snorts all at once. Her future husband kisses her through her tears, his hands on either cheek, both of them radiating love and happiness.

Surreptitiously, I try to wipe my own tears without anyone noticing. Judging by the tightening of Wes's arm and the low, rumbling chuckle in his chest, I fail spectacularly.

"Don't get any ideas, Wes," I say as I try my best to glare at him.

"Still opposed to marrying me, huh?"

"Definitely."

"I've got ten months to change your mind, otherwise we'll have to find somewhere else to live."

"Good luck with that," I grumble, but I can't quite hide my grin.

Wes's eyes sparkle at the challenge, then his lips find mine for a searing kiss.

We're interrupted by squealing as Fiona thrusts her new ring toward Jen and Candice. Extricating myself from Wes's arms, I join my friends in the doorway of our beloved café and restaurant and swoon over Fiona's new ring.

"Never thought I'd marry anyone again," she says with a sigh, running her fingers over the sparkling diamond. "But then again, I never thought I'd meet anyone like Grant."

"You deserve it, hun," I say, giving her a tight hug. When we pull apart, I turn my head and meet Wes's gaze.

My heart skips. Maybe...

That thought is interrupted by Candice clearing her throat. "I also have news."

Jen whips her head around. "You're engaged?"

"No." Candice huffs a laugh.

"Pregnant?"

"God no," she says, horrified.

We laugh, and lean in as Candice takes a deep breath, her eyes sparkling.

CANDICE

"WE HAD a special customer a few weeks ago," I say. "Some big-time Hollywood producer."

"We did?" Jen's eyes are wide.

I nod. "Uh-huh. And he was impressed by the food we have on offer. I didn't know who he was until after, but he talked to me while he was here. Said we should keep Fallon and Jen under lock and key to stop them from ever leaving. Bought a whole box of pastries to take on the plane with him back to L.A."

"He said that?" Jen glances at me, then at Fiona and Simone. I know she knows her pastries are good, but I'm not sure she truly understands what a genius she is at baking. I can't keep the smile off my face as I think of what I'm about to tell her, of just how much this Hollywood bigwig was impressed by her work. All four of us are blubbering messes, but I can't keep the news to myself any longer.

With a deep breath, I smile at my three best friends. "Mr. Big Shot Producer is shooting a movie in the area in a few months. He wants us to do the catering. He sent the proposal to the company email this morning, and ladies, it's a huge contract. Huge."

Fiona stares at me. "Wait. What?"

Simone starts laughing and claps a hand over her mouth. Jen just stares.

I grin. "If we commit to the contract, the profits will keep us afloat for a whole year. We'll need to hire another full-time chef for it, probably, but we have time to find someone before shooting starts on the movie." I glance at Jen, a question in my eyes.

"I'll do it," she says without hesitation, without me even needing to say anything. "If Guillaume won't let me take a couple of months off my restaurant job, I'll quit."

"Holy shit!" Simone yelps, then hops a few times, then gathers everyone in a bone-crushing group hug. "Holy shit! Holy shit! What's the movie?"

"Don't know yet," I say.

Simone lets out a squeal, her blue eyes shining. "I wonder who the actors will be. Hopefully someone hot. I'll never say no to a bit of eye candy." Simone glances over her shoulder, then back at the three of us. "Don't tell Wes I said that."

We laugh and, with tears in our eyes, turn back to the setup for the Fringe Festival. A year ago I was running around, frazzled and overwhelmed. I'd had a harebrained idea to start a pop-up café to promote my yoga studio during the festival. I'd bitten off more than I could chew, and I was desperate. I offered Fiona a temporary job, and I never could have imagined I'd end up here.

Even with a less-than-great date with Rudy under my belt, I still feel like I've grown in the past year. I feel like maybe, Paul is smiling down on me. He'd be proud of me for this. For running my yoga studio while investing in the café. For trusting three other women to start a new business with me. For not letting my own fears and grief stop me from providing for myself and my daughter, from living life to the fullest.

And who knows? Maybe this catering contract will put Four Cups on the map. And if there's some hot Hollywood eye candy for me to ogle, I won't be the one to complain...

Candice meets red-hot movie star Blake Harding when she's thrust into the leading lady role...

Read out Book Three: DIRTY LITTLE MIDLIFE MISTAKE!

EXTENDED EPILOGUE

SIMONE

WITH MY SWEAT-SOAKED sports bra stuck to me and my hair a frizzy mess, I lie back on my yoga mat and let out a long breath. Other yogis are rolling up their mats, and I force myself to sit up and lean against my hands.

Candice smiles at me from the front of the room before walking over. "How was that?"

I blow out a breath. "Tough as ever."

"You're getting better. I remember the first time you came to one of my classes, you couldn't even touch your toes." She sits next to me, cross-legged, posture perfect, and nods at other students as they file out of the room. "All the work you're putting in has paid off."

I glance at the loose waist of my yoga pants and nod. "I've lost weight. If you'd asked me a year ago if that was possible, I would have laughed in your face."

"It's all that walking and yoga. And other activities you and Wes are doing." Candice arches a brow, grinning.

"That and the fact that Wes has a criminally healthy diet. I brought chocolate home last week and he looked at it like it would jump up and bite him. He refused to eat any! I considered breaking up with him for that alone."

Candice laughs. "You balance each other out."

"Maybe." With great effort, I get to my feet and start rolling up my yoga mat. Dabbing my towel over my forehead, I let out a breath. "See you tomorrow?"

"I've got the early shift at Four Cups, so I'll be there when we open." Candice smiles at me.

Gathering my things, I sling my gym bag over my shoulder and make my way out the studio door. Candice moved her studio from her previous space down the street to a room at the back of the Heart's Cove Hotel. Walking through a lush courtyard, I make my way to the lobby and see the twins poring over a computer screen on the other side of the reception desk.

"Hi Dorothy. Margaret."

"Simone." Margaret smiles, a twinkle in her eye. She and Dorothy exchange a glance as they straighten up. Margaret smooths her hands down the front of her wide-leg trousers. "Come here for a moment, would you?"

I angle toward the desk and lean over it, watching as Dorothy spins the monitor toward me. A social media post greets me, and Dorothy asks me a question I answered an hour ago about responding to comments. Frowning, I glance at her. She's usually really quick to learn new things on the computer. She hasn't needed my help with this kind of thing for a while.

I point out what she needs to do, then stop when Margaret puts her hand on her sister's shoulder. They both glance at the lobby doors, then at me.

I frown.

Something's going on.

A shuffling sound behind me draws my attention, and I spy Candice coming through to the lobby. Odd. Usually she goes directly from the studio around the side of the hotel to her car. She sees me and throws me a panicked sort of smile.

Then the bell above the lobby door tinkles, and Wes walks into the room.

His presence fills the space, pressing against me like a physical touch. In his usual faded jeans and simple T-shirt, he combs his fingers through his hair and throws me a roguish grin. His dimples make an appearance, and I forgive him for the chocolate incident. I can just about bear the thought of him not eating dessert if it means he'll look like that while he looks at me.

"Hey." My tongue feels heavy in my mouth. I'm a grown woman, for crying out loud! The man makes me feel off-balance with nothing more than a grin.

"Hey, beautiful." He closes the distance between us and wraps a strong arm around my waist. His lips dip to mine, and I hear something that sounds suspiciously like a longing sigh coming from Candice's corner. Wes's hand splays over my back while his other palm rests against the side of my neck. He kisses me right there in the lobby, tongue and all.

When I fall back, I'm flushed. Overwhelmed. "Wow."

Wes just grins. "I want to show you something." He slips

his fingers into mine and tugs. I have no choice but to follow as he leads me out through the lobby door and across the parking lot.

Then I see it.

A gleaming black SUV with a big red bow stretched over the roof. It's parked against the curb, proud and on display, and I stop in my tracks. Wes pauses beside me, a smile teasing at his lips.

"Wes..."

He reaches into his pocket and pulls out a key fob, dangling it between two long fingers. "Happy birthday, Simone."

"No." I shake my head. "Absolutely not."

He tilts his head. "What do you mean, 'no'?"

"You didn't get me a car."

Instead of answering, Wes flips the fob and presses a button. The locks on the car click as the lights flash. He glances at me again, a smile teasing his lips.

"You got yourself a car. I'm going to get a used car I can afford."

"Simone..."

"Wes." Crossing my arms, I level him with a stare. "You didn't get me a car. It's too much."

"Nothing is too much."

Oh, my heart. I catch my breath, and judging by the curling of Wes's lips, he doesn't miss a moment of it. Grasping my hand, he curls my fingers around the key fob. "At least sit down in the front seat, Simone."

"I'll get fat."

He laughs. "What?"

"I've been walking everywhere and doing yoga and eating chicken and broccoli. If I get a car, I'll get fat." I'm not making any sense. I *know* I'm not making any sense. But I can't stop talking.

"So let's get fat together."

That makes me throw him a flat stare. "You don't eat chocolate, Wes."

Damn it, his grin is too sexy to resist. "I'll love you no matter what size you are, Simone." He gestures to the car. "Just get in the driver's seat and see how it feels."

"It'll feel amazing. That's the problem!"

"Oh, get in the car, Simone!" Dorothy calls out from behind me.

I turn to see her, Margaret, Candice, and—unbelievably—Agnes crowding under the entrance awning of the hotel. They give me encouraging smiles and wave me forward.

"Was everyone in on this?" I ask, turning to Wes.

"I needed to make sure you'd be busy while I went to pick it up."

"You planned this."

"It's your forty-fifth birthday this weekend, Simone." Wes slides his arm around my back. "This summer has been the best summer of my life, and I owe that to you. A car is nothing."

Letting out a long breath, I bite my lip. The best summer of his life? My heart does cartwheels, mostly because I agree. After the Fringe Festival, Four Cups was busier than ever. With the promise of a Hollywood catering contract next year, we're looking at soaring profits and a surprisingly good investment.

But that's not what made this summer amazing. It's the fact

that every night I've gone to sleep next to Wes, and every morning I've woken up beside him. I've walked through the woods most mornings with a mug of coffee in my hands to find Fiona sitting on an Adirondack chair, waiting for me. I've spent my days in the office Wes built, surrounded by friends and loved ones.

For the first time in my life, I've felt more than happy. I've felt at peace. Content. Totally, utterly satisfied.

"Simone..." Wes tugs my hand, dragging me around to the driver's side. We stand next to the door as my mouth dries up, eyes widening as I look at the leather seats, the gleaming dash with high-tech electronics.

"My old car, Bertha, didn't even have power windows," I blurt.

A warm, deep chuckle. Wes's fingers tilt my chin and, hidden from our audience at the hotel, Wes plants another kiss on my lips. He tastes minty, fresh, and exactly like Wes.

I close my eyes and melt into him, my heart thumping so hard I feel like I'm going to pass out. When I part my lips and feel Wes's tongue sweep into my mouth, I let out a low moan.

He smiles, pulling back, his eyes crinkling at the corners as he looks at me. "I love you, Simone. Now get in the car."

Heart banging, I do as he says. He closes the door when I slide in, and I find myself surrounded by that new-car smell, hands on a smooth steering wheel, butt in a leather seat that probably gets warm at the push of a button.

I have a car!

Putting the key in the ignition, I turn it and feel the car rumble to life beneath me. Laughing, I lay on the horn and watch the twins, Agnes, and Candice whoop and scream from the parking lot, their arms in the air. My smile splits my face in half, then, impossibly, widens as Wes slides into the passenger seat.

He hooks a hand around the nape of my neck and crushes his lips to mine. "Happy birthday, beautiful."

"This is too much."

"Nothing is too much, Simone."

"You didn't need to get me this."

"I know." He smiles. "I know you didn't ask for this. I know you don't want *things* from me. But I also know I want you to be safe and independent and able to get around on your own."

"You're just sick of me using your truck."

"That too." He grins, then kisses me again. Hard. By the time he pulls away, my head is spinning.

With a wave and another honk, I say goodbye to my friends and drive down Cove Boulevard toward my beautiful home on the coast. Wes slides his hand over my thigh and squeezes, sending a thrill rushing through my veins. When we make it home, I barely have time to close the car door before I'm being hauled over Wes's shoulder with a squeal.

"Now it's time for part two," he growls.

"Part two?"

"Of your present. It involves my tongue." He smacks my ass as we walk toward the front door. "And less clothing."

Laughing, I let him carry me across the threshold and onto the couch. He tugs my pants off with a violent yank, then kneels in front of me and hooks my bare legs over his shoulders. "Now I want you to lie back against those cushions and enjoy yourself, yeah? No protests. Not one word about refusing the presents I give you."

"I think I can manage that," I reply, breathless, then let my head fall back as his mouth gets to work. His hair is silky in my fingers, his deep moans rumbling through my core, his big, broad shoulders perfectly framed by my legs.

Yes, I can accept this kind of birthday present. I might even look forward to it every year.

ABOUT THE AUTHOR

Lilian Monroe adores writing swoonworthy heroes and the women who bring them to their knees. She loves making people laugh and is eternally grateful to have found people who share her sense of humor.

When she's not writing, she's reading (or rereading) a book, walking, lifting weights, or attempting to play the guitar with very limited success.

She grew up in Canada but now lives in Australia with her Irish husband. He frequently asks to be used as a cover model for her books, and she's not quite sure whether or not he's joking.

Dirty Little Midlife Dilemma

Dirty Little Midlife Drama

Dirty Little Midlife (fake) Date

Brother's Best Friend Romance

Shouldn't Want You

Can't Have You

Don't Need You

Won't Miss You

Protector Romance

His Vow

His Oath

His Word

Enemies to Lovers/Workplace Romance

Hate at First Sight

Loathe at First Sight

Despise at First Sight

Secret Baby/Accidental Pregnancy Romance

Knocked Up by the CEO

Knocked Up by the Single Dad

Knocked Up...Again!

Knocked Up by the Billionaire's Son

Yours for Christmas

Bad Prince

Heartless Prince

Cruel Prince

Broken Prince

Wicked Prince

Wrong Prince

Lone Prince

Ice Queen

Rogue Prince

Fake Engagement Romance

Engaged to Mr. Right

Engaged to Mr. Wrong

Engaged to Mr. Perfect

Mountain Man Romance

Lie to Me

Swear to Me

Run to Me

Doctor's Orders

Doctor O

Doctor D

Doctor L